THE LEGEND

Jennifer Ames was not beautiful but she had a certain something that kept Peter Barrington in willing thraldom for ten years. One day they hoped to marry and to speed the happy day, Jenny takes a job as governess to Lord Barclay's twin children, Michael and Marie. When she arrives at the Worcestershire manor house, Jenny finds herself engulfed in mystery. Why does the tall, good-looking Derek both fascinate and frighten her?

THE LEGEND

THE LEGEND

The Legend

by
Patricia Robins

Dales Large Print Books
Long Preston, North Yorkshire,
England.

British Library Cataloguing in Publication Data.

Robins, Patricia
   The legend.

   A catalogue record for this book is
   available from the British Library

   ISBN 1-85389-677-2 pbk

First published in Great Britain by Hutchinson & Co.
(Publishers) Ltd., 1951

Published in Large Print 1997 by arrangement with Patricia
Robins.

Dales Large Print is an imprint of
Library Magna Books Ltd.
Printed and bound in Great Britain by
T.J. International Ltd., Cornwall, PL28 8RW.

CHAPTER I

'Peter darling, do try and understand. It's only for a year and it would make so much difference to us. It must be worth it!'

The girl's face was strained, frowning a little with the effort of persuasion. Even this way one could not look at her but think—How attractive she is! What character and strength she has!

Strictly speaking, she was not beautiful. In fact, Jenny Ames worried a good deal about her looks and considered herself rather ordinary. But she had just that something about her which perhaps can only be described as sex-appeal, although the word gives far too flighty an impression for Jenny's quiet serene features, her deep, almost black-brown eyes and soft, wavy brown hair. Peter sometimes hummed under his breath, *Jenny with the light brown hair,*' but his Jenny was no sweet little mouse-like creature the song put to his mind. She was strong and vital and passionate and he was finding out now, to his own discomfiture, just how determined was her will.

His own lean, handsome face looked

disconcerted and a little sulky as he turned his blue eyes from her and said:

'Perhaps a year doesn't seem long to you, Jenny. It seems a lifetime to me. Besides, it's another year on top of ten. *Ten,*' he repeated with emphasis. 'Why, it's just utterly ridiculous, Jenny. Anyone would think you were trying to put off our marriage indefinitely.'

A quick retort rose to Jenny's lips, but she quelled it, knowing Peter's accusation was the result of his hurt pride. He must know that for eight of those ten years *he* had demanded *she* do the waiting.

'You're only seventeen, Jenny,' he had said. 'And anyway, I don't believe in war marriages. They aren't fair on the girl—particularly when the man is a sailor and away for long years, maybe, at a time. No, darling, let's wait.' Those had been Peter's own words. 'The war won't last long. It'll give you time to grow up a little more and find out if you really do love me.'

And no argument she could put forward could change his mind. As the years went by, they discussed marriage again, several times, but always Peter, at the point of weakening, would end by saying: 'The war can't last much longer, Jenny. Then we can have all our dreams—a home, children, everything we want. Don't let's take second best now. I've only a week's leave. It would mean a rushed wedding in a registry office, and you know you've always wanted to be married in white! Then a few days' honeymoon and parting—perhaps for six months. Besides, darling, you know how I feel—in case anything happened to me, I mean.'

Yes, Jenny had known. Peter had always had a morbid idea that he would be killed in the war. He was afraid he might, if they were married, leave her with a child to support and no means except a pathetically small pension.

She had not wanted to wait then. As for everyone else, war had increased the tempo of her living and Jenny felt the urge to secure happiness while she could. At least a few weeks as Peter's wife would be better than nothing.

But because he had felt so strongly about it, she hadn't pressed her demands. She didn't want to add to his worries and responsibilities. He was doing some very secret and dangerous work, and she knew that if he were married he would not feel free to take the same risks.

So she had waited until at last the war was over. But then things had become worse instead of better. Peter's firm had taken him back—but only on the same pre-war salary which he had earned as the most junior member of a commercial art department. As a member of His Majesty's Navy, they had told him quite firmly, he could not possibly have gained in experience—in fact, he may well have forgotten all he knew. They were sorry, etc, etc, but it was the old salary or nothing.

Clearly they could not buy a house, have children, furnish a house, or even rent a small flat on Peter's minute salary. Jenny, who had had three years in the Wrens, had returned home and was doing a part-time job as a doctor's receptionist. Her salary for that half day, five days a week, was larger than Peter's full-time pay, Saturday mornings included. They might have managed to scrape enough together on their combined salaries to marry and start a home—provided they both continued working. But Jenny knew Peter well enough not to suggest it. Peter was of Scottish blood—even if he had lived all his life in England. He had been brought up to the old conventional standards—that a man should be able to support his wife—and that a woman's place was in the home. Strictly speaking, Jenny approved his principles. She was not a career woman and her one idea of heaven was to settle down as a housewife and have a large family. But it did seem the most ghastly shame that after all those years of waiting they should still not be able to marry.

'I'll soon get a rise, darling,' he had comforted her. 'Just you wait and see. Confound the beastly editor. One of these days I'll show him!'

Now at last, that day had come. Peter had done some brilliant work both in the office and at week-ends and evenings for other publishers. That he was being grossly underpaid was quite clear to everyone. He earned more in his spare time as a free-lance than he earned full time, in spite of a small rise that the firm had stintingly allowed him. So he had decided to become a full-time free-lance, and he had, this very day, given notice at the office, and having received a tremendous amount of satisfaction from the surprised, anxious look on his ex-boss's face, he had left the office for good and all, collected enough free-lance work to keep him busy for quite six months, and called round at Jenny's home to tell her that at last their moment had come.

Jenny could well see how bitterly her own words had upset and disappointed him. But she was convinced it was for the best. Apart from the fact that if Peter was going to make his way as a free-lance, he ought to be quite unencumbered and free from any worry or added responsibility

11

that might upset his work, there was the question of the house.

An ex-navy friend of Peter had offered them first refusal of a little Tudor thatched cottage about thirty miles from town, at a more than reasonable price. She and Peter had been down two week-ends ago to spend the Saturday and Sunday with Peter's friend and look over the place. They had instantly fallen in love with it and each had confided in the other afterwards that it was their ideal house they had always dreamed about.

'It has so much character and charm!' Jenny enthused. 'And, Peter, that barn which has been converted into a studio—it might have been made for you. Oh, darling, do you think we could ever manage to buy it?'

That had brought them both down to earth. Jenny had a small gratuity from her service in the Wrens—Peter had a slightly larger one, but apart from that and a few hundred pounds they had managed to save towards a house, the total figure did not come within four hundred pounds of what they required.

'We'll raise a mortgage, Jenny,' Peter had said, wildly. 'We can't let it slip out of our hands now.'

But mortgages, it appeared, were not easily raised on cottages with thatched roofs. It would mean borrowing the money at some extortionate rate of interest—or else asking Peter's friend to accept terms of deferred payment and then hope to earn sufficient to pay off the remainder within a year.

'God alone knows how we'd do it,' Peter said doubtfully. 'I start free-lancing next week and even if things go well I've a hundred and one necessities I must get—materials, easels and so on.'

'We need four hundred pounds, don't we, Peter?' Jenny had said. Peter nodded and replied gloomily:

'I'm afraid we'll just have to try and forget about it, dearest.'

But Jenny couldn't and wouldn't forget. She had perused the 'Situations Vacant' column of the *Daily Telegraph* every day and then, just as she was giving up hope, the very thing turned up that was so perfect in every way, she could hardly believe it was true.

'Young ex-Service girl with initiative and ability to take responsibility, wanted for one year as governess-companion to five-year-old twins. Exceptional salary to right applicant.'

And there had been an address and a Mayfair telephone number in London.

Impulsively, Jenny had telephoned and an appointment had been made.

Without telling Peter, Jenny had kept this appointment. A little nervous but determined to get the job, she had found her way to an expensive block of flats. A French maid had shown her into the apartment, and while she sat waiting she surveyed the room to which she had come, trying to form a picture in her mind as to the woman who would be interviewing her. It was beautifully furnished, and it did not need even Jenny's artistic mind to appreciate the quality and value of the various ornaments that were tastefully placed around the spotless room. Personally, she did not herself care for such ultra-modern ideas. The glass table by the window had interior lighting—the rich red and white striped curtains were of sheerest silk taffeta and this brilliant contrast was carried out by matching cushions—a white and red piped settee in which she sat and a pure white carpet that must be worth hundreds of pounds on which she had gingerly placed her neatly clad brown brogue shoes.

Jenny began to wonder whether she had done wrong in dressing down for this interview. She had purposefully avoided wearing her rather exotic 'New Look' light wool frock and the beautiful soft

14

leather brown platform-soled shoes Peter had brought her back from abroad one leave. Instead, she had worn a simple but neat brown coat and skirt, no hat (since the only ones she possessed were rather silly dressy hats Peter liked her in), and the brogue walking shoes. Governesses, she imagined, weren't supposed to look chic.

Her reverie was suddenly interrupted by a clear, rather high-pitched voice saying:

'You must be Jennifer Ames. Funny, but you're not a bit as I imagined you. I suppose I expected someone like my last horror—Miss Simkins—she was just like her name.'

The woman suddenly realized that Jenny, who had risen to her feet politely, was still standing.

'Sit down,' she said in her cool, authoritative tone. 'You look very young. How old are you?'

Recovering from the faint surprise that had overtaken her when this incredibly beautiful and smart woman had drifted into the room, Jenny said quickly:

'I'm twenty-eight. I look a good deal younger than I am.'

The woman shot her a swift glance and then turned towards the glass table, opened an enormous plastic cigarette-box and drew out a Turkish cigarette, which she lit. Then, on second thoughts, she turned to offer the box to Jenny.

'Thank you, I don't,' Jennifer said quietly.

'On principle?' this very abrupt prospective employer asked her.

'No, I enjoy smoking,' Jenny said truthfully. 'Just now I can't afford it. So I find it easier to give it up altogether.'

The beautiful face (that Jenny could only think of as a mask, so perfectly was she made up, so faultless her *coiffure*) showed a faint gleam of interest.

'You're honest, anyway. Old Simkins would never have admitted she couldn't afford anything. Used to make out she was heiress to a fortune—one of these days. Tell me more about yourself. Are you married? Why do you want the job? Are you good with children? I shall expect you to take complete charge. I'm not very often down in the country and when I am I want the children out of the way. I believe children should be kept in the nursery until they are of a reasonable adult frame of mind. Well?' she asked suddenly and impatiently, as if her own quick questioning had not made it impossible for Jenny to speak up earlier.

As she gave a brief summary of her Service career and a few details about Peter and herself, Jenny tried to sort out conflicting emotions. There was something so unreal about this woman that she found it hard—in fact, impossible—to sum her up. That she was very rich indeed was clearly evident—by the room if not by the clothes she wore and the jewellery. But she was not *nouveau-riche*. There was breeding and good taste and that aristocratic, authoritative tone... She was beautiful—very much so for a woman of thirty—forty? Jenny found it impossible to judge her age. But what was underneath that mask? She was hard—the way she had spoken of her children proved so. What was her husband like? Did she love him? It seemed utterly impossible that she could ever feel about her husband the way she, Jenny, felt about Peter. She was too controlled—too cool....

'And so you see,' she said, 'I want a job that only lasts a year because my fiancé and I intend to get married next autumn whatever snags are still in the way. I want the job because we need the money to buy a house. It's no good my pretending it is because I adore children. I do like them, as it happens, but I think it's best to be honest.'

'And you have had no experience of children?' the cool voice asked her.

'Very little,' Jenny admitted. 'But I've studied child psychology, and I passed my school certificate with exceptional marks.

I could give elementary lessons without difficulty. Apart from that, I'm used to disciplining others. As I told you, I was an officer in the Wrens for two years. It also happens I can sew very well should you need anything for the children.'

'Well, there may be some mending, but I think there's a woman in the village who copes with that. The children are dressed by Daniel Neals, so you won't have to "run up anything."'

Was the voice faintly sarcastic, or only amused? Jenny wondered.

The woman stood up and walked slowly with her long, graceful strides to the window and stood staring out at the view across London's rooftops. For a while there was no sound except her deep inhaling. Then she said without looking at Jenny:

'Are you a nervous person?'

'Nervous?' Jenny asked. 'I don't quite understand.'

'Easily frightened?' the voice said. There was no mistaking the impatience this time.

'No, I don't think so,' Jenny said. 'I'm rather too practical to be frightened very easily.'

There was a question in her last remark and she was glad when it was answered.

'The simple-minded locals seem to think Marleigh Manor is haunted. So do all my servants, for that matter. That's why that

18

silly Simkins woman left. You might as well know because I don't want all the trouble of engaging you to have you run back to London on the next train.'

'If I accept the job—and that of course depends on whether you engage me, as you say,' Jenny replied coolly, 'then I certainly shouldn't quit for any ghost or spook or whatever it is that haunts the place. You must forgive me if I am harping too much on the subject, but so far you haven't mentioned a salary. Whether I take the job will depend on that for the reasons I told you earlier.'

The woman turned then and there was a faint disconcerting smile on her face.

'How much do you want?' she asked bluntly.

For a moment, Jenny's composure left her. Then she remembered Peter and the darling little cottage and courage returned.

'I should want eight pounds a week—and my keep!' she said, and held her breath.

Of course, she didn't expect to get it. It was utterly absurd to suppose she would. But somehow she felt that with this woman she was expected to drive a hard bargain. It was as if her own value depended upon the value she gave herself.

'I'm not worth four hundred a year!' she thought. 'I'm not worth half that. But she might offer me, say, five or six pounds a week. She's too rich to notice that....'

'I see you're a very determined person, Miss Ames. However, I have nothing a against that. You want four hundred pounds to help this future husband of yours buy the cottage with the roses round the door, and you intend to get it. I can understand that. Once I make up my mind to have something, have it I will. I think you and I will understand each other very well—that is when we see each other at all, which won't be often. You're a refreshing change from that Simkins woman. I'm sure the children will appreciate it. Perhaps it will knock some sense into them. I shall expect you to start next week. And by the way, there will be occasions when you will be expected to dine with us. I entertain occasionally, and you can be of some help. But you'll have to get yourself some smart clothes. I can't stand dowdy people around me. I'll write you a cheque now and you can fit yourself out before you go down to the country. Buy at least three evening dresses and one smart cocktail outfit. I'll make the cheque out for sixty pounds. No doubt you'll manage on that.'

This time Jenny's control really was shaken. She could find no words at all. Four hundred pounds—eight pounds a week! It was ludicrous—fantastic. This woman must be mad! Why, she hadn't even had a governess's training. And now a cheque for sixty pounds to buy some clothes....

'I presume you will want to see this fiancé of yours from time to time. You can have every alternate week-end off provided Mrs Minnow, my housekeeper, is available to look after the children. I shall expect you to forgo such occasions as Christmas and Easter. You can take two weeks' holiday in the year some other time when it suits you. Is there anything else you'd like to ask before you go?'

Jenny realized this was her dismissal and stood up.

'I still don't know the address,' she said, feeling that this was without doubt the most important of the many questions that were seething in her mind.

'Get it from my maid,' the woman said carelessly. 'Good-bye, Miss Ames. I hope you'll settle down and that we shall suit each other. Mrs Minnow will tell you the routine for the children.'

Jenny had left the flat in a whirl and returned home to try and gather her emotions into some kind of order. Before Peter arrived, she had one thing quite clear in her mind. She had been engaged for the job and, year or no year, she intended to go through with it. Neither ghosts, nor her imperious, rich, frightening employer, nor

Peter's pleadings were going to alter it. She was quite certain in her mind that this was the solution to all their problems. Peter's friend had said he would accept a year's deferment of pay. That meant Peter would have twelve months to get on his feet—twelve months free of financial worry. And at the end of it...

She went across the room and sat down beside Peter, turning his head slowly towards her and keeping her cool hands cupped round his head.

'Oh, darling, darling!' she whispered. 'Don't you see the waiting will be just as hard for me—just as hard. And a year won't seem so terribly long to you. Wait and see. You'll be so busy the months will just fly by. And Peter, no matter what happens—even if I'm sacked and we lose the cottage and you don't have a penny to your name, we'll be married this time next year. I promise.'

His arms went round her then, and his mouth came down on hers in a strong, passionate, demanding kiss.

'Oh, Jenny!' he whispered, his voice husky with feeling. 'I love you so much. I can't think when I hold you like this in my arms. I expect you're right. I don't care. I only know I love you, I love you.'

And so the matter was settled, except

for a teasing remark made by Peter, much later.

'Suppose you meet some other fellow down there in that haunted manor,' he said. 'Suppose he entices you away from me with his enormous wealth and aristocratic family tree?'

'The only person I'm liable to be enticed away by is a ghost!' laughed Jenny. 'A dashing cavalier without a head.'

'It's far more likely to be a wailing nun!' said Peter. 'I wonder if our cottage is haunted.'

'Only by terribly happy people,' Jenny replied, her eyes meeting Peter's in a long look. 'Oh, darling, to think that we can talk about it now as ours—our own. It'll be worth it, won't it, darling?'

'Anything is worth anything for you,' was Peter's somewhat enigmatic reply.

But Jenny knew what he meant.

CHAPTER II

Jennifer hardly noticed the length of the three-hour journey to Marleigh Manor, so deep was she in a variety of thoughts. First there had been Peter and their parting at the station to think about. For several days previously she had been pent-up with a peculiar excitement and the week between her interview with Lady Barclay and today had seemed to drag on leaden feet.

Peter had been a little resentful of her excitement but he understood. It was her first *real* job and in a way it was an event. It meant a year away from home in new surroundings and that tantalizing challenge which appealed to her adventurous spirit of whether or not she would succeed at her post as governess-companion. After all, her experience of five-year-old children was very limited. She had only her common sense to rely on. But she would manage somehow. As to the ghosts...well, that was just amusing, and it would be fun to write and tell Peter if there really were a 'wailing nun'!

But when it came to their final parting at the station the excitement had dropped away from her and she had felt only a queer, horrid sensation of dread. She put it down to the fact that Peter was looking so forlorn, so woebegone.

'I'll be seeing you the week-end after this, darling,' she had told him, but even that could not comfort him or make herself feel any better. These last two years they had been seeing each other nearly every evening without exception. Naturally they would miss each other now. Besides, as Peter said, it was doubtful whether either of them could afford frequent railway fares when they were so terribly expensive.

'I'll manage it somehow next Saturday week,' he had told her. 'I want to reassure myself that you're all right.'

'Why on earth shouldn't I be all right?' Jenny had asked.

Peter held her tightly in his arms for a brief moment as if by doing so he could protect her against his unnamed fears.

'I don't know, darling. It's just that that woman you saw sounds so peculiar—and the place is such miles away...and these ghosts...oh, I don't know what it is. I just have a nasty taste in my mouth when I think about it. Perhaps it's saying good-bye to you when I'd hoped so much I would be saying "Hullo" to my wife!'

'I'll write him a long letter tonight,' Jenny thought, as the train sped her on her way. 'I wonder if I did right to send a telegram to the Manor announcing my arrival.'

From what little information she had been able to furnish from a travel agency, it seemed that Barclay Manor was some three or four miles from the station. They could give her no information about buses.

'Someone's bound to meet me,' Jenny consoled herself. 'And if not, I can get the village taxi or something. I wonder what the house is like. If only Lady Barclay had been more communicative! But I suppose it's her prerogative to do all the questioning. I'll find out all I want to know soon enough!'

She smiled at her own curiosity and tried to settle down to her magazine. But her thoughts soon wandered again to the little thatched cottage and how she and Peter would furnish it; the interview as she tried to recall any scraps of information Lady Barclay had let fall about the house, the people in it, the children. But she realized she did not even know her future charges' names. The only name she could recall was Mrs Minnow, the housekeeper.

'Well, I hope she's a nice friendly person,' Jenny thought vigorously. 'I should hate it if she were like that Mrs Danvers woman in *Rebecca.*'

Almost before she realized it, it was

time to change from the main line to the little local train that ran slowly and dreamily from one tiny village to another, until, fifteen minutes later, it came to a grinding, groaning stop at Little Mills.

Jenny hastily collected her three small suitcases and climbed down to the platform. Nobody else seemed to be alighting at her stop and she had had the carriage to herself. She stared around the tiny station, feeling a little lost—rather as she had felt when she was posted to some new station in the Wrens.

Then a smart uniformed man came walking towards her and touched his peaked cap.

'Miss Ames?' he asked.

Jenny nodded, wondering what it was about this man that struck her as faintly disagreeable. His manners were polite, his expression friendly and respectful, and yet his eyes...

'I've been sent to meet you, miss. I'm the chauffeur at the Manor.'

He stooped to take her suitcases and Jenny followed him out to the tiny sunlit car park, surrounded by flower beds, in the centre of which stood incongruously enough in so rural a surrounding an enormous black Rolls.

The chauffeur pushed her suitcases into the boot and held open the door for her.

Jennifer climbed in and was glad that a glass partition made conversation with the chauffeur impossible. She wanted to look around her and see the countryside undisturbed. First impressions, she felt, were so important.

But there was nothing she could possibly find to dislike in the beautiful Worcestershire landscape. She could imagine how glorious must be the orchards they passed in blossom-time—in the spring. Even now, it was lovely. The leaves were turning their faint yellow and golden brown, and the quiet lanes were like any other part of England in the autumn—soft, sleepy, drowsing in the all too soon departing warmth of the sun.

Presently, the car took a sharp turn past a rather pleasant-looking lodge where Jenny assumed the chauffeur lived, but her eyes were on the magnificent pair of wrought-iron gates and the long sweeping lawns that stretched away into the distance, following the line of the drive into a graceful curve. She waited expectantly as the Rolls swung slowly round and the Manor came into view.

'Oh!' gasped Jenny, unable to keep silent at such a huge and glorious mansion. Marleigh Manor was half Georgian, half Victorian. It had been newly painted white, and it stood out from the soft green of the lawns and brilliant reds and yellows of the dahlias that were massed in huge flower beds along the walls. It was startling—so much white against such contrasting colours, and yet it did not look wrong.

It was a three-storied house—and because of its great length it looked low and rambling. As they drew closer Jennifer saw a long terrace with a trelliswork of wistaria overhead.

'How lovely that will look in the spring!' she thought, seeing in her quick imagination the heavy drooping bunches of soft violet against the whiteness of the walls.

The car stopped and the chauffeur opened the door for her. As Jennifer stepped out the massive oak front door was opened by a maid and a short fat little woman came hurrying on to the terrace towards her.

'I'm Mrs Minnow, the housekeeper,' said the fat little woman with a wide, friendly smile. 'I hope you had a good journey. Jones, would you put Miss Ames's suitcases in the blue room, please?'

She turned again to Jennifer and Jenny smiled and held out her hand.

'You're not a bit as I imagined you would be,' she said. 'Somehow, I expected you to be very small and rather pale!'

Mrs Minnow laughed delightedly at this description.

'No doubt my name put that in mind,' she said. 'Come to that, you're not very like what I imagined you to be, Miss Ames. You look so young. The last governess, Miss Simkins—'

'I'm not really so young,' Jenny said hastily. 'I'm nearing thirty.' (She thought this sounded older than twenty-eight.) 'People always think I look younger than I am.'

'Well, well!' said Mrs Minnow, and then recalling herself, she said: 'Dear me, whatever am I doing keeping you standing out here. Come inside, and I'll show you to your room. I expect you'd like a cup of tea.'

'I would, very much,' said Jenny gratefully.

She followed Mrs Minnow into the house with a glow of well-being. Mrs Danvers, indeed! Why, Mrs Minnow was a sweet old woman—of good country stock, judging by her Yorkshire accent. And the house was beautiful. It was so important, thought Jenny, to like your surroundings when you have to live in them for a year. It made all the difference to the job.

Inside, the house was just as beautiful— particularly the six-foot wide Georgian staircase with its long gallery overhead.

They went straight upstairs, so she did not have time to see the downstairs rooms.

At the far end of the gallery Mrs Minnow opened a door and stood aside for Jennifer to enter. As Jenny did so another insuppressible gasp came from her lips.

Indeed, the room warranted the admiration she felt.

It was large, though not over large, and of the same period as the Georgian entrance and staircase. The beautiful arched window was hung with glorious sky blue corded silk curtains, the divan bed was covered to match, and as she stepped forward she felt the deep soft pile of a deeper toned blue carpet. The blue room! It was really beautiful beyond description. She moved quickly over to the window and stood staring down into the garden below. There were few trees to block the view and she could see for several miles around her—gentle undulating countryside, sleeping quietly in the mellow afternoon sun.

'It *is* a nice room, isn't it?' said Mrs Minnow. 'I'm afraid Miss Simkins didn't appreciate it. Said blue depressed her, so she had the primrose room along the other end. Not near so nice as this—Victorian, you know. But then, so was Miss Simkins—' She broke off as if this disloyalty to the poor departed Miss Simkins was hardly fair. 'M'lady said to put you in here,' she added.

'That was very kind of her,' Jenny said, running a comb through her soft brown hair and bending to look into the triple-sided mirror that stood on a beautiful antique Georgian chest-of-drawers. The rich red-brown of the walnut furniture harmonized perfectly with the soft blue furnishings, and yet one might have expected the modern and the antique to clash! She was soon to discover that the whole house was a blend of the same combination—modern comforts and antique beauty. Whoever had been responsible for the interior decorating must have had great skill—and great taste, thought Jenny, and to Peter she wrote later, *How you would admire it, my darling, with your artistic mind.*

'I'll just ring for Winnie and ask for your tea to be sent up,' said Mrs Minnow. 'Then, while you're drinking it, I can tell you a bit about things. I expect you'll want to know.'

'Yes, there's a lot I'll have to learn,' Jenny said ruefully. 'I don't even know the twins' names!'

When Jenny's tea arrived in a beautiful Wedgwood china tea service, she sat down and listened while Mrs Minnow talked.

'Well, first I'll tell you who's in the

house, like,' said Mrs Minnow. 'There's the twins, bless their dear little hearts—Master Michael and Miss Marie. The young master likes to be called Micky, though! They're in the nursery wing now; they just can't wait to see you. When m'lady wrote saying you'd be coming, she didn't describe you at all, and they that plagued me with questions about you I couldn't answer! Never mind, they'll see for theirselves soon enough.'

'You're very fond of them, aren't you?' said Jenny, who had noticed the adoring expression on Mrs Minnow's face when she spoke of the children.

'That I am!' said Mrs Minnow. 'Nursed them from birth, I did. That's how I came here—as Nanny to them. Now, of course, they are a bit too old for a Nanny. Last winter Miss Simkins came—' She broke off and swallowed as if she could not bear to talk about handing over her babes to Miss Simkins' care.

'It must have been very hard for you to give them up,' said Jennifer sympathetically.

Mrs Minnow nodded.

'Yes. I cried myself to sleep for weeks afore Miss Simkins came. But the children—bless them—they still came to me with their little troubles and worries—until Miss Simkins put a stop to it.' Mrs Minnow sighed.

'Quite right, really. I can see it undermined her discipline. However, I was lucky to be kept on as housekeeper. At least, I still see the children. Fortunately for me, the last housekeeper left just before Miss Simkins came. M'lady agreed to keep me on in her place.' (She gave another sigh and then pulled herself together with a visible effort.) 'Dear me,' she said. 'I'm going off the track. That's what happens when you're getting old! Now, what was I saying...oh yes, the twins! Then of course there's m'lord and m'lady, though m'lady isn't down here a great deal. And then there's Miss Amelia—'

'Amelia?' Jenny broke in. 'Who is she? I don't think Lady Barclay mentioned her.'

'Like as not!' was Mrs Minnow's mysterious, caustic comment. 'Miss Amelia is m'lord's daughter by his first marriage. She's fifteen and—well, rather quiet and plain. Not that it's her fault. She can't help it, and m'lady will—' She broke off abruptly and hurriedly changed the conversation. 'There I go, rambling again. Then there's Mister Derek, m'lady's son by *her* first marriage,' she added, seeing Jennifer's puzzled look.

'Lady Barclay told me there were only two children to look after,' Jenny said with a little frown.

'So there are, Miss Ames. Only the twins. Miss Amelia has a tutor to see to her lessons. Otherwise she doesn't have any looking after. Winnie sees to her clothes and that, of course. And Mister Derek's older than you are, miss, or else about the same age.'

'But I don't understand,' Jenny said weakly. 'Surely Lady Barclay can't have a son in his late twenties. Why, she looks well under forty herself.'

'M'lady takes very good care of her looks,' said Mrs Minnow. 'She's only just the right side of fifty. Mr Derek was born when she was seventeen.'

'I see!' said Jenny.

'Well, apart from the servants, that's all,' said Mrs Minnow. 'I won't worry you with all their names.'

'Are there so many?' asked Jenny with a smile.

'Ten living in and three come in from the village,' said Mrs Minnow.

'Ten!' gasped Jenny. 'To look after six—seven people?'

'Well, it's a big household, and m'lady likes things just so,' said Mrs Minnow. 'There's Cook and Winnie, who's the children's maid, and m'lord's and Mr Derek's valet, and Annie, the house-parlourmaid, and Jones, the chauffeur, and old Tom, the gardener, and Marianne, m'lady's French hussy, and myself and Robert, the butler. It's not really so many, seeing all the work there is in such a big house. And m'lady entertains a great deal when she is down. Huge parties, she gives.'

'Yes, Lady Barclay told me,' said Jenny. 'Well, thank you very much for being so helpful, Mrs Minnow. I think I'd like to see the children now—that is, after you've told me their routine.'

'Not much to it,' said Mrs Minnow. 'Half past eight they get up and you supervise their dressing if Winnie's not there to do it. That depends on how much work there is downstairs. Then they have breakfast in the nursery. After breakfast they have lessons till twelve, then half an hour in the garden if it's fine until lunch-time. After lunch they lie down for an hour—with their picture books. Then mostly their father takes them riding in the afternoons. If it's wet, they just play indoors or else in the squash courts if Mister Derek isn't playing there. Four o'clock their tea. After tea they play about until half past five, then it's reading-time. M'lord insists on their having some of the easier classics read to them until bedtime. They're in the middle of *Alice in Wonderland* now. Quietens them down before going to sleep. They have milk and biscuits when they're in bed. That's really as it is most days—unless m'lady is down and wants them down to the sitting-room for tea. When that happens they have to be dressed up real smart. Whenever m'lady wants to see them they *must* be washed and smartened up first. If it's m'lord who wants them, they can stay in what they are in. He doesn't notice.'

Jenny digested all this in silence and tried to commit it to memory. Anyway, there would always be Mrs Minnow to refer to, she consoled herself.

A few minutes later Mrs Minnow was leading her along to the nursery wing. This consisted of day and night nurseries, the twins' own bathroom, and the schoolroom. It was, she saw in a swift glance, as expensively and ostentatiously decorated as the rest of the house. It was like the sort of nursery one would expect a film star's child to have—elaborate friezes on the walls—miniature furniture, huge dolls' houses, rocking-horses, indoor sandpits—everything duplicated in pink and blue. The money that must have been spent on the place... Jenny didn't even have time to consider it. Two diminutive figures were flying across the room, from where they had been kneeling on the window-seat staring out into the garden, and stood looking up at her.

'Are *you* our new governess?' asked Micky, a puzzled frown on his small angelic-looking face. He had, Jenny noticed, his mother's beautiful hazel-green eyes, but where hers were veiled and inscrutable, his were childishly open and full of expression. She was to learn that the hardest task Micky ever had to face was hiding anything from anybody. Whatever his lips said, his eyes always spoke the truth.

'You don't look any older than Meely!' said his sister Marie.

Marie, amazingly like her twin, and yet curiously different, was staring up at Jenny from exactly the same green eyes with their long curved fringe of dark lashes. But where Micky had met her glance—almost defiantly—Marie looked away immediately and a faint colour stole into her cheeks. Jenny was not long in discovering that where Micky's shyness and uncertainty showed itself in defiance, Marie's always showed in that faint flush and the hasty fluttering of her lashes as she refused to meet a glance.

Jenny smiled and bent down, sitting back on one heel so that she was almost level with them. She held out her hand and said:

'I *am* your new governess and I *am* older than Meely—that's your sister, Amelia, isn't it?'

'Half-sister,' Micky corrected her, but he put his small hot hand into hers and gave her a half-smile. Marie turned to look at him and said in a whisper that was clearly audible to both Jenny and Mrs Minnow as well as to her twin, for whom it was meant:

'Don't do that, stupid. You know you said we weren't going to like her!'

'Well, I've changed my mind,' said Micky loftily. 'And you can jolly well change yours, because I'm not going to change back.'

His voice was quite definite and Marie must have realized it. There also seemed to be an understanding between them that they never hold different points of view.

Marie, her head still downcast, put her hand in Jenny's and said in a small, resigned voice:

'Orright. I'll like you,' and then with a swift gesture, shyness gone and in its place a pleading, anxious look, Marie turned to Mrs Minnow and said:

'Do *you* like her, Nanny?'

Mrs Minnow smiled her broad, comfortable smile and said:

'Yes, Marie. I think she's going to have lots of ideas for fun and games and stories...and I think she's nice and safe.'

At Mrs Minnow's last words the twins glanced swiftly at one another and then away again. Had Jenny not been watching their faces she might never have noticed it. What was it Mrs Minnow had said—safe? Safe! What a funny word to use! And why that glance between the children?

She was left no further chance of reflection, for the door opened behind them, and as Jenny turned her head she saw a tall, dark and extraordinarily handsome young man standing there looking at her.

'So you're the new governess,' he said in a deep, curiously compelling voice. 'Jones told me you'd arrived. In the absence of my mother, I'd like to welcome you to Marleigh Manor.'

CHAPTER III

As Jenny murmured polite replies to his enquiries as to her journey, she was struck anew by the curious resemblance of Lady Barclay to all her children. Without being in the least effeminate, Derek Barclay had inherited her amazing beauty—there was no other word to describe the perfectly moulded features, the incredible green eyes with their dark lashes, the full mouth.

Where the twins were still too young to show any of her graceful movements and dignified manners, Derek Barclay had both qualities without either detracting from his masculinity. They were in keeping with his tall lithe body, his long tapering fingers and deep, high forehead.

But the most compelling of all these attributes was his eyes. They held her gaze now in a deep, penetrating look and try as she might she could not drop her own glance from those faintly smiling, curiously hypnotic pools of green. It was an aristocratic face, almost haughty, and yet his words were friendly and not in the least patronizing.

'You're a very pleasant surprise, Miss

Ames,' he was saying. 'My mother omitted to describe you in her letter. I might add that after Miss Simkins you're a most refreshing change.'

The scarcely veiled compliment caused Jenny to drop her eyes quickly, conscious that Mrs Minnow and the twins were watching her. She felt a little angry with Derek Barclay for making his remarks too personal. The son of the house should surely not pay the governess compliments, she told herself sharply.

'By the way,' she heard his voice continuing, 'I would appreciate it if you would dine with us tonight. I know Lord Barclay would like to meet you.'

Although his words were spoken courteously enough, Jenny detected the faintly authoritative tone and took this request to be an order. Actually she was feeling a little tired after the excitement of the journey and she had been looking forward to an early night. She wanted to sit quietly for a little while, sorting out her first impressions—and above all she wanted to write that promised letter to Peter. She felt, however, that she had no choice but to accede to this request.

'Thank you very much,' she said briefly.

Derek Barclay turned to go. At the doorway he looked round and with a curious little half-smile, he said:

'We don't dress for dinner, you know—not when my mother is away.'

'I see. Thank you,' Jenny said again. And then the door closed behind him.

'That's an honour, I'm sure,' said Mrs Minnow, breaking the silence that followed his departure. 'Poor Miss Simkins was never invited downstairs to dine all the time she was here.'

Poor Miss Simkins! Jenny could feel truly sorry for her. It seemed as if she had been disliked by everyone.

'Oh, *her!*' came Micky's voice, full of childish scorn. 'She was dreadfully dull and ugly and Derek only likes beautiful things.'

'Like that Cynthia woman!' supplemented Marie.

'Well, I don't like her either,' announced Micky. 'She smells!'

'Master Micky!' came Mrs Minnow's scandalized voice.

'Well, she does!' Marie defended her twin. 'It's perfume, like Mummy's, but not just a little sniffy bit like Mummy uses. The Cynthia woman has lots and lots and you can smell wherever she's been.'

Jenny could not help but be amused by this childish observance of someone who evidently overdid the use of perfume. But at the same time she felt the twins, young as they were, should not be allowed to speak about their elders in such a fashion.

'I'm sure this Cynthia you speak of is very nice if she's a friend of your brother,' she said, 'and I don't think you should talk about her in that way. It isn't polite.'

'Well, it's true, anyway,' said Micky. 'I hope she doesn't marry Derek. I'd hate to have her as an aunt.'

'She wouldn't be your aunt. She'd be your sister-in-law, Master Micky,' said Mrs Minnow.

'What's that?' asked Marie.

While Mrs Minnow was trying to explain this relationship, Jenny found herself thinking, with curiosity and the tiniest tinge of disappointment:

'So Derek Barclay is engaged to be married. I wonder what Cynthia is like! She must be very beautiful, and yet I don't like the sound of her. She sounds as if she is one of those sophisticated society girls with long red talons and a perfectly coiffured head and exquisite clothes.'

She shook herself out of her reverie and said to Mrs Minnow:

'Well, I wish I hadn't been invited down to dinner. I had been hoping for an early night. I suppose dinner will be late?'

'Half past eight, Miss Ames. Why not have a little lie-down until then? I'll see to the twins for the rest of today. I'm

44

sure m'lady wouldn't expect you to start work now.'

Jenny gave Mrs Minnow a grateful smile.

'That's very kind of you. I think I will,' she said.

But there was a sudden unexpected outcry from the twins.

'I want Miss Ames to put us to bed,' Micky said forcefully.

'So do I,' said Marie, stamping her little foot.

'Now, children,' came Mrs Minnow's voice anxiously. 'Don't start being naughty just as Miss Ames has arrived. Whatever will she think?'

'I don't care,' shouted Micky, his little face going red with temper. 'I *want* Miss Ames!'

Although Jenny might have felt pleased by this tribute to her new popularity, she could see that it was clearly not right to give in to the twins. It appeared that they liked to have their own way.

'Now, Micky,' she said sternly. 'You heard what Mrs Minnow said. She will put you to bed and I will start looking after you tomorrow.'

'I won't go to bed, I won't, I won't!' screamed Micky, with Marie's voice echoing his.

'It's no good reasoning with them,' sighed Mrs Minnow. 'Once they get into one of their tantrums there's nothing can be done with either of them. You'll just have to give way.'

'I'll do nothing of the sort,' said Jenny sharply. 'It sounds to me as if they've been used to having their own way too much.'

'Their mother spoils them!' said Mrs Minnow in an undertone. Jenny frowned. Somehow it did not fit in with her picture of Lady Barclay. Had she not said she wanted the children kept out of her way as much as possible?

'It's lack of the right sort of discipline,' went on Mrs Minnow. 'One minute m'lady is petting and spoiling them in the drawing-room—that's when she has guests and is showing them off. The next minute she's sending them upstairs and getting furious because they won't do as they're told. The children never know where they are with her.'

'Surely Miss Simkins had some method of controlling them?' Jenny said, her voice and Mrs Minnow's all but drowned by the twins' screams.

'None at all,' said Mrs Minnow. 'The twins managed her. They did just as they liked.'

Jenny squared her shoulders.

'Well, it's going to be quite a different kettle of fish now,' she said firmly. And to the twins:

46

'You can scream from now until to-morrow. It won't make any difference to me.'

For a second the noise stopped. Micky looked at her angrily.

'Yes, it will. Mummy doesn't like us screaming. Miss Simkins 'ud do anything to keep us quiet. We'll scream and scream until you say you'll put us to bed.'

He opened his mouth to start yelling again, but Jenny, giving a sudden amused laugh, caused him to hesitate, staring at her open-mouthed.

'What are you laughing at?' asked Marie sullenly.

'Well, at you two, of course,' said Jenny. 'You're both being such very silly children. To start with, you know your mother is away, so even if I minded her hearing you scream it wouldn't matter tonight, would it? So you just scream away until you're both hoarse. Then Mrs Minnow can give you some medicine—rather nasty stuff, I know—but you'd have to have it for sore throats.'

'I won't have any medicine,' Micky said, his face screwed up in one big pout, his eyes watching Jenny's face intently.

'Oh, but you will if I say so,' said Jenny. Something in her tone convinced Micky that she was right. He changed his tune.

'If I don't scream until I've a sore throat,

I won't have any,' he said.

'Well, no, of course not,' agreed Jenny pleasantly.

She pretended not to see the look he shot at Marie—a look which all too clearly said:

'What are we going to do about it? Are we going to give in?' Their good behaviour hung in the balance for a moment or two. Jenny turned the tide by saying:

'After Mrs Minnow has put you to bed I'll come and tell you a story.' The tears dried like magic and the twins edged closer to her and said:

'What sort of story? An adventure story? Will it be 'citing?'

Jenny smiled.

'That depends on how good you are. The better you are the better the story will be,' she said.

They flung themselves upon her, eyes shining, small hands clinging to her.

'We'll be *ever* so good!' said Micky.

'We won't splash in our baths *at all*,' said Marie.

'I should hope not!' said Jenny, wondering whether she should have bribed the children with the promise of a story if they were good, and determined to show a little authority, 'Why, you've been behaving just like babies, when you're quite grown up.'

'Grown up?' Micky asked, puzzled.

'Mummy says we're only babies.'

'She says "you must meet my two enchanting babies",' said Marie, her voice so exact an imitation of that Lady Barclay might use when addressing a room full of guests, that it was all Jenny could do not to laugh.

'That's just drawing-room talk,' she said, biting her lip to keep from smiling. 'But you know you aren't babies, and Mrs Minnow knows and I know. After all, babies don't have much fun, do they? Grown-ups have much more fun and can do all sorts of exciting things.'

'What sort of things?' asked the twins.

But Jenny refused to be drawn into answering questions of that sort, and left the children to Mrs Minnow while she hurried back to her room.

She slipped off her travelling costume and lay down on her bed, pencil and a pad of paper beside her. She wrote the address and started her letter:

Darling Peter.

And then her pencil ceased writing and she was lost in thought. Clearly the twins were going to be a handful. They had, without doubt, been dreadfully spoilt. She saw exactly how Lady Barclay treated them. They were show pieces when it pleased her to exhibit them to her friends. It suited her to pet them and give way to them so that they hung about her, asking prettily for another sweet or cake, affectionate loving children whom her friends would admire. But when there was no one to witness this child-like devotion and charm the twins were of no use and were relegated to the nursery. Clearly, too, Miss Simkins had been afraid of Lady Barclay, afraid to thwart the twins' wishes in case their tantrums should reach Lady Barclay's ears and annoy her.

It was no way to discipline children.

'And what am I going to do?' Jenny asked herself. 'Lady Barclay said I was to keep them out of her way and yet that will be impossible if I let them scream until they're tired of it. It's not going to be easy!'

But she wasn't afraid of the coming conflict. There was a challenge in it which she was ready and eager to take up. She was certain that the twins were good underneath. All children, to Jenny, were born good and only spoilt by outside influences. Tonight she had had her first success. She sighed and turned her mind again to her letter.

I arrived safely this afternoon...

Once again the pencil lay idle in her hands. She was tired, sleepy with a curious relaxed feeling of contentment. Whatever else it might be, she was certain this job would not be dull. Her eyes closed and a minute later Jenny was fast in a dreamless sleep.

When she woke an hour later she glanced at her watch and saw it was seven o'clock. The letter to Peter, barely started, had fallen to the floor.

Jenny gave it a wry smile.

'Fancy falling asleep like that,' she chided herself. There would be no time now to finish the letter before dinner. She would barely have time to change into her new soft wool frock after a bath and keep her promise to tell the twins a story.

Jenny took particular pains with her dressing that night. It was not only that she wished to create a good impression—on Lord Barclay of course, she assured herself quickly, as if some inner voice had suggested she might be making herself beautiful for Derek Barclay—but that she had not often in the past had the opportunity of wearing such lovely clothes—clothes she had been able to buy with that cheque from Lady Barclay.

She brushed her hair vigorously for five minutes and was rewarded to see it shining in soft curly waves about her neck. Her cheeks had a warm rosy colour that her deep sleep had induced and her eyes were bright and sparkling. All traces of her tiredness had vanished, and staring at her reflection in the mirror she knew that the new dress became her. She would wear it when Peter came down on his first visit.

It was half past seven when she made her way back to the nursery. Mrs Minnow was in the play-room, tidying the toys that were scattered about helter-skelter.

'They're in bed waiting for you as good as gold,' she told Jenny.

Jenny smiled.

'I'm glad they weren't any trouble,' she said. 'And I think, as from tomorrow, Mrs Minnow, I'll start them on the job of tidying their own toys.'

'A very good idea, Miss Ames, if you can get them to do it,' agreed Mrs Minnow in a dubious voice.

'They'll do it,' Jenny said confidently.

A call from the night nursery reminded her that the twins were waiting for her story.

There was something very disarming about the two little pink-clad figures sitting up in bed, Micky with his hair brushed smoothly off his face, Marie with her long curls tied in a pink bow. Their faces were scrubbed to a rosy cleanness, and touchingly they held hands across the gap between the tiny twin beds.

One day, thought Jenny with a moment's swift tenderness, she and Peter would be standing together at the door of their own children's nursery. The thought was gone in an instant.

'Sit on *my* bed,' Marie pleaded.

'On *mine!*' begged Micky. So she sat on Micky's bed and allowed Marie to snuggle under the blue eiderdown beside her.

'Ooh, you do look nice!' said the little girl. 'I think you're just as pretty as Mummy.'

'I think she's nicer,' said Micky.

Jenny quickly reproved him for this remark, but he held his point of view until Marie changed the conversation.

'Must we call you Miss Ames?' she asked. 'It's such a funny name.'

'What's your other name?' Micky enquired.

'Jennifer!' she told them. 'Jenny for short.'

'Jenny Ames, Jenny Ames!' said Micky. And then, after a moment's thought, he said, 'I think I'll call you Jamie.'

'But that's a boy's name,' Jenny laughed.

'It's nice,' said Marie. 'I never heard any little boy called Jamie.'

So Jenny invented a little story about a wee Scots laddie called Jamie, and they listened entranced until a loud gong announced that it was eight o'clock and dinner-time.

They clung to her as she stood up, but she remained firm and reminded them of their promises to be very good. Reluctantly, they released their hold of her and she bent to kiss them good night. Then she hurried away with a last promise to look in on them before she herself went to bed.

As she ran down the wide staircase Jenny caught sight of Derek Barclay and an older man she took to be Lord Barclay, standing in the open doorway to the left of the entrance hall. She felt a moment's shyness and then, recovering her self-possession, she walked down the remainder of the stairs more slowly.

Derek Barclay heard her footsteps and turned towards her as she reached the hall. He came to meet her and stood for a brief instant staring at her with that penetrating gaze of his.

'How—lovely you look!' he said in a low voice.

Once again Jenny felt shy and annoyed that he should be so personal. After all, she was only an employee here. He had no right to make such remarks. And yet, woman-like, she could not help but be the tiniest bit flattered. Derek Barclay must move in a very smart and *soignée* set. That he should find her—plain Jenny Ames—attractive—well, it *was* pleasing to one's vanity.

He took her arm and led her into the

54

drawing-room and introduced her to Lord Barclay.

'My stepfather,' he said briefly. 'This is Jennifer Ames.'

'I'm very glad to meet you, my dear,' said the old gentleman, staring at her shortsightedly over a pair of spectacles. He had snow-white hair and a white military moustache which gave him the look of a retired army man. For all he must be nearing sixty, Jenny thought he looked amazingly strong and athletic. She recalled that Mrs Minnow had said he rode a good deal and could see that his straight back had the markings of a good horseman well used to the saddle.

'How do you do?' she said politely.

Derek Barclay went over to a small table to pour out a glass of sherry. Meanwhile, Lord Barclay said:

'I don't think we've met before, have we? Do you live round here?'

Jenny felt a moment's bewilderment. Then, realizing that he had mistaken her for one of Derek's personal friends, she said quickly:

'I'm the new governess, Lord Barclay. Your son asked me to dine downstairs tonight.'

Lord Barclay coughed and shot Derek an angry little glance.

'The boy should have told me,' he said.

'I'd no idea you had arrived. I hope you are quite comfortable, Miss Ames? I'm afraid my wife is still in London. If there is anything you want please ask Mrs Minnow, the housekeeper.'

Jenny knew immediately she was going to like Lord Barclay. He was 'one of the old school', a Colonel Blimp without the drossness, which had been replaced by a calm, gentle courtesy.

'That's very kind of you. Mrs Minnow has been looking after me.'

Derek rejoined them and handed Jenny a glass of fine old sherry.

'Smoke?' he asked, pulling out a thin gold cigarette-case.

Jenny shook her head.

Derek shot her a quick look.

'A woman of virtue?' he asked with a light laugh.

'I've given it up for a while,' Jenny said, almost defiantly. Once again she felt resentment at Derek's remarks.

'Very good thing too, if I may say so,' said Lord Barclay. 'Don't like to see women smoking myself. Old-fashioned, I expect. Well, dinner will be getting cold. Where's Amelia?'

'Deep in a book, no doubt,' said Derek in a light, amused tone. 'In fact, deaf to the world as usual.'

'Reading is a very fine pastime,' was

Lord Barclay's faintly rebuking comment. 'Ring the bell and ask Robert to go and find her.'

The butler was sent in search of Amelia, and Lord Barclay, followed by Derek and Jenny, went into the dining-room.

If Jenny had thought the first floor of the house lovely, the downstairs rooms were even more strikingly beautiful and lavish in their luxury. A huge shining refectory table more than fifteen feet long stretched the length of the dining-room. It was laid with exquisite lace mats and lit only by candles in long silver holders. Georgian plate had been laid in four places. At the far end of the room the french windows, opening on to the lawn, were hung with deep-red velvet curtains. It seemed to Jenny, used as she was to the small suburban house she shared with her mother, to be a vast room more like a banquet hall than someone's private dining-room.

They were half-way through the soup before Amelia arrived. She came hurrying into the room, peering about her over the rim of her horn-rimmed spectacles. Seeing her father she hurried over to him and kissed him on the cheek.

'I'm sorry I'm late, Daddy,' she said. 'I didn't even have time to change.'

That was evident, for she wore an untidy tweed skirt that showed no sign of its original expensive cut and good cloth. The blue twin set also seemed untidy, and Jenny realized that it was more the fault of the girl's figure than the clothes themselves.

Amelia Barclay was immensely tall for her age—five foot ten to be exact. She was thin, lanky, scraggy, with all the faults of an overgrown, gawky schoolgirl, and not a trace of the beauty so apparent in the other Barclay children. And then Jenny remembered that Amelia was Lord Barclay's daughter by his first marriage and realized that it was her father she took after and that there could be no possible family likeness to Lady Barclay.

Her thin, pale face was not exactly enhanced by the horn-rimmed spectacles, and she was at the spotty stage Jenny herself had been through at fifteen and knew so well! Added to this not very prepossessing general effect, Amelia's nose was scarlet, which fact Derek seemed to notice.

'Couldn't you even powder your nose before you came to table, Meely?' he asked.

There was that faintly mocking tone in his voice, and hearing it Jenny felt vaguely resentful. She found herself taking Amelia's part.

'If Amelia's only fifteen, I imagine she

doesn't use make-up yet,' she said.

'No, I'm afraid she doesn't. My mother has been trying to teach her this feminine art, but I'm afraid Meely is still too much of a schoolgirl to be interested in her looks.'

Jenny saw the girl's face flush a dull red. But she didn't speak to Derek. Instead she peered across the table at Jenny and said:

'I'm so sorry. I didn't see you when I came in. Are you the twins' new governess?'

'Yes,' said Jenny gently. 'I arrived this afternoon.'

'Nobody told me,' said Amelia. 'Or I'd have come to see you were all right.'

'I'm very comfortable, thank you,' said Jenny.

'There was a very peculiar noise upstairs when I was changing for dinner,' said Derek into the silence that followed. 'I suppose the twins were playing you up, Miss Ames?'

'Derek, you know they are always like that at bedtime,' Amelia spoke with unaccustomed courage. 'Don't make out it's just because Miss Ames has come—'

'Keep your hair on, Meely,' Derek broke in calmly. 'I only meant the din seemed louder than usual.'

'Let's hope you'll be able to knock some sense into them, Miss Ames,' said Lord

Barclay, as he motioned to the parlour-maid to take away the soup plates. 'My wife seems to think Miss Simkins couldn't control them.'

'She certainly couldn't,' Derek said. 'However, I'm sure Miss Ames will have more success. I imagine the twins will fall ardent slaves to her beauty and do everything she tells them.'

Jenny bit her lip angrily. It really was unfair of Derek Barclay to be so consistently personal. Even if she were not the usual type of governess, the fact still remained that she was an employee here and he ought to treat her as such.

Neither Lord Barclay nor Amelia, however, seemed to take any notice of Derek's remarks.

The conversation changed to horses and riding and, to Jenny's relief, remained impersonal, although she could not help but notice that Derek referred all his remarks to her. Perhaps it was natural, since Amelia and her father seemed to address all their remarks to each other! It was clear to see that there was a very deep affection between father and daughter and that Amelia, when deep in conversation with her father, was quite a different person from the awkward, shy schoolgirl that she seemed when Derek addressed her. The girl's face took on a glow all its own and she was, Jenny decided, watching her, no longer plain or dull.

Perhaps that is the answer to most of us, she thought. We are what the people we love want us to be. It was true that Peter always brought out the best in her. He seemed to think her incapable of an unpleasant thought or action or, indeed, any unpleasant quality at all. And invariably, when she was with him, she was her nicest. For Jenny knew that, like anyone else, she was by no means perfect. She had her faults and weaknesses but somehow they never seemed to appear in Peter's presence.

After dinner, coffee was served in the drawing-room. Presently Amelia put down her coffee cup and started to question her father about some autobiography she was reading, and before long the two disappeared into the library to find a book.

Seeing her opportunity to finish her letter to Peter, Jenny said:

'Will you excuse me if I go upstairs now? I rather want to—'

'No, don't go, please,' Derek said, jumping to his feet and putting a detaining hand on her arm. 'Once Meely and my stepfather get to talking books they'll be shut up there in that library all evening. Please stay and talk to me, won't you?

It's confoundedly lonely in this house, you know, especially when my mother is away.'

There was a boyish appeal to his request that immediately struck an answering chord in Jenny's kind heart. Besides, she need not stay long—just a half-hour or so.

'Haven't you many friends round here?' she asked as she sat down again in the settee and Derek pulled out a pipe and stood, legs astride, in front of the huge blazing log fire.

'No, it's very isolated. Of course, people come down weekends a good deal. The trouble is, I haven't enough to keep me busy. My stepfather seems to think I'm necessary down here as a kind of glorified bailiff, but there isn't enough work for my liking. Besides, as I said, it's lonely. Meely's no company, as you can imagine. And one can't ride or play squash all day, every day and evenings as well.'

'No, I suppose not,' said Jenny.

'I'm hoping my mother will persuade my stepfather to employ some man to act as bailiff,' Derek confided in her.

'Don't you like it down here?' Jenny asked curiously.

Derek gave a short, bitter laugh.

'I suppose it's all right, but I want to be a soldier. My father—my real father, I mean—was in the army and, in fact, all my paternal ancestors. Believe it or not, my six years in the army during the war were the happiest years of my life. It's in my blood, I suppose. Soldiering!' His voice softened and became wistful. Jenny listened to him puzzled.

'Couldn't you stay in the army,' she asked.

'No! I was offered a permanent commission but had to refuse. You see, this estate is a big one. My stepfather is getting on in years and the time will come when he has to hand over the running of the place to someone else. Me! Of course, it's really young Micky's inheritance, but he's only a kid and it'll be years before he can look after the place. So that leaves me.'

'But that's not fair if the place isn't to be yours in the end,' Jenny burst out impulsively.

Derek gave another laugh.

'Perhaps not! But to be fair to my stepfather I must admit that I owe him a tremendous amount. This is all I can do to repay him. You see, when my father died, he left my mother and myself penniless. I was only a child at the time—ten, I think. My father had, of course, sent me to a good preparatory school prior to going to Eton and then Sandhurst. Of course, it was impossible for my mother to afford to carry out those plans. When she married Lord

Barclay he paid for my education—Eton and then the University. You see, the former Lady Barclay had died at Amelia's birth. There was no son to carry on the name and inherit the estate. Nor was it imagined that one day the twins would arrive. I was, therefore, the son and heir. My stepfather accepted me as his own son and brought me up to step into his shoes. There was nothing I could do about it. I don't think I realized until I was years older how much soldiering meant to me. By that time my education was nearly completed. Then the war broke out and soon after that the twins were born. Of course I imagined that would let me out, but my stepfather had too much to do running the estate practically single-handed during the war. His health has gone and he must give up a little more each day. My duty clearly was to take over from him until Micky comes of age.'

'I see,' said Jenny. 'Is that why you took your stepfather's name?'

Derek nodded.

'I suppose I'll survive,' he said with a sudden smile. 'In any case It'll be different now you've come. I think it was jolly decent of my mother to choose someone so young and pretty. I guess she realized how fed-up I was getting stewing away down here on my own. I hope we'll be good friends. May I call you, Jennifer?'

Jenny bit her lip.

'I really think as I'm a governess now that your mother might prefer you to call me Miss Ames,' conscious of the fact that the words must sound horribly prim to the man beside her. 'You see,' she added hastily, 'I'm sure your mother didn't—well, was only thinking of the twins when she employed me!'

Derek smiled.

'Perhaps! Still, we're living in a socialist world. There's no reason why we shouldn't be friends, is there?'

Jenny shook her head.

'Then suppose I just call you Jennifer in private? Please?'

Again that boyish appeal; but the position was awkward for her. Whatever Derek might think, she was sure Lady Barclay wouldn't approve of her son getting too friendly with her.

Feeling unable to cope further with this conversation, Jenny felt it would be an opportune moment for her to go. She stood up saying:

'I suppose it won't matter when we're alone. Now, if you don't mind, I think I will go upstairs. I have one or two things to unpack—' she ended vaguely.

'If you must go, won't you say good night first?'

Puzzled at first, but seeing his outstretched hand, Jenny assumed he wished to endorse his words of friendship with a handclasp. She held out her own hand, and then, before she realized what was intended, Derek had grasped it firmly in his own and pulled her roughly towards him. His arms went round her in a hard, forceful grip in which it was utterly useless to struggle, and his mouth came down on hers, crushing the angry protest she had been about to make.

CHAPTER IV

For those few seconds' duration of that kiss Jenny was prey to many different emotions. At one and the same time, she wished to struggle until he freed her and yet she wanted to return that passionate embrace. She was also quite horrified at her own reactions.

He released her suddenly so that she had to take a step back to avoid losing her balance. He saw how deathly pale her face was and then, as her eyes came up to meet his half-amused glance, saw the brilliant flush of red as it spread upwards to her cheeks.

'I...you...perhaps you didn't realize that I was engaged to be married!' she said at last, her voice ice-cold with anger which was contempt for herself as much as for him. 'And that I am aware of the fact that you, also, are engaged.'

And before he could detain her, she turned and ran from the room.

Lying full length on her bed, oblivious to the creases she would make in the lovely dress she wore, Jenny buried her head in the pillow and tried to still the racing beat of her heart and the trembling in her limbs. The back of one hand against her lips, she felt again the warmth and passionate demand in the kiss that Derek Barclay had so recently planted there; felt deep within herself a renewal of the exquisite sensation of weakness that had spread over her as his hold on her had tightened. Never, at any time, had Peter's kisses aroused in her such a storm of emotion, such a wealth of response that was entirely of the body and quite out of control of the mind.

Memory of Peter brought the colour rushing to her face again.

'Oh, how could I? How could *he!*' she whispered, horrified at the thoughts which now assailed her. 'It was a despicable thing to do...even had he not realized I was engaged to another man.' Was it his custom to kiss any girl on so short an acquaintance just because the idea amused him or the mood struck him?

Perhaps Jenny would not have hated him quite so fiercely in that moment had she not hated herself so much, too.

'Oh, Peter, Peter,' she cried aloud. 'What would you have said if you had been there...if you knew? I didn't mean it to happen. He gave me no chance. I was taken unawares...and then...somehow, I couldn't help myself!'

Would he understand? Would she write

and tell him and beg his forgiveness or would it be better not to mention it? Far better not, on second thoughts, for then he would surely not permit her to stay in the house. Did she still wish to stay, now, after what had just happened? Perhaps it would be better to go as soon as possible.

'Now I'm being melodramatic!' she chided herself as her normal common sense began to get the upper hand of her emotions. 'Derek Barclay didn't know that I was engaged. He isn't altogether to blame. And besides, no doubt in the set he moves amongst it is their way to go around calling even mere acquaintances 'darling' and, quite probably, kissing is looked upon by them in the same unrestricted light. It isn't so much his fault as the fault of his upbringing. His mother probably spoilt him and his good looks have probably entitled him to a lot of spoiling from any woman he smiles on. He must be used to attracting the opposite sex and taking what he wants from them.'

For his kiss had left her in no doubt as to the fact that he didn't lack experience with women. Rough as he had been, so that her lips still felt bruised, there had been an instant reaction in her to that primitive fierceness.

'Now I *am* being silly!' Jenny thought, with a slight smile fleeting across her face as she turned to lie on her back. And yet it was, in a way, quite true. When Peter kissed her, it was always such a considerate and gentlemanly sort of kiss. He never allowed his feelings to get the upper hand and so her own had very seldom been out of control. Just once or twice—last Christmas Eve, for instance, when they had stayed up so late... Peter's prolonged love-making had worn them both down until he had crushed her fiercely against him and said:

'It's all so damned silly. We ought to be married—to be able to belong to one another as we want—not just messing around like this!'

His voice had been constrained and full of angry frustration. She, too, had felt frustrated—felt a longing to be able to surrender herself completely and without reservations to the man she loved. Peter's sudden loss of control had shown her that he, too, was feeling the strain of their long engagement. And yet it had been of his own making....

And now, in spite of all Peter meant to her and all their memories, she had let herself be kissed by another man and...had liked it.

'For I did like it!' she told herself, suddenly honest. 'And what is far worse, I liked it in spite of the fact that I dislike the way he went about it!'

Perhaps she and Peter had allowed their love-affair to become too static, too commonplace. Things had to go forward—or back. And since convention did not permit them to carry on to new delights of love and companionship—so they had drifted backward, in a sense, so that their everyday companionship and the good-night kisses were just ordinary and a little bit dull and matter-of-fact.

'I can see that now,' Jenny thought. 'I can see, too, that it suited us to have it so. It meant less wear and tear on our nervous systems to cut out too much emotion. And since we had to wait...then it was best to put such thoughts out of our minds and temptations as far as possible out of the way.'

She gave a sigh which was almost of relief. It did, after all, excuse the fact that she had enjoyed being kissed with such fierceness and passion. But did it excuse Derek Barclay from such behaviour? What would happen tomorrow? How could she bear to face him in the daylight? Was he, too, a little ashamed? Would he, too, be embarrassed? Would he treat the whole thing as if it hadn't happened—or try to kiss her again?

With sudden determination, Jenny jumped off the bed and started to undress. Let tomorrow take care of itself. It had been a terribly long and tiring day, fraught with excitement such as she had not been used to of late, and she was tired—deathly tired. A kiss wasn't so important when one looked on it sensibly. It couldn't have meant anything to Derek Barclay and she had already explained to herself, quite satisfactorily, her own reactions and the reason for them. Derek was just a rather bored young man with nothing better to do than kiss the governess. No doubt he would have kissed one of the maids in just the same way had it taken his fancy. Men with his background, his social advantages, could get away with such behaviour.

'But not with me!' Jenny told herself firmly, as she climbed wearily into bed and laid back against the pillow. 'He'll soon find out just how much I dislike him and what little chance he'll get to repeat the performance.'

Reassured, Jenny closed her eyes and allowed sleep to snatch her quickly into its soothing grasp. But she could not control the dreams that troubled her rest—dreams in which Peter became hopelessly confused with Derek Barclay and her own heart lay torn and undecided about them both.

When Jenny awoke, it was to find the sun streaming in through the open windows into the beautiful room which for a moment seemed quite foreign to her. Then remembrance of where she was returned to her and a smile illumined her face as she recalled that she was now a governess and that fortune had blessed her undoubtedly by providing her with more luxury and comfort than she would have imagined possible in such a situation.

The smile left her face as quickly as her thoughts raced backward to last night and the way Derek Barclay, son of her employer, had kissed her. Her happiness vanished and a frown crossed her forehead. Already it was today and she must meet him face to face. How awkward it was going to be!

But again her natural good spirits and common sense took the upper hand. Unless expressly asked to dine downstairs, she was to have all her meals in the day nursery with the children. The chances were she wouldn't even see Derek Barclay for a day or two. By then they could treat the matter as if it hadn't happened. Or she would, anyway.

The sound of two bright cheerful voices outside her room caused her to glance quickly at her watch. Half past eight! She had overslept.

'May we come in, Jamie?' asked a piping treble through the keyhole of her door. 'It's us—me and Micky. Mrs Minnow said we weren't to wake you, but we want to talk to you.'

Jenny smiled. What a wonderful, mischievous little pair of monkeys were these two small charges of hers! She might so easily have found herself with two overgrown, unattractive, 'lumpy' children. At least she would not be bored by the twins—even if they did keep her busy.

She jumped out of bed and, pulling her dressing gown round her, opened the door for them.

They flung themselves on her, each demanding to be kissed first.

'Well, really!' Jenny laughed, but she gave them each a hug and they curled themselves either side of her on the edge of her bed.

'You overslept!' Micky announced almost reproachfully. 'Old Minnow said you were tired but we've been awake for ages and ages.'

Jenny bit her lip and, with a brave attempt not to smile, her face assumed a serious expression.

'Whom did you mention, Micky?'

He gave her a look from under his incredible lashes that was both scowling and laughing.

'Oh, Mrs Minnow, then. I say, aren't you jolly well hungry? We had our breakfast hours ago. Mrs Minnow—' he stressed the 'Mrs' and gave Jenny a knowing little smile full of mischief as if to say 'just this once I'll say it'—'she said she'd bring you in a tray today as a special treat, and you're to ring for it when you're awake. But we saved you this in case you couldn't wait.'

He pulled out an incredibly messy piece of buttered toast which had crumbled at the edges. Various particles of dust and fluff had adhered to the melted butter. Marie in turn produced two sticky prunes. Jenny looked helplessly from one to the other.

'She doesn't really like prunes!' Micky said.

Marie turned on him like a small tiger-cat.

'Yes I do! At least, I wanted the stones to make it come to This Year, and I minded saving them just as much as you did the toast, so there!'

'Children!' Jenny cried, hoping her voice sounded sufficiently stern and did not betray the laughter behind it. 'I'm very grateful for your little offerings, but I'd rather you ate your own breakfasts. And Marie, prunes are good for you.'

Marie gave her a smile that was full of sweetness.

'I know!' she said. 'But I don't really like them very much. Still, if you're *sure* you can wait for your brekky, I'll keep them.'

Not waiting for Jenny's reply, she popped one into her mouth, irrespective of its state, and after a bit of concentrated chewing went to the window, spat out a pulpy mess, and turning back to Jenny, gave her another brilliant smile and, producing the prune stone, said, 'There, now the other prune will make it This Year.'

'Marie!' Jenny cried aghast. 'You're not going to eat the other one. Why, it's filthy! I forbid you.'

Marie's face darkened suddenly and a look of fear shot into her brilliant eyes.

'But you can't mean it, Jamie. I must eat it. I told you this one makes it This Year.'

Her voice was so tragic, so full of conviction, Jenny withdrew the command that had sprung to her lips and thought quickly.

'You mean—This Year, Next Year, Some Time, Never?' she asked.

Marie gave a sigh of relief and nodded her head.

'But that's only a game,' Jenny said gently. 'You don't really believe—'

'Yes, we do!' broke in Micky, his mouth full of the horrid piece of toast which Jenny had refused with good reason. 'Besides, you never know, it might work and then...'

His voice trailed away into a sudden

dead silence. A chill seemed to have come over the room, and looking from one child to another, Jenny sensed a curious tension between them. It was strange—and a little frightening. They were so deadly serious.

'And then what?' she prompted gently.

There was another silence while again the children exchanged glances. Then with another brilliant smile, as if her next words explained everything to their mutual satisfaction, Marie said:

'Why, then it'll be This Year.'

A further question rose to Jenny's lips, but she thought better of it. It was too soon to expect them to place very much trust in her. Whatever this 'thing' was, she felt determined to discover in due course. There had been something fearful and ominous in the twins' voices—something secretive and furtive and strangely frightening. Whatever they hoped would happen This Year mattered to them—a lot.

Meantime, she said:

'I'd rather you didn't eat that second prune, Marie. I'll give you one of mine when my breakfast comes to replace it. And Micky, you shall have a piece of toast. Now go and throw those things away like good children.'

They looked at each other, a barely perceptible nod of assent passing between them, and went in silence to the window and, before she could stop them, threw the unwanted remains away.

'Next time find a better place for rubbish,' she reproved them, but her voice was gentle, for she did not wish to discourage them after their obedience.

She rang the bell for her breakfast and the children started chattering again as if nothing in the world mattered to them except their plans for the day. They wanted to show her the grounds—their secret hiding-places, their camp, their house in the tree; the ponies, their pets—everything. Only lessons were not mentioned.

Disliking to damp their enthusiasm, Jenny compromised and promised they should spend the morning exploring and then they could both tell her in their very best English, everything they had seen and done. She would give them words to spell—names of their pets and so on. It would be a good lesson in English.

The twins were delighted.

'That'll be heaps and jeeps more fun than old Simkins' lessons,' they twinkled.

The arrival of one of the maids with Jenny's breakfast tray interrupted her little lecture on politeness to elders. She took the tray and then, with her face burning a sudden scarlet, saw that there was a letter addressed to her—in fine, forceful handwriting—a writing she did not know but which she was quite certain was Derek's. The letter had not come by post and there was the Barclay crest embossed on the back of it.

She bit her lip and turned quickly to the children, who, happily, had not noticed her concern.

'Here's your toast, Micky,' she said, and to Marie she handed the promised prune. 'Now run along to the nursery and let me have my breakfast in peace. I shall be up and dressed in ten minutes and by then I want to see your nursery as tidy inside the cupboards as out. Now...I mean it,' she added as they looked at one another and then appealingly at her. She smiled, and they capitulated and smiled back, running quickly after the maid. She could hear their eager little voices from outside the door saying:

'That's Jamie, our new gov'ness. Isn't she nice? We *do* like her!'

The smile left her face as she lifted the envelope and carefully opened it with a knife.

'Dear Jennifer!' it began. Her face flushed again, this time in annoyance—when she had refused him permission to call her that—on his mother's account. It wasn't fair! She read on, her heart beating quickly.

I felt I must drop you this note with your breakfast so that you did not pass through the day as well as last night thinking too badly of me. Had you given me a chance, I would have apologized at the time I behaved so unforgivably. It was unforgivable of me, I know, and yet I am asking your forgiveness, and in all sincerity, I think I am a little to be excused in the face of such temptation. If this again offends you, please remember that it is but the truth and as I am sure you would wish my small brother and sister, your charges, to tell the truth at all costs, may I not do the same?

I did not know that you were engaged—how should I? You wore no ring. As to my own engagement, it is unofficial and more probably than not will not materialize. It has been broken so many times in the past, once more is more probable than not. Under the circumstances, I consider myself quite free, although I am aware now that you are not. In any case, I had no right to presume on so short an acquaintance.

Forgive me, Jennifer, and believe me when I say I do most sincerely wish to be your friend.

It was signed boldly with his Christian name.

The closely written pages left her with mixed feelings. Was this man always to

80

arouse such controversy within her? More than anything she was vastly relieved. He was sorry and he wished to be her friend. It had been a flash of weakness on his part and he had apologized. Now they could both forget it. Nevertheless, it was hardly the letter she would have expected her employer's son to write to her, the governess. It might be a socialist world nowadays, but she felt certain that Lady Barclay would not uphold such ideas, and to be honest, she did not, herself, think that it was the best relationship. It was her duty (and she was paid) to look after the children. That was the sole reason for her presence in this house. She was not here to make friends, and no doubt if Lady Barclay ever learned of last night's interlude she would at once be sacked. For all its apologies the letter was a little too personal. In fact, it would have been better left unwritten—the whole thing ignored.

She sighed deeply. Perhaps, after all, she was making a mountain out of a molehill. At least now she could accept Derek Barclay's apologies and forget him and the whole stupid business. She would show him, by her behaviour when they next met, that she had no intention of letting their 'friendship' pass the barriers of mere acquaintanceship. She would say 'good morning' and pass by, and that would be that.

All the same, she hoped very much that she would not meet Derek for a day or two at least. Then she need not be afraid of that tell-tale colour which might, at his name, rush unbidden to her face.

Jenny sighed again, and putting the matter out of her mind, dressed quickly and went along to the nursery to find the twins.

During the morning's ramble through the grounds, stables and myriad outbuildings, Jenny was amazed at the size of the place. It was bigger than she had imagined, seeing only the front of the house on her arrival. Although fairly cold there were still bright shafts of autumn sunlight streaming through the beeches on to the house and dappled patches on the beautifully kept lawns and flower beds.

The trees were very lovely in their autumn guise but already the leaves were beginning to fall and, watching the twins as they scampered about trying to catch them and gain a wish, Jenny felt a moment's grief. Soon it would be winter and the trees would be bare and the garden, now a glowing mass of chrysanthemums, would be deserted and colourless. Then, indeed, might this mansion, for it was surely that, seem lonely and a little forbidding. The trees were too near the house, and for all their beauty must cast shadows and prevent what light there might be during the day from cheering the large rooms.

Shall I be lonely in the winter? Jenny asked herself. Perhaps a little afraid in that huge house, in such a deserted place? And then the children came running to her, their faces alight with laughter, their voices shrill and a little wild with exhilaration, and an answering smile lit up her face, chasing away sombre reflections. No, with these two handfuls it was doubtful whether she would have time to be lonely or afraid. Besides, of what need she be frightened?

Little Marie, with one of her sudden changes of mood, slipped her hand into Jenny's and said with a childlike wistfulness:

'Isn't it a pity that the flowers are going to die and the leaves fall off?'

'They will all be here again in the spring,' Jenny said, giving the little hand a reassuring squeeze.

'Yes, but that's not for ages and ages. And I don't like the winter. I'm afraid...'

Her voice trailed away, and Jenny felt a quick shiver run over her. That their two unsimilar minds, living in such different worlds, should have the same thought!

'Of what are you afraid, Marie?' she

asked gently, keeping the anxiety out of her voice.

'Of when it's dark!' said Marie, and as if aware that she had said too much, or perhaps that she might say more, she tugged her hand free and with a shout that Jenny felt sure was falsely cheerful, ran after her twin, calling:

'Catch me! Catch me! Catch me if you can!'

Jenny followed them at a distance lost in her own thoughts, and it was only the sound of other voices that made her look up to the long paved terrace at which she had arrived, to find Derek Barclay with his sister Amelia.

The colour raced into her cheeks and receded swiftly in anger. He might have spoken sooner instead of letting her wander along in a day-dream looking, no doubt, like a sleepwalker or something equally silly. She nodded her head to him with a barely audible 'good morning' and turned to Amelia, who was smiling at her shyly.

'What a beautiful place this is,' she said, addressing the girl. 'Your father must be very proud of his estate.'

Amelia looked pleased.

'Yes, he is. He loves it very much. It is beautiful... Did you have a good night, Miss Ames?'

'Very comfortable, thank you,' Jenny

replied, her gaze averted from the glance she knew Derek had cast in her direction.

'It's nearly lunch-time,' Amelia went on. 'Father won't be back, so I...we...thought we'd lunch with you in the nursery. I hope you don't mind.'

Jennifer cast a quick look at Derek, expecting that this idea had been his and not Amelia's. But his eyes were twinkling, and presently her own eyes lost their seriousness and she found herself smiling back at him.

'After all, Jennifer Ames,' she told herself, 'although you've taken on the job of being governess there's no need for you to become too staid and prim.'

Derek Barclay was holding out a hand of friendship, so why not accept it? He might have been very surly or difficult to manage, or he might have been unbearably rude—many things in fact that were far worse than this open-handed friendship. It seemed now as if he had given that kiss only in a kind of schoolboyish daring—perhaps for a whim.

'Come now, Miss Ames!' (was it on purpose that he was addressing her so formally?) 'Why so much hesitation? We won't incite the twins to naughtiness, will we, Amelia?'

Amelia gave him a half-smile, then, turning to Jennifer, said:

'I do wish you would agree, Miss Ames. Derek is in such a good mood and—'

'He hopes I won't spoil it,' Jennifer finished the phrase for Amelia. What a queer household this was—all undercurrents and emotions! Perhaps that was understandable between two children with a half-brother and half-sister, neither of whom were blood relations at all!

'Inferring that I'm not always in such good spirits?' Derek asked Amelia. 'Well, it's no doubt true. And why should I not be happy on such a clear, sunny morning in the company of two such pretty women!'

Amelia's face flushed a dull dark red and Jenny's retort to Derek gave way to a quick:

'Now don't blush, Amelia, when a compliment is paid you. I know I usually do, but I never think it is as becoming as the poets say. Besides, it's quite true. Blue suits you very well and you do look pretty in it.'

This, in part, was true. Blue suited Amelia's fair skin and forget-me-not eyes. But for all that she was scarcely pretty— only coltish, clumsy, untidy. Poor Amelia. Had Derek been making fun of her?

'Do you really think I look nice?' Amelia asked, her eyes suddenly hopeful as they gazed into Jenny's. Her voice was now all

86

child and it was not even the vanity of a woman that had prompted the words. 'I did try this morning. I had a letter from my mother. She said you dressed so well she hoped I wouldn't shame her by looking too ghastly. So I tried.'

Jennifer walked up the steps on to the terrace and took the girl's hand with a gesture of friendliness that concealed the pity she felt for her.

'You know you don't make the best of your looks, my dear,' she said. 'Would you like me to help you? You could look so—well, so attractive if you chose.'

'I know I don't make the best of myself,' Amelia said. 'Mother is always telling me so. But...well, Miss Ames, do *you* think clothes matter?'

Jenny hesitated before answering. The girl was so serious, so really anxious to know her opinion.

'In a way, I do,' she said. 'I think if one can look chic it gives one self-confidence even if it won't alter the personality within. Do you see what I mean?'

'I...I think I do,' Amelia said hesitantly. 'Perhaps if I knew I was well dressed I shouldn't be so shy, and then I could talk better to strangers and perhaps interest them even though I am so dull!'

'Come now, Meely, you're not as dull as you make out. You and Father like to hide yourselves under a cloak of dimwittedness—just so that you can shut yourselves in the library and be at peace.'

Derek's words were teasing, but Amelia's reply was quite serious.

'Yes, that's probably true, Derek. But Father and I haven't your and Mother's gift for attracting people and entertaining them. I wish I had—then I wouldn't be such a disappointment to her.'

'I'm sure you're not that, Amelia,' Jenny cried, hearing the hopelessness in the girl's voice.

'No, it's just that you don't bother, Meely, and you know how Mother likes to show off the family. You always turn up looking such a sight, no wonder she's cross, and she's quite aware of the fact that you don't even try.'

'Then we *will* try—together,' said Jenny firmly. 'I know I'm only here to look after the twins, but after they are in bed, Amelia, I shall take you in hand. We might try out one of those home perms on each other—you do me and I'll do you. That would be fun.'

'And probably burn your heads off,' Derek said, laughing indulgently.

Amelia gave Jenny a brilliant smile, so that for a moment she did look pretty.

'I'd love that,' she said. 'And I am glad

you've come to stay here, Miss Ames. We're very lucky to have you.'

Jenny was touched by the formal little speech, and even Derek's 'hear, hear', followed by his faintly mocking laugh, could not spoil the tribute.

Lunch started badly. First the twins could not be found and then Micky turned unaccountably sullen and said he didn't want any lunch. Marie echoed him, and it was all Jenny could do to persuade them, cajole them and finally bully them to the table. Their behaviour was quite inexplicable, and she sat puzzled and silent while the twins, with downcast heads, played about with the soup. It was only when Derek said crossly, 'Stop playing about, kids, and eat that up at once as Miss Ames told you,' that they set to and swallowed as if their lives depended on it.

'I do believe you're the only person in this house with any influence over them,' Jenny said to him.

Derek gave her a curious glance. Then he laughed, saying:

'Well, so I should have—an elder brother to a couple of kids that age.'

'They must love having an elder brother like Derek,' Jenny thought. He was tall and handsome and no doubt excellent at cricket and tennis. Micky and Marie were at the age to hero-worship. And yet—the thought nagged at the back of her mind—they seemed almost afraid of him. In awe of him anyway. Or was it just that they respected his authority?

Derek was being both courteous and charming. Amelia, quite different from the silent person who had graced last night's dinner-party, blossomed forth surprisingly under Derek's gentle teasing and smiled shyly and eagerly from one to the other. The three of them embarked on a discussion about painting and Jenny noticed from the corner of her eye that once attention was removed from the twins, they, too, showed themselves more lively and were chattering between themselves in some quite unrecognizable language.

'That's what they call the "Egg Language",' Amelia informed her with a smile. 'I think you put the word "egg" before every sounding vowel, but I'm not certain. Anyway, they speak far too fast to understand.'

Derek requested Jenny's permission to smoke and offered her his cigarette-case. Jenny refused on account of the twins but they, their meal now finished, were begging to be allowed to get down and go to their rest.

'We always have half an hour on our beds,' Marie informed her gravely.

Jenny laughed.

90

'Run along then. When you're rested, we'll go for a long walk.'

'They're queer children,' said Amelia, more to herself than to anyone else. 'Last week, nothing and nobody on earth could persuade them to have their rest.'

'It's Miss Ames' influence,' Derek interposed quickly. 'You know, Amelia, I can't help wondering if the Mater knew quite what a bargain she was getting when she employed Miss Ames.'

Jenny smiled.

'Perhaps your mother won't think so.'

'I wonder when the Mater will come down,' Derek mused.

'Didn't she say tomorrow?' Amelia asked.

'Yes, but you never know with Mother,' Derek replied.

His words proved correct, for when Jenny returned with the twins from a long walk in the beech woods for nursery tea, the maid who brought it upstairs informed her that Lady Barclay would be home to dinner and Sir Gerald had asked if she would be so good as to dine with them tonight.

'Sir Gerald,' Jenny echoed quickly.

The maid nodded.

'Yes, miss. He and Miss Amelia were in the library and rang for me to tell you.'

'Thank you,' said Jenny, and felt strangely happier for knowing that this time the invitation came from Sir Gerald and not from his son.

CHAPTER V

After tea, which she had alone with the twins in the nursery, Jenny was thankful to find that they were happy to play quietly together, leaving her free to finish her letter to Peter. In fact, the letter was so much on her mind that she did not notice at first that the children were almost too subdued. However, for the moment she was content to forget them, and drawing out her writing pad and leaning on the scrubbed nursery table, she read what she had written.

Darling Peter,

I arrived safely this afternoon... She crossed out *'this'*, altering it to *'yesterday'*, and proceeded:

...and so much has happened that I really haven't had a moment until now to write to you, although I did just begin to write yesterday evening. I was so tired by then that I fell asleep on my bed, pen still in hand, and nearly overslept through dinner. As I had been invited to dine downstairs 'en famille', that would have been a bad beginning.

Well, my darling, it is hard to know where to start. First the house. It is very large, very beautiful, half belonging to the Georgian era and half Victorian. My first impression was of grandeur and sunlight and—in fact, that I had come to one of the original 'stately homes'. But I must admit that when I was walking in the grounds this afternoon I had a moment's qualm as to what it would be like during the winter. Rather lonely, I imagine, and a bit gaunt. I suppose I shall think longingly of our little cottage and the sitting-room all cosy in the light of a big log fire. However, the nursery is a friendly enough room, and as I expect to spend most of my day there I shan't mind it very much. I have a dream of a bedroom—looks like something in a Hollywood film...pale blue, and sumptuous rugs. Walnut Queen Anne furniture and pale blue satin curtains with a pattern of silver stars.

As regards the children, the twins are darlings...full of character, and I know I'm going to love them both. Little Marie is the female image of young Micky, and they are very attractive children, full of spirit—and mischief!—and with endearing ways. You must somehow manage to meet them when you come to visit me, as I know you'd enjoy them as much as I do. No doubt I shall have my work cut out managing them. As far as I can see, they managed the last governess, and their mother's discipline, from what I hear, was so inconsistent that it was definitely a drawback. So far, Lady Barclay has not been here but she arrives this evening and I have a feeling that the whole house, which has a lazy, sleepy atmosphere when she is away, will spring into life as she opens the front door. Sir Gerald Barclay is charming—real old Col. Blimp type—and if vague, very kind and positively adores Amelia, his daughter by his first marriage. She's a rather plain gawky child in her teens and, I believe, the bane of her stepmother's life. Amelia is rather pathetic in her way. I think she admires Lady Barclay but is also afraid of her tongue, and the child has a dreadful inferiority complex about her clothes and appearance. I'm sure I can help her. She is otherwise very like her father and has his literary interests, so that they spend hours locked up in the library perusing books together.

There is one other member of the household —Lady Barclay's son by her first marriage—a young man about your age called Derek Barclay. I think he changed his name when his mother first married Sir Gerald Barclay and it was understood that Derek would be heir to the estate. Then the twins were born and of course, Micky being Sir Gerald's real son, it has cut Derek out, or so I imagine. He doesn't seem to bear the child any grudge, though, and although the children are a little in awe of him, he treats them very well. He is very like his mother to look at, and I suppose you would call him attractive....

She broke off, wondering whether to score this last sentence out and then decided to leave it. After all, she might as well be honest with Peter. He would perhaps meet Derek Barclay in person when he came down to visit her, and he would be far more suspicious if she hadn't mentioned him.

Suspicious of what? she asked herself then, and thinking, bit her lip. Last night's little interlude was over and forgotten. There was surely no need to tell Peter about it—to worry him. He would be anxious enough without her making him jealous too.

She resumed her writing with sudden energy.

Oh dearest (she wrote), *if you knew how much I was missing you—even although it is only a day since I last saw you. Come down and see me soon and I shall do my best to get a weekend off soon to come to town. It may be a bit tricky next week-end as Lady Barclay is home and I gather she entertains a lot. But failing this one, then I'll certainly wangle the next. I wish I wasn't quite so far away. I'd give a lot to be able to slip on a coat and run round to see you this very minute, to be in your arms and hear you say you love me. Write to me as often as you have time, darling, and I'll do the same.*

You have all my love, Peter, my very dear and only sweetheart, and I think about you constantly. Don't worry about me—I've landed on my feet and think I shall be happy here—as far as I could ever be happy without you.

Your own,
Jenny.

She sighed as she folded the sheets of paper and slipped them into the envelope. Writing to Peter brought him closer and, in so doing, made her the more lonely that she could not turn to him now and hear his voice, feel the touch of his hand. She *did* love him...so very much, and even the strangeness of this new adventure and the grandiose surroundings could not entirely make up for the fact that she would no longer see him every evening—in fact, their meetings would, from both financial and work reasons, be few and far between.

Still, she comforted herself, it would be well worth it when one considered that this time next year they would be married—and have their adored little cottage, too.

She scribbled Peter's name and address and then turned to the children. They were very quiet, heads bent over a large picture book, bodies nearly submerged beneath the nursery table. She watched them for a moment in silence and then, surprised that they did not turn over the page, said:

'You're not asleep, children?'

They raised white, startled faces to hers. A flush spread over Marie's pale cheeks as she said:

'Oh no! We were looking at our picture book.'

'We're being very good, aren't we?' Micky said.

Puzzled still more by the wistfulness of his voice, Jenny nodded her head. They were strange kids! Pulled from one mood to another without any logical reason so far as she could see. She glanced at her watch and said:

'Goodness, it's past your bedtime. Put that book away and tidy up while I go and run your bath.'

Her words were greeted with an icy silence.

'Did you hear me, Micky? Marie?' she asked, a tone of impatience creeping into her voice.

The two little faces looked up at her with identical fathomless expressions.

'Do you think, as we've been *very* good, we might stay up a little longer?' Micky asked.

So that explained why they were so

quiet. Jenny smiled and shook her head.

'I'm afraid not tonight, darlings, because your mother's coming home, and I'm sure she'll expect to find you all tucked up in your beds when she comes to say good night. Tomorrow you can have an extra half-hour.'

Marie jumped to her feet and stood defiantly in front of her new governess.

'But tomorrow night isn't the same!' she cried, her voice tense and shrill. 'It's got to be tonight. And Mummy doesn't come to say good night to us, anyway.'

Jenny felt very perplexed. Was this just rank disobedience or was there something more behind it? There was such a wealth of feeling in Marie's voice that she could not imagine it to be just a mere whim.

'Why don't you want to go to bed, Marie?' she asked the child curiously.

Marie shot a quick look at her twin and Micky gave an almost imperceptible shake of his head.

Their mouths set in thin, stubborn lines of silence.

Jenny put an arm round the little girl and drew the stiff small body against her own.

'Come, Marie, you can tell me,' she said. 'You can trust me, you know. I could keep a secret. What is wrong?'

'You're not to tell her!'

Micky's voice rapped out, forbidding and definite.

Suddenly the small body relaxed and to Jenny's consternation the child burst into tears.

'Marie!' she said. 'Tell me what it is. Are you frightened of the dark? Is that it? You needn't be ashamed to tell me if it is.'

The child continued to sob piteously and Jenny turned to Micky.

'Is that it, Micky?' she asked gently. 'Why don't you want to tell me? I shouldn't laugh at you. I wouldn't tell anyone.'

He gave her a long, calculating stare. His voice was very quiet and strangely adult as he said:

'Well, what if we are frightened? It isn't any good, is it? We have to go to bed sooner or later.'

'But, Micky, you weren't frightened last night, were you?'

'No-oo...not last night,' Micky admitted, his eyes averting her gaze.

'Then why tonight?'

'We can't tell you. We just are!' was Micky's comment, in a tone so final that Jenny knew it was no good pursuing the question.

'Do you want to tell me what you're frightened of?' she asked him. 'You don't have to if you don't want to, but I might be able to stop it—to find out what it was and explain it to you. There isn't anything to be afraid of, you know.'

Neither of them spoke. The only sound in the room was Marie's sobbing, now quiet and infinitely hopeless.

'Look!' Jenny tried again. 'Suppose I gave you a nightlight?'

Micky shook his head.

'Miss Simkins wanted us to have a night-light but Mummy said no. She said we were grown-up now and not babies any more and it was pamping us.'

'Pampering you,' Jenny corrected automatically, while she was thinking.

'I can't belittle her authority by going over her head!' But mentally she resolved to take it up with Lady Barclay at the first opportunity. It was sheer cruelty to deny these two small infants the comfort that a little ray of light would give them. As to their being grown-up, they weren't, and even then, there were plenty of adults in the world who were afraid of the dark. It was absurdly old-fashioned to treat them in such a way. Something had frightened the twins and their fear, however unfounded, was very genuine to them. She would insist on a night-light. If she were going to look after these children then she wanted complete authority. Indeed, Lady Barclay had made it quite clear that she was to have it, and to keep the children out of her way.

'Perhaps when I ask Mummy she will agree to your having one,' Jenny told the children, but their response was negligible. 'And as for tonight, suppose I promise to look in on you after supper and sit with you both till you fall asleep?'

Marie turned a radiant tear-stained face to Jenny and flung her arms round her neck.

'Oh, would you? Would you really?' she asked.

'And before *you* go to bed?' Micky asked, jumping up and leaning against her knee. 'You don't go to bed till awfully late, do you? By then it would almost be morning....'

'I promise,' Jenny said, and her heart twisted at the enormous sighs of relief that came from them both.

From that moment they were as docile and manageable as anyone could have wished. Within half an hour they were sitting up in bed, rosy and warm from their baths, eagerly attacking their trays of milk and biscuits.

Jenny left them eating like two young lions at the Zoo whilst she went to her room to change.

One of the maids had informed her that a long frock would not be worn as Lady

Barclay would be arriving so late, so Jenny chose another of her new dresses—this time a plain but smart black wool with which she wore a triple row of imitation pearls. No doubt Lady Barclay would notice that the pearls weren't real, Jenny thought with a wry smile, but anyway, a governess wasn't expected to have real jewellery, and she was otherwise simply dressed in a way to which her employer could not possibly object.

She looked very young in the sophisticated frock, but she wore it well and was reassured by the knowledge that it was one of the most expensive in her new wardrobe. She felt in need of 'bolstering', for in spite of herself she was a little in awe of Lady Barclay.

She called in to tuck the children up for the night and on a sudden impulse left the communicating door to the day nursery open and one of the lights in it full on. The shaft of light fell across the little twins beds, and even while she doubted that Lady Barclay would approve of this substitute for the forbidden night-light, she knew that it was worth any reproof she might receive when she heard the two little voices say:

'Oh, thank you, Jamie!'

'That's absolutely smashing!'

She kissed them both good night and

closing the door went out to the long gallery and made her way downstairs.

Lady Barclay was in the drawing-room with her son when Jenny opened the door and joined them. They broke off their conversation immediately, and Jenny had the feeling that she had intruded on some private discussion at an inopportune moment.

Derek, however, hastened over to her side and drew her into the room with a smile of friendliness.

'Well, Mother,' he said, 'you seem to have hit the jackpot all right when you engaged Miss Ames. Father must be taken with her because he has insisted she join us for dinner tonight; Amelia has promised to let Jenny do something about her hair, the twins are her ardent slaves and I'm quite overcome!'

He linked his arm through Lady Barclay's and at the same time offered Jenny a drink from the silver tray of cocktails on the table by their side.

'Good evening, Miss Ames!' Lady Barclay said, a faint smile crossing her face for a moment. 'I'm glad to hear you've won the household over so soon. It'll be a great relief if you can do something with Amelia. She looks such a ghastly mess as a rule, I despair of introducing her to my guests.

And no doubt if the twins have taken to you they'll be much more manageable. Maybe your youth will turn out to be an advantage after all, although I must admit it gave me some doubt when I considered giving you the post.'

'Nonsense, Mother-Mine!' Derek said. 'Miss Ames' youth is in itself but another qualification.'

Lady Barclay shot him a quick look of suspicion which Jenny could not possibly have misinterpreted. She felt her face redden and was relieved when Lady Barclay gave a quick little laugh and said:

'Oh, well! No doubt you know best, my dear. I'm sure you're a very competent judge.' She turned to Jenny and asked graciously but without any real interest: 'And how are you settling down, Miss Ames? Do you think you'll enjoy being here?'

'Very much indeed, thank you,' Jenny answered. 'I'm more than comfortable and I've quite settled down already.'

'Good!' was Lady Barclay's disinterested reply. 'Now perhaps you would be so good as to try and find Amelia. She's sure to be late for dinner and to arrive looking a sight. I really cannot stand having that child sitting near me at table much longer. There's another ten minutes before Robert rings the gong. See what you can do.'

An excuse to be rid of me? Jenny wondered, and then, as she left the room obediently, she gave herself a wry smile. Well, she was an employee now, and it was Lady Barclay's privilege to order her about.

Amelia was in her room when Jenny knocked, and as she bade her come in Jenny saw that she was near to tears in a hopeless effort to untangle her long hair.

'I came to see if you were ready,' Jenny explained. 'Here, let me do that for you. I love doing people's hair. Do you mind?'

'No! Thank you!' Amelia said gratefully, passing the comb to Jenny. 'Has...has Mother come?'

'Yes, she's in the drawing-room with your brother.'

'Oh, with Derek!' Amelia's voice was full of relief as if she were now, at any rate, safe from her mother's comments.

Skilfully, Jenny unravelled the knots and, then, seeing that Amelia really had a beautifully shaped face she swiftly plaited the long hair and twisted it into two braids round the girl's head. The result was quite transforming. Except for the shiny nose Amelia looked almost a young woman.

'Now, isn't that nice?' Jenny asked, admiring her own work.

Amelia's doubtful expression changed

into a slow smile as she surveyed herself in the glass.

'Why, I think it does look better! Yes, it really suits me! Oh, thank you, Miss Ames! You *are* kind.'

'Suppose you call me Jennifer when we're alone like this,' Jenny suggested. 'After all, I'm not so *very* much older than you are and we might be friends.'

The girl's response was immediate.

'Oh, I'd love that. You see, the twins are really much too young to talk to seriously, and Derek...well, it's not like having a woman to talk to and do things with. May I really call you Jennifer?'

'I don't see any reason why not,' Jenny said, 'unless you think your mother might object.'

Amelia's face fell.

'Perhaps she mightn't like it,' she said with childish honesty. 'All the same, when we're alone—'

'Well, that's settled then,' said Jenny. 'Now stand up and let's have a look at you.'

A touch of powder and the briefest outline of lipstick, a twist here and there to Amelia's plain grey wool frock, and she really looked quite charming.

'Haven't you any jewellery?' Jenny asked. 'A necklace?'

Amelia looked surprised.

'Well, yes, though I don't often wear it.'

She unlocked a little drawer in her dressing-table and pulled out a jewel case for Jenny's inspection. Jenny gasped.

On the velvet beds lay jewels of priceless worth—emeralds, rubies, diamonds which many women would have given their souls to possess. Among them was an emerald-and-diamond necklace with ear-rings and brooch to match. A set worth thousands of pounds.

'But...how magnificent!' Jenny cried.

Amelia looked pleased.

'Yes, aren't they? They belonged to Mummy. Father gave them all to me when...when she died. When he married again he said I was to keep them, and he bought new ones for my stepmother. He loved my mother very much, Miss...Jennifer. I don't think he really would have married again except that there wasn't a real heir. I mean I was a girl and didn't count. Besides, he always believed that great wealth and estates and things could only be a disadvantage to a woman. So Derek was to be his heir, though of course he couldn't inherit the title. At least, I think it was always Father's hope that one day he'd have a son of his own. Then of course Micky was born and he was terribly pleased. You'd have thought he would have spoiled Micky dreadfully, wouldn't you, and left poor little Marie out of it? But do you know, I really think he's just as fond of Marie.' Amelia gave a happy little laugh. 'I think perhaps Father likes *me* best of all because I'm the only one that looks like him, although he says sometimes that I look like Mummy—my real mother, that is.'

Her voice softened as she spoke of her dead mother, and Jenny listened in silence. It seemed as if the girl had had these thoughts penned up in her mind and welcomed this opportunity to express them to a confidante. They were very personal, and yet surely it could not matter her, Jenny's, hearing them? They were safe with her.

'But I'm not really like Mummy,' Amelia was adding. 'She was very lovely. In a funny way you remind me of her. She was soft and sweet and kind, like you, I think; I was only a baby when she died but Father's told me all about her.'

She fell silent and Jenny felt the sense of loss which the thought of her mother gave Amelia. She looked quickly into the jewel case and drew out a necklace of well-matched corals.

'Oh, Amelia, this would look perfectly sweet with your grey dress. May I put it on?'

Amelia nodded; the corals did in fact improve the *ensemble*.

'Finishing touches are so important!' Jenny said with a smile. 'And now I think I hear the gong.'

Lady Barclay and her son were moving towards the dining-room as Jenny and Amelia descended the stairs and they all met in the hall. Jenny felt the girl's hand tighten about her own and wondered.

Lady Barclay looked her step-daughter up and down, and the slight frown on her face vanished. Her voice was quite kind as she said:

'Well, you really do look presentable for once, Amelia,' and turning, went into the dining-room on Derek's arm.

Jenny felt her face flush in sudden anger. She might so easily have left out that last barb. No wonder Amelia suffered from an inferiority complex! In that moment she was certain that she was not going to like Lady Barclay.

Amelia's face, however, was radiant.

'Oh, thank you, thank you for helping me!' she whispered, and pulled Jenny forward into the dining-room with quick, eager steps.

Her face soon fell, however, when she observed that her father's chair was empty. She cast nervous glances around the room as if she hoped to find him amongst the shadows that lay outside the circle of candlelight on the polished table.

'He's sure to be late,' Jenny heard her anxious whisper.

'Shall I go and find him?' Jenny asked, puzzled by the girl's anxiety. But Amelia shook her head, and they sat down.

Derek soon drew Jenny into the conversation, which was about some show in London, and he and Lady Barclay seemed unaware of Amelia's distraught silence.

Jenny sensed the girl's tension and wondered if everyone in this house suffered these nervous undercurrents. She was soon to understand, however, the reason for Amelia's anxiety. Shortly before the sweet was served Sir Gerald appeared in an old tweed coat and a pair of riding breeches.

'Sorry, my dear!' he mumbled. 'Didn't realize it was so late!'

For a moment no one spoke as he took his chair at the head of the immense table and the butler served his soup. Then Lady Barclay said in an icy voice:

'I do think you might have a few manners, Gerald. It's really quite unforgivable on my first night home. You must have heard the gong. I consider your behaviour quite insulting.'

The baronet continued to suck in his

soup. Between mouthfuls he mumbled:

'Very sorry; really most apologetic. In the library.'

'That's no excuse!' Lady Barclay's voice was now shrill with unconcealed irritation. 'If you must choose to annoy me, at least you might show a little consideration for your guests. I understand it *was* you who invited Miss Ames to join us tonight.'

'Please, really, I don't—' Jenny gasped in an agony of embarrassment at being drawn into this marital upset. Really, Lady Barclay ought not to talk to her husband like that in front of the butler, Amelia and herself.

'Did you invite her or didn't you?' Lady Barclay broke in on Jenny's words.

Sir Gerald raised his head then and gave Jenny a sheepish smile which was half apologetic, half conspiratorial. It might have been Micky it was so ingenuous.

'Of course I invited you, Miss...er... Ames. Yes, indeed I did. You must excuse me. Getting rather deaf in my old age. Never heard the gong.'

Jenny smiled back at him, and heard Lady Barclay give an annoyed 'Tch!' and saw her toss her head. She was white with anger, and for a moment Jenny was really afraid she might lose all control. No doubt she was even more aggravated because her husband had apologized to the governess and omitted to do so with the same good grace to his wife!

'Before Father interrupted, you were telling me about the party last Saturday,' Derek broke in, tactfully regaining his mother's attention. 'Do finish the story. I was so interested.'

Jenny saw Lady Barclay's face soften as she looked at her son. In that moment she looked almost beautiful. The thin line of her lips, so carefully painted, curved into a smile. Her whole expression seemed to alter—to become gentle and adoring.

'She really loves her son, whoever else she doesn't love!' Jenny thought.

Then to her relief the sweet, now finished, was cleared away and Lady Barclay announced that they would have coffee in the drawing-room.

'Are you sure you won't mind being left,' she asked her husband icily.

'No, indeed!' he replied quite cheerfully. 'Amelia will sit and talk to me—won't you, my dear?'

Amelia gave her mother a swift pleading look, then went quickly round the table to her father's chair. With a shrug of her shoulders Lady Barclay again took Derek's arm and went quickly out of the room.

Jenny sensed her employer's relief when she excused herself from coffee, saying she had things she wished to do upstairs. No doubt, she thought, as she climbed the stairs to the gallery, she is pleased to have Derek all to herself again. A strange woman! Beautiful in a hard way, but I don't like her. I just don't!

True to her word, she looked in on the twins, who were almost asleep. She sat between them, lost deep in thought, until she was quite certain that they would not wake again, and then she tiptoed through the nursery, turned off the light and went quickly along the gallery to her room.

So it was still quite early, Jenny thought, but she was tired, suddenly and unreasonably tired.

'I'll go to bed!' she told herself. 'I could do with an early night.'

When at last she turned off the light and lay back against the soft pillows, it was to Peter that her thoughts turned. She fell asleep picturing him in her mind as he sat alone in his studio painting some picture and thinking of her. And in her sleep she smiled.

CHAPTER VI

That first sleep was so deep that it was some few minutes before Jenny became aware of the muffled screams from beyond her door. She sat up quickly, rubbing her eyes, trying to force herself back to full consciousness.

When at last she realized that she was not dreaming, that the children were crying, she sprang out of bed and, pulling her dressing-gown quickly over her shoulders, opened her door and raced out of her room along the gallery.

It was almost pitch dark. At the far end of the gallery a shaft of bright moonlight shone through a latticed window and Jenny's heart gave a sickening lurch and a cold shiver ran up her spine. She stopped dead in her tracks. A shadow crossed that moonlit patch, a dark unrecognizable shadow, moving swiftly into the concealing darkness beyond.

Its very swiftness seemed unearthly and in that terrified second Jenny wondered if indeed she had seen a ghost. Then, as suddenly, fear receded and a desire to *know* took the upper hand. Without further hesitation she ran swiftly after the shadow, passing the night nursery, from whence came the now low sobbing of the twins—a dreadful, hopeless, utterly uncontrolled sound of sheer terror.

She was past the door in a flash and into the patch of moonlight, where she stood still, able to see to the end of the gallery, and to note that there was nothing there...only the closed swing-door shutting off the servants' staircase that led to the floors above and below. Again a shiver crept over Jenny and she found that she was trembling. With almost forced courage she walked towards the door and opened it. It was almost a relief to find the little stone passage and staircase deserted.

Jenny frowned, beginning to doubt now the fact that she had really seen that ghostly figure. Surely she had imagined it?

She let the door swing to behind her and stood at the end of the gallery. Immediately on her right was Amelia's bedroom. The door was closed and no sound came from it. Was it possible that the girl had not been awakened by the crying of the twins? Hardly! Jenny thought, since she herself had been roused from a deep sleep at the other end of the gallery. She hesitated outside Amelia's door, wondering whether to knock and go in.

Then she decided against it. Tomorrow would do to question Amelia.

On her left was the door to the day nursery and beyond the door to the twins' bedroom. Between them and her own room was one of the enormous double spare rooms. At the end of the corridor lay her own room, then Sir Gerald and Lady Barclay's suite, and their private bathroom. On the floor above, which Jenny had not yet seen, she knew that Derek slept and had also his own sitting-room; there were other spare rooms and bathrooms and linen cupboards. In a separate wing lay the servants' quarters.

'Could one of the maids have come down the back staircase and in through the swing-door to the children's room?' Jenny asked herself, her mind racing. 'And yet if so, for what reason? What point could they have in coming here? Theft? But there is little or nothing to steal from the twins! A practical joke?'

She rejected the idea instantly. All the servants were middle-aged, staid, stolid retainers like Mrs Minnow, whom she imagined had been with the Barclays for years. They were not the type to play practical jokes—to 'take liberties', as no doubt they would put it. They were of the old-fashioned, faithful domestic types to whom the new socialist outlook was as unwelcome as it was impossible in a household like this. And Lady Barclay was not the type herself to stand any familiarity or impertinence from her staff.

These reflections flashed through Jenny's mind in the space of a few minutes. Then she ran quickly to the twins' room and opened the door, switching on the light.

Two pale, tear-stained faces gazed at her in a moment's abject terror.

'What,' Jenny asked herself, 'did they expect to see?'

Then they were out of bed, throwing themselves upon her, hugging her and crying incoherently.

She pulled them gently but firmly back to their beds and tucked them in together side by side, wrapping the warm bed-clothes round their shivering little frames. Slowly their tears dried. At last very gently she was able to question them.

'What was the matter, darlings? What frightened you? Tell Jenny. She'll soon scare away whoever it was.'

Their faces relaxed a little but the strange, remote look of fear came back into their faces. Neither spoke.

Jenny looked from one to the other feeling hopelessly in the dark. There was something here she did not understand. Under normal circumstances a child would gabble out the truth—a bad dream, a ghost, a bogy...but it was as though *these* two children were too frightened to speak.

She sat down beside them and cuddled them close to her.

'Come, darlings, tell me all about it,' she said gently. 'Did you have bad dreams?'

The twins looked at one another, and Jenny was again aware of that almost imperceptible nod that passed between them. It reminded her (ludicrously in view of the circumstances) of two dogs she had once had as a child. For no apparent reason they would look at one another from where they had been lying dozing through an afternoon, and with no further passage of canine words that were audible to a human being would rise slowly to their feet and the next she saw of them was of two wagging tails before they disappeared through a hole in the hedge on one of the forbidden hunting expeditions. Often Jenny had wondered how such perfect understanding flashed from one to another without more than a look. She had pondered about some canine sixth sense not known to humans. And now it was the same between these two children. Did the fact that they were twins give them some kind of telepathic understanding? Were they identical twins? she wondered.

'Yes, yes, we had a bad dream,' Micky

was saying. And Marie echoed him, 'Ever such an awful bad dream, Jamie!'

'They're lying,' was Jenny's immediate suspicion, but then doubt set in. Suppose they were identical twins? Wouldn't it be possible for them to dream alike as their thoughts in conscious moments were twin paths running in the same grooves? Who was she with her little knowledge on such subjects to stand as their judge? Besides, what did it matter beside their fear?

'Tell me about it?' she suggested. 'Perhaps that will make it better.'

But they shook their heads and she did not force their confidence. After all, she told herself, she had only been here forty-eight hours. She could not expect them to trust her fully yet. She must win their complete confidence first and then they would be open with her in all their dealings.

'Better now?' she asked them. 'You ought to go to sleep again.'

Marie's grip on Jenny's arm tightened.

'You won't leave us, will you?' she asked, her small voice strained and pathetic in its appeal.

Jenny hesitated. Would this be spoiling them—creating a precedent?

Micky sensed her hesitation. He said:

'Please, Jamie, please!'

She capitulated. There would be plenty

of time later to get to the bottom of this mystery, and if anyone were frightening them it was better that she should stay.

'All right!' she said. 'You and Marie can sleep together and I'll sleep in Marie's bed. I'll just run along and get my clock. I shan't be long.'

Two white faces stared at her distrustfully.

'*Promise* you'll come back?' Marie said insistently.

Jenny smiled.

'But of course I will, Marie. You don't think I'd break my word, do you?'

'Cross your heart and cut your throat?' Micky put in swiftly.

Jenny did as she was bid. How anxious they were! How frightened still! Could this be what Mrs Minnow called 'one of their tantrums'? If so, it was time someone with a few modern ideas took over their care. With fear such as this—and Jenny knew that it was not pretended—punishments would have no effect.

Closing their door behind her she went swiftly along the gallery which was still plunged in darkness.

'I'll get a torch tomorrow!' she thought with a wry grin. She was not really frightened and yet nevertheless she was glad when she reached the comparative safety of her own room. Hastily she found her clock and switching off her own light plunged once more into the darkness of the hall.

She had moved but a few paces when she heard footsteps. This time she felt the blood congeal in her veins and goose pimples cover her flesh. She felt an insane desire to rush back into her room...or else race along to the twins' room, but she didn't move. The footsteps were coming nearer, descending the big staircase, she thought, as her heart pounded suffocatingly in her throat.

Then a light flashed in her eyes, blinding her, and as she felt that she must indeed faint in sheer terror a voice said almost in her ear:

'So it's you, Jennifer! I wondered who was creeping about.'

She let out a long-drawn sigh of relief.

'Oh, Derek!' she gasped. 'How you frightened me! I've never been so glad to see anyone in my life before!'

'Hey, steady up,' he said, taking her arm, his voice slightly mocking but with amused sympathy. 'Why, you're trembling! Poor Jenny! What's frightened you so much?'

Reaction had set in, and Jenny was trembling violently. She gave a nervous laugh.

'It was you...your footsteps. I don't know what I thought.'

'Surely I didn't wake you up?' Derek said. 'Or did you hear the twins, too?'

Jenny nodded. It was ridiculous but she had never been so thankful to see anyone in her whole life.

'I came down to see what was up,' Derek said. 'Are they all right?'

'They're very frightened. I've promised to sleep the rest of the night with them.'

Derek laughed. It was a very reassuring sound in the darkness of the passage, for he had put out the torch as soon as he had recognized her.

'Hardly seems as if you're going to be much consolation to them! Why, I think you're more frightened than they are, my sweet.'

She felt the blood rush to her face and was suddenly glad that the darkness hid her blushes. She was very aware now of his nearness, of his arm round her shoulder, although she had not noticed when he placed it there, and of the casual endearment 'my sweet'.

'I—I ought to go to them. I promised,' she said weakly, trying to draw away from him.

'No, wait a minute!' Derek said. 'You're in no state to go to them yet. You'll only frighten them more. You know what kids are. They always sense your feelings—especially the twins. I'll swear they have some instinct no one else has got. They're much too highly strung. Comes of being born of old parents, I dare say....' Then he added with a laugh: 'Not that the Mater would approve of that remark. Still, she was in her forties.'

Although his words were unimportant the sound of his voice steadied her. How stupid she had been to give way to fright in such a manner! It was coming on top of the twins' fear, she supposed. She might have known someone else would have heard them and come to see what was the matter.

'Here, let's sit down a minute,' Derek was saying. 'There's a window-seat at the other end of the gallery and we shall be able to see each other.'

'Really, I think I should—'

'Now, no arguments,' Derek said authoritatively. 'A few minutes won't hurt and I expect you could do with a cigarette!'

Jenny gave in. Derek seemed to understand exactly how she felt, and she did need that cigarette, badly.

She allowed him to lead her along the gallery to the window through which the moonlight still streamed. As they walked through it she was tempted to tell him what she had imagined she had seen on this same spot a few minutes ago. But she thought better of it. Derek would think her a stupid, fanciful girl utterly unsuited for the care of two highly strung children. For all she knew he might report the whole scene to his mother, who had already stated that she thought Jenny too young for the post. And in spite of all that had happened she wanted to stay here. It was like a challenge. It seemed as if the house, Derek, the twins...were all saying to her, 'Don't you dare stay now you know us!'

As if reading her thoughts—in part anyway—Derek said as he offered her a cigarette.

'I hope this won't put you off staying here, Jennifer. We should all hate to lose you now—even although you have only been with us such a short time. Why, the Mater is really pleased with the results so far; Amelia has quite a schoolgirl crush on you, the twins adore you, my stepfather, as far as he is aware of anything, seems to like you, and as for myself, well, you've made all the difference to my life here.'

Her vanity could not but help being pleased by such praise. In a moment of weakness that she soon regretted she allowed herself to ask curiously:

'Why should it make any difference to you?'

He turned to her then, and in the moonlight she saw that his face was flushed and eager, boyish, even while there was still that faintly mocking glance from those incredible green eyes. She stared at them fascinated, unable to look away, even when his arm went round her pulling her against him.

'Don't you know, Jennifer, that you're terribly attractive?' he asked, his voice low and deep with a strange urgency. 'Last night you swept me right off my feet so that I *had* to kiss you, to risk your disapproval. You were wearing a blue dress, and you looked demure and young and utterly enchanting. This evening you were a different Jenny. You were a woman in black, fascinating, sophisticated, remote. And now...Jennifer, if you could see yourself, with your hair tumbling about that pale little face, your eyes exactly the colour of the dressing-gown you're wearing, still a little surprised from being woken so suddenly from your sleep. Jennifer...*Jenny*....'

She began to struggle then, but already his lips were on hers, bruising her mouth as they had done in the library last night, travelling down her cheek to her throat, to the smooth creamy skin where her dressing-gown had parted to reveal the delicate pink of her chiffon nightdress. She tried to pull the wrap around her, fought to push him away but with steadily weakening efforts. There was something about this man, about the way he made love, that stirred her even against her will to response. Every nerve in her body seemed to answer to his touch, to thrill to those wild, passionate kisses. Her heart was racing not with fear now, unless it were fear of the power he seemed to have over her. His hands were gripping her wrists, holding her arms prisoner so that she had no weapon with which to fight him, no protection against those deep, searching kisses.

'Jenny, Jenny,' he cried as he sought again for her lips, 'if you only knew how you drive me crazy with longing for you! Kiss me! Kiss me!'

He forced her head upwards so that she was again looking into those brilliant green eyes and this time his expression frightened her back to her senses. There was so much passion in them, so much fierceness and hunger and determination.

She brought up the hand he had freed and pushed fiercely against his chest.

'Let me go!' she breathed. 'Oh, please, let me go!'

'Not till you kiss me—one kiss!' Derek said hoarsely. 'One kiss will buy your freedom!'

She might have laughed at such dramatic words had the moment not been so fraught with uncontrolled passions, had she not known that every moment this man held her, she was weakening to his will. Peter, herself, convention—nothing seemed to matter any more except the man beside her.

She gave a deep sigh, capitulating suddenly, lifting her mouth to receive his kiss—to return it. For those few seconds the world stood still and she knew nothing but the swimming of her senses and the fierce pounding of her heart—or was it his?—against her breast.

Then he let her go and she ran from him while there was strength in her legs—ran to the twins' room, where with a superhuman effort she forced herself to calmness, to still the trembling of her limbs, and closing the door quickly behind her, knew the feeling that now, at last, she was safe.

For the remainder of that night Jenny had no rest at all. It was some time before the twins slept, but she was unable to find the same release. She lay in the darkness, her hands against her flushed cheeks, hating herself, hating Derek, wondering how she could ever face Peter again.

Twice in two days she had been disloyal to him. Oh, it was useless putting all blame on Derek Barclay. He was the cause, but she had a will of her own, and in this moment of complete honesty she admitted that she had not made best use of it. In spite of the loathing it gave her to see herself as she really was, Jenny knew now that she was a woman with passions as deep and demanding as Derek's. It had not seemed to matter that she was engaged to another man...that she loved him. Sheer primitive instincts had gained the upper hand of her, and even had she disliked Derek it would have made no difference. She was attracted to him physically, in a way that she had never believed to be possible. He had by his own uncontrolled desires aroused her to a sensualism that she had never experienced with Peter, even during the most intimate moments of love-making.

Did that explain it? she asked herself wearily. When one loved a man, did one's respect for him, one's affection and mental feelings, put a different construction on to it? Did it raise primitive feelings on to a different plane above the baseness of human nature? Or could it be that she didn't really love Peter after all?

'No, not that! That isn't true!' she told herself fiercely. 'I do love him. I always shall. I'm going to marry him.'

She knew that she still wanted to marry him...that was if she could ever again consider herself worthy of his love and devotion. She knew then that she hated Derek Barclay—hated him for making her dislike herself so intensely. What right had he to invade her privacy and cause this emotional crisis? She had been happy and contented with Peter. She hadn't wanted anyone else to come into her life and spoil everything.

But had it spoilt everything? Could she not forget it—forget Derek and those moments—put them behind her as if they had never been? Or would they make her dissatisfied now with Peter—with the man she really loved? Could she ever again react kindly to Peter's love-making—which was so kindly, so considerate, so guarded?

That's not true! she argued with herself. At times, Peter and I have wondered how we could bear to stay unmarried—the strain of wanting each other the way we were meant to want each other.

But never, said truth, had she felt like this before—never been so near to losing control as well as will-power, never had she known such frightening and ecstatic moments.

Oh, Peter, Peter! she thought. If only you were here now—here to hold me in your arms and comfort me and reassure me. It must be all right between us. It must! We love each other. That's all that matters.

But she was not reassured by her own words. As the dawn lightened the sky and came creeping through the partly curtained windows she was no nearer to answering her own questions. She only knew that she both feared and hated Derek Barclay; the more for the hold she knew now that he had over her—a hold she was not going to allow to continue, even if it meant giving up her post.

When at last the grandfather clock struck seven and she saw that the children were stirring, she slipped quietly from the room, and knowing sleep to be impossible bathed and dressed. Feeling refreshed she went out into the grounds for a brisk walk. In the bright autumn sunlight some of her complexities vanished. It was such a beautiful morning—fresh, sunny, crisp. Somewhere in the direction from whence the sun was rising, Peter lay, still asleep perhaps, Peter whom she loved; Peter who loved and trusted her.

She felt strangely close to him in that moment of solitude. It was almost as if last night had never been.

With sudden resolve, she determined to ask Lady Barclay that very morning if she might have the following week-end off. Today was Saturday...only eight more days and she could see Peter again—know that all was right between them. Because Peter was Peter she could tell him everything, and he would understand...explain everything to her.

She resolved, too, that no matter what happened, last night must never be repeated. If necessary she would say so outright to Derek Barclay—tell him that if he persisted she would have to go. When he realized that she meant it he would soon tire of her and leave her alone.

Jenny smiled, her natural resilience and good spirits coming again to the fore. Everything was going to be all right, she thought, and with an appetite that was completely unspoiled by lack of sleep she went in to have her breakfast with the twins.

As breakfast ended Amelia came in with a message from Lady Barclay. 'She would like to see you in the sitting-room as soon as you're ready, Jennifer,' she said, giving Jenny a friendly smile.

For a moment Jenny wondered guiltily whether Lady Barclay had learned of last night's escapade, and then she rejected the idea. No one knew of it but Derek and herself, and he would not be likely to tell his mother, who would most certainly be very angry.

'I'll just get the twins settled with some

sums and I'll be right down,' she said to Amelia. 'Will you wait for me?'

This would be an excellent opportunity for questioning Amelia as to whether she had heard anything last night. Derek was not so important in the cold grey light of dawn, but Jenny did intend to get to the bottom of the mystery and discover what had scared the twins.

Amelia admitted without hesitation that she had been woken by the screams of the twins.

'Then why didn't you go to them?' Jenny asked.

Amelia hung her head.

'I expect you'll think me a dreadful coward—and I suppose I am—as well as stupid. But...well...oh, Miss Ames—I mean Jennifer—we were all made to promise not to tell you in case you left, like Miss Simkins.'

Jenny gave the girl a quick look. So there was a mystery, after all!

'Well, seeing that I've already discovered part of it, don't you think you might tell me the whole?' she asked.

Amelia gave her a frightened look.

'Mother would be dreadfully cross...' Her voice trailed away.

'I believe she's afraid of her mother now,' Jenny thought. What a household of fears she had come to!

'Then I'll ask Lady Barclay myself,' Jenny said, not wishing to get the girl into trouble.'

'Oh, I shouldn't do that,' Amelia said quickly. 'She might be cross with you.'

Jenny smiled.

'Well, suppose she is. I'm living here now and I have a right to know what's happening in the house.'

Amelia looked both surprised and dubious and Jenny, herself, was not quite so confident as her words sounded. However, as soon as she was alone with Lady Barclay her courage returned. The worst this woman could do would be to give her notice, and although that would mean an end to Peter's and her plan to get the little house, it might in other ways be a good thing, she thought grimly.

Lady Barclay told her to be seated and immediately launched into details of a large house-party she was giving during the week-end.

'There'll be twenty guests,' she said with a sweep of her hand. 'Mrs Minnow has full instructions as regards the rooms and the food, but I'd like you to go round after her, checking the little details—ash-trays, flowers, and so on. She's too old to bother much now, I'm afraid. And I'd like you to do all the flowers. I really haven't time myself. Get Adams, the head gardener, to pick what you want. There'll be dancing in the sitting-room, writing-room and hall, so you might give those special attention. The library you needn't bother about. I dare say some of the men will retire there in dull groups and drink whiskey and smoke. Oh, see that there are plenty of ash-trays. And I shall want you to attend the dance and help receive the guests. Amelia is useless—she's far too shy and awkward, heaven knows! Show them their rooms and so on. And Amelia is to come to this dance. I've invited a young man especially for her. I want her to make a good impression as he's rich and it would be a good match.'

Jenny took advantage of this pause to say:

'Isn't Amelia a little young yet to—'

'Nonsense! It's time she acquired a few social graces. She's a bit young to be married of course, but I want to get her off as soon as possible. I don't see her making much success as a *débutante* and I'm not inclined to waste a lot of money on a season for her. If there's anything else I'll let you know.'

'And the twins' lessons?' Jenny asked, knowing that Lady Barclay had filled her morning already.

'They can be scrapped for today. After

all, it's the weekend. Well?' she asked as Jenny hesitated.

'There's just one thing,' Jenny said, taking her courage in both hands. 'Last night I was woken by the twins crying. As I went along to them I thought I saw someone in the gallery by the window.'

Lady Barclay shot her a quick glance.

'Well?' she said again, after a brief pause.

'Well, I feel I have a right to know what is going on,' Jenny said on a long breath. 'The twins were very frightened. I can't be expected to cure their fancies unless I know what had caused them.'

Lady Barclay appeared to hesitate and then abruptly made up her mind.

'I'm glad you said "fancies",' she informed Jenny. 'I hadn't meant to tell you because—you're young, and I thought you might be frightened. But it seems you're a girl with a little bit of sense. The Manor is supposed to be haunted. All rubbish of course. My son has been over the house from top to bottom, and there isn't a secret passage or a tomb or a anything in the least suspicious. We even had some members of psychic research down and they reported that the idea of a "haunt" in the gallery is unfounded. No one has actually seen a ghost. But the children, stupid little things, have picked up the servants' gossip and imagined they heard footsteps. Amelia is no better than the twins. As to what you saw, it must have been imagination...a curtain blowing across the window...a shadow. I can assure you, there is *no* ghost.'

'I see!' said Jenny. 'And is there a legend attached to the Manor that might have given rise to the servants' gossip?'

Lady Barclay gave her a quick, almost friendly look.

'Yes, it all started from some such silly story. Anyway, you can take my word for it that there is no truth in it whatever. In fact, no one has *seen* the ghost in living memory—except that absurd Miss Simkins, who was frightened out of her wits...purely a case of auto-suggestion.'

'Then there's nothing to worry about,' Jenny said, reassured now and already convinced that it must have been a curtain *she* had seen. 'But the fact remains, Lady Barclay, that the twins are seriously frightened. I would like your permission to allow them a night-light.'

For a moment Jenny's employer hesitated. Then with a graceful sweeping gesture of one of the red-tipped hands Lady Barclay said:

'It's up to you entirely, Miss Ames. I want the nonsense knocked out of them and I don't mind how you do it. I have faith in your ability and common sense. There's only one thing I will not permit, and that is that you should sleep with them. I consider that is coddling them too far.'

Did she know already of last night's events? Could Derek have told her?

'I'm afraid I did do that last night,' she admitted frankly. 'They were terrified out of their wits. After I had heard them screaming, I decided that it was the only thing that would get them to settle down again. I'm sorry if you disapprove.'

Lady Barclay had already turned away and was sorting some letters on a table beside her.

'You weren't to know, so it's not your fault, but I repeat, I would rather it did not happen again. Now, could you please run along and see how Mrs Minnow is progressing. There's a lot to be done.'

Jenny accepted her dismissal and left the room with a lighter heart. She had scored one point with the night-light and was greatly relieved that Lady Barclay knew nothing of her meeting with Derek last night; relieved, too, that her employer was not proving so difficult to deal with as she had feared.

CHAPTER VII

To Jenny's relief Amelia was in the schoolroom when she returned to the twins and hearing how busy Jenny would be, offered to take them out for a ride on their ponies. With the children out of the way, she was free to give all the time Lady Barclay required of her to check up on the finishing touches for tonight's party, and the household of guests who were due to arrive this afternoon.

She worked with a will, enjoying her task. It was, in spite of those moments' misgivings, the kind of job she had often thought about but never imagined herself lucky enough to land. She had a natural flair for floral decoration and it was perfectly wonderful, she decided, to be able to go round the greenhouses with Adams, ordering him to cut bunches of this and that, entirely according to her own tastes and regardless of the expense.

By lunch-time there were flowers in all the guest-rooms, and the downstairs rooms were a positive bower. Unrestricted, Jenny had spared no effort and had, consequently, achieved a magnificent effect. Huge vases and bowls of greenery and brilliantly hued chrysanthemums brightened the sombre panelling in the hall. Dark corners were transformed by great jars of Michaelmas daisies and autumn leaves. In the drawing-room Jenny had chosen a more formal decoration: carnations, toning carefully with exotic bowls of roses and the rarest varieties of dahlias.

With Lady Barclay's pleased consent she planned to spend the afternoon making shoulder sprays for all the women.

This she did between constant inter-ruptions as people arrived either in their own vehicle or in one of the Barclay cars which periodically, throughout the afternoon, went down to meet the London trains.

The majority of arrivals were from the same smart society set in which it was obvious to Jenny that Lady Barclay moved. The women wore faultless country tweeds and simple but extremely smart hats. They were beautifully coiffured and manicured and had the same 'hot-house' look of their hostess.

Jenny was a little amused by the number of 'darlings' that were thrown about like dust in all directions; by the waves of perfume and the carelessly worn jewellery, on lapels, round slim white necks; the startlingly bright lacquered fingertips. She wondered idly if any of these women had ever done a day's work in their lives—how, indeed, they managed to survive in the present-day world of heavy taxation.

She was not so amused, however, by the pasty, effeminate crowd of young men, who seemed bored and *blasé* and who all, without any hesitation, made for the nearest decanter regardless of the time of day. Was this the crowd from whom Derek Barclay chose friends? she asked herself scornfully. And yet, oddly enough, he did not seem to fit in with them entirely, despite a similarity of smart West-End tailored suits. Derek had strength of character, a strong personality which none of these others seemed to possess. Whether she liked him or not, she had to own that he was more *a man* in every sense of the word. In actual fact most of the male guests were several years older than himself. There was one exception, the rather pimply young man whom Jenny discovered was the *vis-à-vis* Lady Barclay had chosen for Amelia. He was painfully shy, very ill-at-ease, and obviously scared to death of his plump, bejewelled mother with dyed hair, who treated him in much the same way as she might have done a favourite poodle. Jenny felt sorry for him, and as she led him down the long gallery to his room she said impulsively:

'You've never met Miss Barclay before, have you?'

He blushed furiously and looked at her from eyes that reminded her of a frightened spaniel.

He shook his head.

'I think you'll like Amelia,' Jenny continued kindly. 'She's not glamorous in the strict sense of the word, but she's really awfully nice.'

He gave her a grateful look.

'I'm gl-glad she's n-not pretty!' he stammered. 'I mean—well, glamour girls rather scare me, I'm afraid. I s-say, is she awfully much older than m-m-ee?—the Mater didn't say.'

'I should think she's younger,' Jenny said with a smile, judging him to be about seventeen. 'She's really not at all grown up. And she's very shy.'

He looked almost happy.

'I—I s-say, is she? So am I! Perhaps we'll get along, after all.'

He lowered his voice and added confidentially:

'Frankly, I've been dreading this weekend. The Mater's dead keen on my making an impression on Miss Barclay. Quite honestly, I don't think I'm capable of making an impression on anybody. I don't like people very much, especially girls. You see, I only left school last term, so I don't

142

know much about them.'

Jenny knew then that she liked this young man—who told her that his name was the Honourable Charles Vagne. He was a typical public schoolboy with a nice voice and excellent manners and a sincerity lacked by most of the male guests. Whatever his mother might be like (Jenny fancied she was *nouveau-riche*), the son seemed a decent kind of lad. She was glad for Amelia's sake.

On a sudden impulse Jenny asked the stammering Charles if he would care to come along to the schoolroom and meet Amelia unofficially. The twins would be there too, she explained, and they could get over their mutual shyness unobserved by their respective parents.

Charles Vagne accepted with an eagerness Jenny found quite pathetic.

As she had imagined, Amelia was looking most untidy, although not unattractive in her Jodhpurs and polo-neck jersey. She was demonstrating to the twins some technicality of jumping by means of a nursery chair when Jenny and her young companion appeared. Amelia blushed furiously, but the twins rushed forward with questions.

'Who are you? Are you one of the people 'vited to the party? What are you doing here? Are you one of Derek's friends?'

It was only a matter of minutes before the young Charles, for he was only just past his eighteenth birthday, was quite at his ease with them, telling them he had a kid brother just their age and one a bit older; asking them about their ponies and admitting under their battery of questions that he had just won a jumping prize at the local gymkhana.

Then Amelia broke in, herself an enthusiastic rider, and Jenny finally left all four of them, sprawled on the thick, curly, black schoolroom rug, talking and laughing as though they were old friends. She only hoped that the more formal evening facing them would not undo all the good.

Mrs Minnow was enlisted to put the children to bed that night, for there was little time for Jenny to do more than bath and dress before cocktail time, at which she was to continue acting as part hostess. She was already exhausted, but after her bath she felt refreshed and more willing to undertake the evening's duties.

She managed to find ten minutes to help Amelia put the finishing touches to her appearance—braiding her hair again and persuading her to wear one of her more valuable necklaces with the pink tulle dress which Lady Barclay had ordered the child to wear. With one of Jenny's tiny sprays of pink rosebuds in her hair Amelia looked almost pretty.

'At least I *know* someone at the party now,' she said to Jenny as they walked down the wide stairs together. 'Charles has asked for the first dance and says he'll take me in to supper. You know, Miss Ames—I mean Jennifer—he's really awfully nice. He's fond of reading as well as riding, and I'm going to show him Father's library. I think Father will like him, too.'

Jenny nodded and smiled.

Charles was downstairs in the hall, obviously waiting for them. He gave them a wry grin and tugged at his collar. His young face was red and perspiring, his hair shining with brilliantine.

'This stiff shirt is the...end,' he said, clearly not liking to use the word 'devil' in front of ladies! 'Gosh, you do look nice, Amelia! I know I look a ghastly sight. I do so hate tails.'

Jenny left them together and went in search of Lady Barclay to see what else she could do to help. Her employer gave her an approving glance. Jenny wore an emerald green light wool dress embroidered with gold sequins. It had a full pleated skirt and a tight bodice glittering with sequins that did credit to her lovely figure. The governess certainly looked smart, thought Lady Barclay, without being too obtrusive. But the green wool frock fell into insignificance behind her ladyship's own daring dress—a recent purchase from Paris. It was oyster-grey satin, exquisitely cut, exposing one white shoulder. The skirt was narrow and draped at one side, in the very latest fashion. It clung so tight to her figure that every line showed—and to advantage. Lady Barclay had no doubts as to the magnificance of that figure for a woman of her age with three children. Diamonds sparkled round her long white neck and on her finger, and the greying hair, skilfully blued, was a smooth helmet round the white face with the brilliant slanting green eyes and scarlet mouth.

Jenny was forced into a murmur of admiration. Lady Barclay did indeed look 'stunning', as Peter might have described her. She was a Vogue cover—startling, different, exotic, and a diamond pin fastened to her belt the spray of palest mauve orchids which Jenny herself had made.

'You look charming, my dear,' Lady Barclay murmured. She was disposed to be gracious to Jenny, knowing she could afford some praise. The girl had done magnificently today. The house looked superb and the guests had all remarked on the little additional comforts in their rooms and questioned Lady Barclay as to who her new 'little find' might be. Yes, Miss Ames was proving her worth, Lady Barclay told herself, and was more than ever delighted when she learned that Amelia and Charles were, safely and surprisingly, paired off through Jenny's tactful behaviour.

'I want you to enjoy yourself too,' she added with mixed kindness. (It would pay her to see the girl enjoyed her job...she would be more likely to remain.) 'I'm sure my son will want to dance with you, and I would like you to consider yourself one of my guests tonight.'

Jenny gave a little bow but mentally decided that she would not give Derek a chance to dance with her. As soon as supper was over and she could decently do so, she intended to slip quietly off to bed.

The buffet dinner, however, laid out on the long table in the dining-room and perfectly served by the butler and maids, did not commence until nearly eleven o'clock. By that time a considerable amount of drink had been consumed, and the party was in full swing. The band—specially brought down from London for the evening—was playing enthusiastically for couples who were dancing languorously in true night-club style. Tired of watching them, Jenny decided to slip up to the twins' room to make sure they were asleep before supper was announced. At that moment, however, she saw Derek at close quarters for the first time that evening. He was coming across the brightly lit room towards her.

Without deliberately cutting him she had no choice but to wait for his arrival.

He looked very distinguished in his 'tails'—very attractive she was forced to admit as he moved towards her. His perfectly cut evening clothes showed off his physique to best advantage. He had inherited his mother's height and slenderness, and like her he wore his clothes so that they seemed moulded to him. Not many men here tonight looked as casually yet perfectly turned out as Derek. He wore a white carnation in his buttonhole.

For a brief second Jenny thought of Peter, who loathed evening clothes as much as poor Charles Vagne....Peter always looked hot and flustered and a little too 'square' in them. He was at his best in flannels—sports attire, or riding kit. How different they were, she reflected in that moment, without being aware that she was comparing the two men—Peter and Derek.

Then Derek was beside her, saying:

'Not dancing, Miss Ames?' in that amused, mocking voice of his. He swept her a bow. 'Then please may I have the pleasure?'

Jenny flushed a little under his long, deep gaze. It seemed as if those penetrating green eyes pierced through her—through to *her fear of him;* and she wonderd if he was aware of the pounding of her heart.

'I was just going up to see if the twins were all right,' she said firmly, taking a grip on herself. 'Perhaps later.'

'Never put off until later what can be done at once,' Derek said, misquoting shamefully. His face softened and he put a hand lightly on her arm and pleaded: 'Oh, come on, Jenny. Don't be so hard on a chap. I'm truly sorry about last night, you know I am. It isn't fair to hold it against me. You were as much to blame as I was, and you know it. Besides, you shouldn't have been so damnably attractive.'

'Really, I've no—'

'No desire to hear all this!' Derek broke in, imitating her voice exactly. 'Now, Jennifer, be honest. Admit that as a woman you must be a little vain, and therefore a little pleased with some flattery. And anyway, even if you don't give a tinker's cuss for me there's no reason to spoil my whole evening by refusing me one dance. In fact'—he gave her an impish grin which again reminded her of Micky—'my fond mamma ordered me to dance with you.'

Suddenly Jenny smiled. She really was being a little absurd. And why be frightened of him in this crowded room, where Lady Barclay would probably be watching them along with dozens of others? And Derek was trying to be friendly. It would give him much less satisfaction if she appeared not to mind whether she danced with him or not, than if she flatly refused, thereby admitting a fear of him.

Before she could change her mind Derek had put his arm round her and was leading her out on the floor as the band started a samba. She tried to pull away then, saying quickly:

'I can't samba. Let's wait till the next one. Please.'

But he didn't appear to be listening and his hold on her tightened, and almost before she was aware of it she had drifted into the dance with him, following him as if she had been his partner in some dancing contest.

He danced superbly, his lead so strong that she could not help but follow. The samba over they drifted into a tango. Now with the beating of drums, gradually she relaxed, gave herself up to the pleasure of the intoxicating rhythm. She did not often have the chance to dance, and

Peter wasn't any good at it anyway. She had been tremendously keen once, and now all her passion for it returned. She realized that she was lucky that her steps matched Derek's so effortlessly. He was as smooth and easy to follow as a professional partner.

Awareness of the people around them—of Derek's own identity and hers—faded as they glided along to the haunting melody. It was a sad, lovely tune, and as she closed her eyes she glided in a kind of dream such as only born dancers understand.

When at last the music ceased and their feet halted as one, they stood for a moment in silence; Jenny's eyes were still closed and she was unaware of Derek's gaze on her rapt young face. She knew nothing of her strong attraction for him in that moment with her flushed cheeks, her red parted lips, her breath coming in swift sighs. His eyes narrowed suddenly, and he bit his lips. He knew that he longed to possess this girl in a way he had never before experienced with any other woman. There had been no lack of affairs in his life—and always they had been perfectly satisfactory. Conquests had been too easy for him, with his looks and charm, and all too soon he tired of the latest fancy, grew bored, and as time went on became almost immune to feminine charms.

And now this girl had come into his life. Jennifer Ames—a girl from a different set—an 'employee' his mother had chosen to be governess for the twins! He could almost laugh, remembering Miss Simkins and what, at the back of his mind, he had originally imagined Jenny would be. But when he had first seen her that afternoon in the nursery he had known the difference and felt her strange attraction. Later that evening he had known that he was seriously affected. Her very antagonism when he had kissed her in the library had only served to increase his interest, and to warn him to go more carefully. What had been just another 'girl' whom he had wanted to hold and kiss began to mean much more. He knew that he liked Jenny for herself—liked her strange prudery mixed with passion such as he had discovered in her last night in the gallery. There was something both virginal and yet fierce about her, and the combination had disturbed him more than he had intended or realized until this moment.

Now, holding her limp body in his arms, he knew that he was determined to get her—no matter what it cost him. His very impatience made him the more cautious, and when she opened her eyes and smiled up at him his face showed none of his violent inner feelings—only a friendly smile.

'That was perfect,' he said as he led her back to the doorway. 'And you dance the samba and the tango beautifully. I do hope you'll let me have a waltz later on.'

Some queer inner instinct warned Jenny to refuse. But she knew that she couldn't. She wanted to dance with him again—know a few more moments of such rare perfection. Derek personally had no part in it—he was only a dancing partner without whom she could not achieve her longing. Some other man might offer to dance with her but he would not be perfect. Such ecstasy could not be repeated.

'Maybe—a waltz—after supper,' she said briefly. 'Now I must go. I'll see you later—and...thank you.'

He stood watching her as she disappeared into the hall, reappeared again going swiftly up the wide staircase and along the gallery. Again her elusiveness fascinated him. He wanted to run after her—to pull her down on that seat where they had been last night at the end of the gallery, and kiss her as he had kissed her then.

Instead, he lit a cigarette and moved off slowly in search of Cynthia.... Perhaps if he showed enough interest in another girl Jenny might be a little jealous, he mused. Women were odd creatures. To Jenny's fiancé he never gave a thought.

To Jenny's relief the twins were sound

asleep, their little night-light burning cheerfully in the saucer of water on which she had placed it. She looked at the two rosy little faces with a sudden rush of tenderness. It was really surprising how fond of two children one could get in a matter of days, she thought. Perhaps it was a natural response to their own uncomplicated devotion. They had hugged her tightly when she kissed them good night, confessing themselves terribly happy because *she* had come to look after them. They loved her much more than Mrs Minnow—they had said—more than Mummy, too. Quickly correcting them Jenny could not but find it a little pathetic that they cared so little for their beautiful mother. It was hardly surprising, since Lady Barclay had not even been to see them since her return—nor sent for them. Too busy! Jenny reflected grimly. She did not deserve their love. All the same it was her duty to try and foster some filial affection whatever her private thoughts.

Tucking the bed-clothes a little closer round them, Jenny felt a sudden renewed pang of longing. If only Peter were here beside her at this moment; that these two children were their son and daughter! How proud—how happy they would both be!

She switched off the light and stood

silent in the darkness, her eyes closed in a sudden longing for Peter, who seemed so very far away. If only he could be here now—not to dance with her, perhaps, but so that they could steal away somewhere together, to talk, to tell one another how much they loved, wanted each other; to feel his lips on hers and return his kiss!

She did not realize that she imagined Derek's kiss from Peter's lips and her response a repetition of last night's.

With a resolve to write to Peter when she came up to bed, no matter how late it was, Jenny closed the night-nursery door and went slowly back downstairs.

Lady Barclay had been watching for her and called her over.

'There's not a sign of Amelia or that stupid Charles Vagne. See if you can find them. It's almost supper-time. They may be in the library with Sir Gerald. And if they are they're all to come out—Sir Gerald as well. It's high time he did his duty as host.'

She speaks of him as if he were a servant, thought Jenny, wondering how she was going to 'order Sir Gerald out of the library'—if he were there.

She hastened in that direction and knocked on the door.

As no one answered she opened it and saw the three of them—Amelia, Charles and Sir Gerald—squatting on the floor round a globe of the world, faces raised to hers with the expressions of children caught stealing jam.

Amelia gave a little laugh and jumped up. They all started talking at once.

'We thought it might be Mother!' Amelia said frankly.

'Thought it might be *my* mater,' put in Charles.

'Well, well, well!' came from Sir Gerald.

'We were having such fun,' said Amelia. 'Father was showing us where the *Amethyst* escaped. Charles is going to join the navy when he's of age, although his mother has forbidden it. Isn't it exciting!'

Jenny longed to sit down among them, seeing them suddenly as an oasis, cool and refreshing, amongst the smoky, drinking crowd and the noise in the reception-room. In here it was cool and dim and strangely happy. She hated having to break the little party up.

'Lady Barcaly sent me to tell you all it's supper-time—or nearly,' she told them, her voice apologetic.

'Gosh, I'm hungry,' said Amelia, and Charles nodded his assent.

'Dare say she wants me to do a few duty dances, too,' said Sir Gerald with a sigh, and gained his feet and smoothed his hair.

'Oh well, better get it over and done with!'

The strains of a waltz drifted from the band, and Charles suggested that he might attempt it with Amelia.

'About the only thing I can do,' he said ruefully.

'Me too,' she agreed. They went off happily together. Sir Gerald turned to Jenny.

'Pleasure before duty,' he said. 'What about this one with me, my dear?'

He danced surprisingly well; Jenny found him most amusing—enjoyed his short gruff comments on his guests. He was only serious once—when he spoke of his daughter.

'By the way, my Amelia is very glad you've come to live with us,' he said. 'Very fond of you! Good girl really, for all her stepmother says....must have a talk sometime, you and I, eh?'

'Having a good time, Father?' Derek's voice broke in as he danced past with a dark-haired girl who wore a flame-coloured velvet dress. She was held tightly against him, his cheek pressed close to hers.

'Beastly American habit,' said Sir Gerald with a sigh as he negotiated another turn. 'Odd girl, Cynthia!'

Jenny looked after the couple with a queer pang. How startling that girl looked with her raven-black hair and red, strapless dress! Her lip-rouge was a scarlet gash across her white haggard young face; she was incredibly thin. The effect both fascinated and repelled Jenny. She wonderd who the girl was, and then recalled with a flash of insight that this Cynthia was *Derek Barclay's fiancée.* So *that* was the girl he was going to marry? Or would he marry her in the end? Judging by the way he danced with her it looked a serious affair. But then, that might be just 'their way'. Typical of the rest of the party, some of the couples sat around in corners or on the stairs, holding hands, making light love to each other irrespective of onlookers.

Jenny tried to give her attention to the waltz but her mind kept seeing those two dark heads so close together. Derek's and Cynthia's. Does she dance as well as I—better? She's far lovelier—and yet I wouldn't be her... Thoughts chased around in her mind. Then the couple passed her again and her heart jerked as she saw that across the girl's shoulder Derek was looking *at her,* his eyes seeming to mock her with their strange tantalizing greenness that caused her inexplicable fear.

She looked away without smiling and was glad when, with a roll of drums from the band, the butler announced that supper was ready and would the ladies and gentlemen proceed to the dining-room.

Jenny joined Charles and Amelia in a corner, spending a cheerful quarter of an hour with them while they all ate like kids on a school outing. Jenny did not realize she was so hungry—for she had eaten little lunch or tea in the general rush to get things done—until Charles heaped caviar and smoked salmon sandwiches and a variety of extravagant pastries on to her plate.

It was barely possible to talk above the noise in the room. Trays with glasses of champagne were passed round but Jenny and her two young companions had iced fruit-juice and coffee. Jenny had barely finished hers when Derek made his way through the crowd and stood beside them.

'How about that dance now, Miss Ames?' His voice was friendly, impersonal, correct. 'The floor isn't too crowded and we could try out a few steps.'

'Go on, Jennifer. He's a wonderful dancer,' said Amelia shyly.

Derek gave his young sister a brilliant smile and a mocking bow.

Rather than cause comment, Jenny could do nothing but accept the invitation.

In the reception-room, now entirely deserted, even by members of the band, who had gone to their own supper, a large radiogram was playing a soft rhythmic melody that she did not at once recognize.

' "Near you",' Derek said immediately. 'One of my favourites. Come on, Jenny, quickly.'

His arm went round her, and again Jenny felt the same spell upon her. But this time there was a difference. This time Derek's lips were against her hair, his deep voice humming softly against her ear, the words of the song searing into her mind. She knew he was quoting them *for her.* Her glance, sweeping quickly round the room, ascertained that there was no one there, and again she felt a nameless fear of this man—a fear that was closely bound up with some extraordinary attraction. His nearness set her heart pounding and she could not be sure if it was her own heart-beats or his, so close did he hold her. She felt it was useless to struggle against him—nor did she wish to as their two bodies moved in time to the music as if they were one. His hand was round her slim waist, burning through her dress until every nerve in her body trembled.

She felt that she could not bear the steadily mounting tension of this dance, and when at last the music ended she no longer had the strength to draw away from Derek's arms. He held her in silence, standing still and alone in the centre of the floor, and it seemed as if they were suspended in space in a timeless moment.

As her arm fell to her side his hand went under her chin, forcing her face upwards so that her eyes looked into his. She knew a moment's swift fear and then as his mouth came slowly down to hers awareness of herself, of him, of Peter, brought strength back to her whole being. With a gesture that was lightning-quick her free hand came up to his face and she struck him across the cheek.

His reaction was utterly unexpected. Instead of releasing her, his hold on her tightened and he gave a short, sharp laugh.

'Really, Jenny, that was hardly the gesture of a lady—and you know, my dear, it was very betraying,' he said.

And without another word he turned on his heel and walked quickly away, leaving her standing there, one hand against her mouth, her heart hammering wildly; she felt a hopeless uncontrollable desire to cry.

When she was certain he had really gone she slipped into the hall, up the stairs and into the welcome privacy of her bedroom.

But once she was alone she found that

the tears would not come. Sitting by the window staring out into the darkness of the night, there was nothing but a hard lump in her throat and a nameless anxiety in her heart. She was sure of only one thing as he sat there—that even if it lost her her job she must see Peter again soon—tomorrow...*she had to see him....* Peter, Peter, her Peter.

Outside her window the great beech trees rustled in the wind and seemed to join with her in whispering his name.

CHAPTER VIII

The following day, Jenny found herself relegated to the schoolroom and was glad to be free of the social round that continued throughout yet another afternoon and evening downstairs.

Amelia and Charles joined her and the twins at church, for Sir Gerald was adamant in his wish that even when he and his wife were absent, the children should attend Divine Service. Jenny sat between them in the family pew, conscious of the many eyes surveying her with the usual curiosity of the 'local inhabitants'.

After lunch Amelia and Charles took the twins riding, and Jenny settled down to another long letter to Peter. Although at first she had some difficulty in starting the letter, soon her pen was racing over the thin sheets of paper, describing in detail all her impressions—*all with the exception of Derek Barclay*. Of him, she found she could not write without hesitation. Her own feelings were not yet clear enough.

It would be asking too much of Peter's understanding merely to say that Derek both attracted and repelled her. Nor could she write to him about last night's incident of the dance and those kisses. It would have to be a spoken confession where she could explain to Peter that she had been kissed against her will; where she could make him see how it had all happened.

She wrote one brief line of the subject, saying:

...I don't think I like Derek Barclay very much.

That was all. And she wasn't happy about it, for she had no real reason for disliking Derek...one could not dislike a man only because of the strange powers of fascination he held over her; or because he was attracted to her and had tried to make love to her. She had to remind herself that to a man, especially with Derek's background, free kisses were given and taken lightly, and with much the same meaninglessness of the 'darlings' his crowd seemed to use so incessantly.

No doubt to Derek those moments so phenomenal to her had been just a method of passing the time...unimportant...scarcely disturbing. He was not to know how upset she had been; how greatly his kisses disturbed *her* peace of mind.

'But I'm not going to let him do so again,' Jenny said to herself firmly. 'He shall not come near me again.'

The letter was just completed when Mrs

Minnow came in with her tea-tray.

'The children are having their tea in Miss Amelia's room,' she told Jenny. 'Miss Amelia peeped in when they came back from their ride, and seeing you were busy she thought best not to disturb you.'

'How kind of her!' Jenny said. 'Are they all right?'

'Quite, miss! I saw the younger ones were changed out of their clothes into nice dry ones. Now Miss Amelia's young man is working their Hornby train for them, and they'll be out of mischief for a bit.'

She was about to go when Jenny on impulse called her back.

'Stay and talk to me while I have my tea, Mrs Minnow,' she pleaded. 'There's so much I want to ask you.'

Mrs Minnow beamed and sat down obediently at the nursery table. She always enjoyed a good gossip and she liked Miss Ames.

'What did you want to know, miss?' she asked, smiling.

Jenny sipped her tea thoughtfully. Had she any right to ask these questions? With a little shrug of her shoulders she decided that curiosity had the upper hand and she *must* know.

'It's about this house,' she began. 'Is it very old?'

'Well, parts of it are, miss. This part

we're in is older than the new wing, as they call it. That's Victorian and was added by the present Sir Gerald's father, the old baronet. But the Georgian part is hardly altered from the days when the first Sir Gerald was given the estate by King George II for some service rendered to the Crown. I'm not sure what it was. But since then the Barclays have always lived here, in Marleigh Manor.'

'Hasn't it been restored at all?' Jenny asked.

'Well, the roof was done in places, but not otherwise that I know of. But I've never seen the plans. They got lost soon after the present Lady Barclay came to live here. His lordship was ever so upset and m'lady had new plans drawn up. But that's not the same.'

'No, I suppose not,' Jenny agreed.

Mrs Minnow lowered her voice confidentially.

'Some in the village says there was a secret passage leading out into the grounds,' she said. 'But if it's true no one has found it. Once when Amelia was a little girl I heard her ask her father if *he* knew where it was, but he told her he thought it had all been walled up long ago in his grandfather's day.'

Jenny took a deep breath.

'And the ghost?' she asked.

Mrs Minnow gasped.

'What do you know about *that*, miss? M'lady vowed she'd sack any of the servants who mentioned that ghost again. Who's been passing on such tattle?'

Jenny smiled.

'Lady Barclay herself told me she thought the servants and no doubt the villagers thought the place was haunted. I suppose there was some legend to give rise to such an idea?'

'Oh, well, seeing her ladyship told you,' Mrs Minnow said. 'Not that I'm altogether sure I do believe in ghosts. I've never seen it anyway, and may the good Lord preserve me from doing so, too. But one of the housemaids left because she said she'd seen something—too hysterical to say what. And Miss Simkins left saying *she'd* seen someone in the gallery. But Cook's not seen nothing, and she's been here since Sir Gerald was but a little lad.'

'What is one supposed to see?' Jenny persisted.

'The legend says that it's the ghost of a murdered highwayman,' Mrs Minnow said, her voice low and confidential. 'Seems that one of the past Lady Barclays had a lover. He was a highwayman and used to come and visit her in the dead of night by way of this secret passage. Then the Master—that was to say the baronet of those days—apparently found out what was going on. One night he locked the door outside when the highwayman was in with her ladyship and lay in wait for him in the passage. As he comes back the baronet pierces his heart with a sword, and then has the passage walled in with the body in it. M'lady never knew that happened to her lover, and it's said he haunts the place, trying to tell her that he was murdered and did not voluntarily forsake her.'

Jenny took a deep breath.

'How romantic! But how wrong, too, or was the baronet in those days a wicked man?'

'No one knows to be sure, miss. They say everyone was in sympathy with the two lovers, for the old baronet was many years her senior and it hadn't been a love marriage, if you know what I mean. Sort of arranged between the families. The young man she'd always loved was so upset he turned highwayman to rob other rich men like the one who'd stolen the girl he loved. Then he met her again and that started everything off.'

'And did Lady Barclay never find out the truth?' Jenny asked.

'Apparently not. That was the way the old baronet decided to punish her. Some say she was reputed to have seen the ghost. But you can never tell what's true and what isn't. After all, most village gossip improves with the telling, doesn't it?'

And I suppose I ought not to be listening to it,' Jenny thought with an inward smile. 'Still, it has been interesting and it does clear up one or two points. Funny that without knowing the story I should have imagined a shadow in the gallery.'

The reflection gave her a qualm of uneasiness. It was all very well in broad daylight to convince oneself of one's stupidity, but when night fell and the house was plunged in darkness...

'Are you ever frightened, Mrs Minnow?' she asked the older woman abruptly.

Mrs Minnow's reply was very reassuring.

'Bless you no, dearie. Why, I've lived here ever since I was fourteen and first came into service at Marleigh Manor. I reckon if that ghost had intended me any harm then he'd have done it by now.'

'Then you *do* think there's a ghost?'

'Couldn't say for sure, miss, could we? But I haven't ever seen one, and I've been living in this house nigh on sixty years now.'

Jenny whistled.

'Oh, that does seem a long while.'

'Well, a lifetime, really,' Mrs Minnow agreed. 'And my mother was Nanny to Sir Gerald before me. She married the butler of those days, and we lived in one of the cottages on the estate when I was very small. Then when I was fourteen I came to live in the house. Sir Gerald would have been about ten years old in those days. Fine sturdy young lad he was too. Very fair and English-looking—not at all like Master Micky.'

'I think Amelia is more like her father than the twins,' Jenny agreed.

Mrs Minnow nodded.

'Twins do take after their mother in looks, same as Mr Derek.'

'She's very pretty,' Jenny said.

'There's some as say so. But the first Lady Barclay—that's to say Sir Gerald's first wife, Miss Amelia's mother—now she *was* lovely. Fair as a lily and as dainty as a piece of china. I recollect that day Sir Gerald first met her. At one of the big dances it was. He was twenty-two and she seventeen. Fair bowled off his feet he was—in fact, it was love at first sight for both of them. "Oh, Minnie," he says to me that evening, "do you think she would ever care enough to marry me?" "Well," I replied, "I don't see no reason why not"...for he was a handsome lad and real good at heart. Next year they was married—such a wedding. I shall never forget it...the whole village turned out and celebrated, and the church was crowded to overflowing. Not seen anything like it since. But Miss Amelia was not born for many long years. Sir Gerald had wanted a son, of course, and my lady had one miscarriage after another. Sir Gerald was fifty and she was forty when the little girl came. After that she tried again every year. She'd wanted a son so bad for his sake. Miss Amelia was five years old when m'lady died, after a final failure—poor lady.'

Mrs Minnow wiped her eyes unashamedly.

'I've never seen a household so cut up. Everyone loved her—down to the last child in the village. The servants fair worshipped her...and of course m'lord and Miss Amelia—well, they were inconsolable.'

'I can believe it,' Jenny said in sympathy. 'How very sad! It seems strange that under those circumstances Sir Gerald at his age should have married again.'

'In a way. But then there were several reasons. For one, Amelia needed a mother's love and care. Then tradition played a strong part. Sir Gerald had always counted a lot on traditions and observed them as if they were among the Commandments. Wanted everything to be the same as it was in his father's days and his grandfather's. So you see, it meant a lot to him to have an heir. We weren't really very surprised when he returned from a holiday in France with his new wife, who was a Miss Lydia

Carlyle, and young Mr Derek. He'd be about eighteen then and just left school. Sir Gerald hoped he'd be company a bit for Miss Amelia, but they didn't really ever make friends.

'Too great a difference in their years and in their natures; Miss Amelia's slow to think and move and reads and dreams a lot. Mr Derek is more like quicksilver—always acting impulsively and yet with lots of thought put into whatever he's doing. Same as m'lady. Between you and me, I don't think she ever has been quite the mother to Miss Amelia that Sir Gerald hoped. Her first words to me when I laid eyes on her were: "I'm glad Amelia has her old Nanny to look after her. It'll seem less strange for her if her routine continues as usual and you have complete charge of her." Right kindly thought, I told myself then. Now I think it was just to leave her free for her own whims and fancies.'

Jenny felt she ought to stop this somewhat disloyal discussion of her employer, but Mrs Minnow was well set now and Jenny could not easily interrupt without being rude.

'Wasn't parties and things at first, though. Not till later. Only fads about the house. She wanted to have *her* room where the children's rooms are, but Sir Gerald wouldn't hear of it. The ladies of the Manor had always slept in the bridal suite and he was firm about it. Tradition meant more to him than sentiment by then. Besides, he wanted to keep his old room naturally. He was real fond of Mr Derek in those days—took the lad everywhere with him. Then as two years went by with no heir seeming to be on the way, he decided to make Mr Derek the heir to Marleigh—had the boy's surname changed by deed poll from Carlyle to Barclay and everything. Mr Derek had the eldest son's room in those days—that's the children's night nursery now. Fearful scene there was when it became known the twins was expected. Sir Gerald wanted Mr Derek to move upstairs and leave the room for the future rightful Barclay heir. M'lady fair shouted the place down—saying she wouldn't have Mr Derek disinherited. Threatened all sorts of things—even though she was carrying her own two children. It's been the same ever since the twins were born. One would think they weren't hers! She's never forgiven Sir Gerald, for she blamed him for it instead of thanking the good God for blessing her with another son and daughter so late in life—'specially when m'lord was so set on an heir of his own. But then Mr Derek has always meant more than anything else to her. If there's one person she does love, it's him. Nothing he can do or say is wrong. I think it's a kind of jealousy on his behalf that makes her act the way she does to the other children.'

Jenny sat still and thoughtful. Whether she had been wrong to listen to all this talk, nevertheless it was very enlightening, and it helped her to understand the personalities of the people amongst whom she was to live for the next year. It made her own job with the twins much easier. And it helped, too, to understand Derek himself. She could sympathize with him, in a way. It must have been hard to imagine yourself the heir to this huge estate and immense wealth and then suddenly find you are ousted by another son after twenty years. In actual fact Derek did not seem to bear the little boy any grudge. He had never yet been unkind to him. Clearly he did not blame his mother, either, for presenting him with his half-brother. Perhaps he, too, laid all the blame on poor Sir Gerald. Yet he was civil enough to his stepfather.

Had she misjudged him? Jenny wondered. There were qualities in him—good ones— that she had not suspected when she vowed she hated him. Was it then only his treatment of her that aroused her dislike?

Mrs Minnow gave a little exclamation.

'Goodness, look at the time! I must be off. It'll soon be the twins' bedtime. Will you be putting them to bed tonight, miss?'

174

Jenny stood up.

'Yes, I will. And thank you for our little talk. Naturally, I shan't repeat any of it.'

Only to Peter—she thought, for it could do no harm to tell him and he would be very interested. The family history read like a book full of intricate characters, all fascinating and strangely bound up in each other by family ties, notwithstanding their vast contrast one to the other.

Jenny did not write this little story to Peter, for after the week-end house-party had dispersed she obtained permission from Lady Barclay to have the next week-end off so that she could go to London to see her fiancé. Surprisingly, Lydia Barclay agreed without hesitation. It so happened that Jenny had caught her in one of her rare good moods. The party had gone very well, and Jenny's help at the dance and with the arrangements had been considerable. Then, too, she had brought about the desired friendship between Amelia and young Charles Vagne. Lady Barclay, although not prepared to give Jenny the credit to her face, had not missed the fact that it was Jenny who had been primarily responsible for this furthering of her own ends. She was well aware that if she herself had tried to persuade Amelia to be civil to the boy the answer would have been a sullen reluctance. The girl's appearance had changed for the better, too—another mark in Jenny's favour.

And, Derek had remarked to her casually, that the new little governess was indeed a god-send in all directions. His opinions counted for a lot, and although Lydia Barclay suspected that they were not altogether unbiased (for the girl had a certain amount of charm in a quiet, innocent sort of way), she was quite content that Derek should find some amusement at the girl's expense. It pleased her to have him in a good frame of mind, happy to stay here at the Manor near her, where they could talk and discuss their plans to their hearts' delight—all the plans she had made for her cherished son's future.

Recently Derek had grown very moody and difficult. He did not care for work on the estate with his stepfather, and Cynthia...was beginning to bore him. That was a marriage Lady Barclay had known for some time would never take place. She was glad, in spite of the fact that Cynthia was well bred and had a large amount of money in her own right. It would have been a good match. But she did not want Derek to marry yet. He was still young and very attractive, and although she was wise enough to know that she could not expect to have all his love and attention, for there would always be a woman in Derek's life (as there must always be some man in hers), she hoped his affairs would remain casual and passing.

When Derek left her, there would be nothing left in her life—nothing worth living and fighting and striving for. To him, she had transferred all her own strange dreams which had not really materialized. Until he was absolutely settled she did not wish Derek to be serious about any woman; still less married. When the Cynthia affair had started Lydia had been very apprehensive. But she refrained from attacking him outright. She had played her cards well entertaining Cynthia, showing the girl up in her worst light, throwing the two together so that he should get bored by her, whilst appearing agreeable to their marriage in the future. As she had thought, Derek soon began to tire of the girl, who was possessive and difficult. She felt thankful and relieved that he was back in her power again for a while at least.

It suited her nicely that Derek should now be interested in the little governess. Marriage she knew he would never contemplate, for the girl was penniless and nobody of consequence, and Derek was far too ambitious to lose his head over Jennifer Ames. But it would keep him amused to flirt with her, without damage to his own heart.

So when Jenny asked for a week-end off, although she had only been in the house a week, Lady Barclay agreed readily. The girl was too good to lose.

'I wouldn't have asked, except that my fiancé wants to reassure himself that I'm happily settled down. He worries about me and—'

'Naturally!' Lady Barclay cut in with a yawn. 'But wouldn't it be a better plan for him to come down here? You wouldn't have to waste so much of the week-end travelling. He could get a very nice room and private sitting-room at the local inn, and the charges are absurdly small. It would give him a chance to see the locality and I'd have no objection to your inviting him here to tea on the Sunday. You could have a little tea-party in the schoolroom with the children.'

Jenny gave her a radiant smile that was not in the least forced. Had she misjudged Lady Barclay, too? For this was really both considerate and even unnecessarily kind!

'How awfully good of you! I'd adore that! I'm most grateful, Lady Barclay,' she exclaimed.

It was, indeed, an excellent suggestion. Peter's last letter had been quite absurdly concerned. Was she sure she was happy?

Comfortable? Not too lonely? Not over-working? That she liked the children? She wasn't just saying so to relieve his anxiety? There was no need for her to keep the job. They'd manage somehow...and so on.

Now he could discover for himself that she was quite all right and she wanted him to see Marleigh Manor. She felt sure his artist's mind would appreciate all the beauty, the glorious surroundings, the vivid colour in the garden, the beeches turning copper and gold and scarlet, the brilliant display of flower beds so perfectly laid out and tended by Adams.

That same afternoon, Jenny went to the village for her walk with the twins, and saw the landlord, Mr Cottham, of the Marleigh Arms. He was a charming old man, and his wife a typical rosy-cheeked countrywoman who kept the inn bright and shining. They showed her the room which Peter could have and Jenny was entirely satisfied. They could have their meals alone in the little private sitting-room and Peter would be more than comfortable in the white-washed bedroom with the immense feather-bed which the Cotthams were reserving for him.

Promising to let them know definitely next day, Jenny went eagerly home to await the cheap rate time for telephoning Peter. Meantime, the twins besieged her with questions about 'the Man' who was coming. What was he like? What should they call him? Would he really have tea with them? When was he going to marry their Jamie? Was he very old? Would they have babies like Cook's daughter when she got married?

Jenny tried to answer all these questions and told the twins to call him 'Uncle Peter', hoping Lady Barclay would not object.

Of Derek there was no sign. Amelia, however, spent the evening with Jenny in the schoolroom, where, to be more cosy, they had had a fire lit and drawn their chairs close to it.

Amelia was in one of her dreamy moods. It was not long before Jenny guessed, from all the girl's questions about herself and Peter and 'how had they first known they loved each other', that Amelia fancied herself more than a little fond of young Charles. Tackled outright—for Jenny wanted to gain Amelia's complete confidence—Amelia blushed and said:

'I expect you'll think me silly. I know I'm very young. But I do like Charles awfully, Jennifer. He's not like some of the awful people Mother has down here sometimes. Why, he really *likes* reading! And Father thinks he's nice, too, and Father's *awfully* difficult to please.'

'I don't think it's at all silly to be *fond* of him,' Jenny said. 'You are a little young to be "in love", Amelia, but then it's a good thing to love as many people as you can in this world. That's not quite the same as being in love, but it'll be a year or two before you think about that won't it? I don't suppose Charles is thinking about love or marriage just yet?'

Amelia gave a giggle that was wholly childish.

'Goodness, no! Nor am I, really. It's just that I like him so much. You see, there's not an awful lot of people I do like. Father, of course, but he's special. And you! But that's not the same as having someone my own age to be fond of, is it?'

Jenny felt a sudden pang of pity for Amelia. She could only mention two people whom she cared about, one her father and the other someone she had known only a week, and liked because she had been kind to her. How awful to be so lonely at her age!

'I'm sure your mother would be very pleased if you invited Charles down here for a visit,' Jenny said. 'Then you would have plenty of time for riding and reading and talking, and getting to know each other better.'

Amelia's face glowed.

'Do you really think she wouldn't mind?

Oh, Jennifer, will *you* ask her?'

She obtained Jenny's willing promise and the two sat in friendly happy silence, dreaming by the firelight, thinking about happiness in store for them.

During the week that followed Jenny was so busy starting the twins on their regular lessons and trying to bring some routine into their lives, that she had little spare time.

In fact Friday came almost before she realized it, and that evening Peter's train was due to arrive from London. After she had put the children to bed she would be free to go and meet him, for Mrs Minnow had promised to listen for them in case they woke or were frightened. Since the night-light had been instituted there had been no further tantrums at bedtime and they had slept soundly every night. Jenny was now convinced that her own fear that night had been unfounded and the shadow but the curtain as Lady Barclay suggested.

She was feeling light-hearted and care-free. Even Derek had not troubled her. In fact she had not seen him since the night of the dance, beyond a brief glimpse of him on horseback when he was riding one afternoon in company with the raven-haired girl Cynthia.... Jenny had convinced herself that Derek had lost whatever interest he had in her personally and returned to his fiancée's society. She was glad that it should be so. She had all her meals in the schoolroom and he had not encroached on their privacy, and Jenny was immensely relieved.

She wonderd now how she could ever have allowed herself even one small act of disloyalty to Peter, far less imagined herself responding to Derek's kisses.

Her peace of mind was not to last, however. Shortly before the twins' bedtime one of the maids came to the schoolroom with a message that Mr Derek would like to see her right away in the library.

Swift refusal rose to Jenny's lips but died unspoken. She was no longer free to refuse such requests. With an effort she remembered that she was an employee now and Derek Barclay had the right to send for her. She could not even excuse herself on the ground that she was putting the children to bed.

Obediently, but with inward trepidation, Jenny went downstairs and into the library.

Derek was seated on the leather chair at his stepfather's desk, feet up on the blotter. He was smoking a cigarette in a long holder. He jumped to his feet as Jenny came into the room and pulled a chair forward for her.

Jenny's mouth was a tight line of anxiety.

What did he want? His face looked serious and he hadn't spoken. She waited in silence. He did not sit down again himself, but stood behind her chair where she could not see his face. Then he said quietly:

'I hope you didn't mind my sending for you like that? It was the only way I could think of, to get you alone. I didn't want to come up to the nursery with the kids there, and you haven't been downstairs much lately. Have you been avoiding me?'

Jenny flushed angrily.

'Certainly not. As you know, my place is upstairs with the children. I'm here to look after them—'

'And not for my amusement!' Derek broke in, his voice holding the mocking tone that aggravated and exasperated her.

She did not reply.

'Have I offended you now?' he asked.

She turned to face him, her face still flushed with annoyance.

'Did you wish to see me about something?' she asked, ignoring his remark.

'I naturally wish to see you now and then,' Derek replied easily. 'Is that such a crime? You've very nice to look at, Jennifer!'

She rose to her feet then, her hands clenched at her sides. This flippancy she need not tolerate.

'If there's nothing else, have you any

objection if I go now? It's nearly the twins' bedtime and I'm anxious to be early as I'm meeting my fiancé's train this evening,' she said tartly.

This time Derek flushed with anger, with acute irritation, because he could not impose his will on this girl, about whom he had been thinking so consistently throughout the week. Her absence had only increased his interest in her, his impatience to conquer her, and now that he had inveigled her down here it seemed that he had progressed no further and that she was about to escape.

'Running away again?' he taunted her. 'You always seem to be running away from me, Jenny.'

Jenny flashed him a look of dislike. He always placed her in the wrong and his jibes were somehow near the truth. She tried to pass him but his arm went out and barred the way. She stood rigidly still and silent.

'Don't be cross!' he said, his voice suddenly soft and pleading. 'I know you don't think much of me, but honestly, I really only wanted to see you.'

There was a humble note in his voice such as he had not used to any woman in his life before. He knew that this girl had an extraordinary power over him. It was a strange feeling for Derek Barclay, who had always had his way with women.

'Now that you have seen me, may I go?' Jenny asked coldly.

He bit his lip, feeling his own powerlessness. Swift anger replaced his momentary weakness.

'I suppose you're in a hurry to get to that damned fiancé of yours. Well, go to him then, and mind you don't forget to tell him how you kissed me the other night; and how deliciously you responded when I made love to you—'

His words were cut short by the sharp sting of Jenny's hand across his cheek. In a moment he had hold of her and his face was close to hers, green eyes flashing, narrowed, almost cruel as they gazed at her.

'All right, hit me, Jenny! It's the second time, but you'll pay for this blow—this way!'

And he kissed her fiercely, brutally, hurting her lips so that she longed to cry out, even while she knew that she would never give him that satisfaction. His hands gripped her arms to tightly that they were bruised. She struggled, trying to keep her mind steady; to think of Peter; trying to fight the slow weakening of her senses that this man's proximity managed always to produce. Then, fortunately for Jenny, he let her go. He wiped his lips with a silk handkerchief, his eyes glittered at her.

'You'll think of that when you kiss *him*,' he called after her viciously.

The door closed behind her and Jenny ran blindly down the hall and up the big carved staircase.

'Now I know I hate him!' she thought wildly. 'He's spoilt *everything!*'

All the carefree happiness of the day had left her. Once again she felt guilty, worried, uncertain. Ought she to tell Peter about this? What could she say? Should she bring him to the Manor after all—risk a meeting with Derek?

At least, she told herself, Derek didn't know how near she had been yet again to surrender. What was this evil fascination he had for her? How was it possible that her body could react to the hard, cruel kisses of a man whom she disliked? That she could be attracted to him in such a way, even while she *knew* herself to be in love with another man?

It was a strangely quiet and yet unusually passionate Jenny who awaited Peter on the little platform—a Jenny who, when she greeted him, threw herself into his arms with an impetuosity and disregard of onlookers which amazed him. He had always thought his Jenny rather shy and reluctant to show emotion before others.

'Oh, darling, darling, *darling* Peter!' she

whispered as his arms went round her tenderly, drawing her close to him. 'I've missed you so much! I'm so *glad* you've come!'

He smiled happily. He was pleased that she had missed him, for he had missed her a great deal, too, and been worried about her as well.

This reception charmed him. Gently his lips brushed hers before he released her, to put an arm through hers as they walked out of the station.

'Happy?' he murmured.

She looked at him from brilliant eyes that were full of an eagerness that touched his very heart.

'Wonderfully happy, Peter!' she said, pressing his arm against her side. 'And to think that we've got two whole days together!'

'And we'll make the best of them,' Peter promised, and quickened his pace as they walked down the quiet country road that led to the Marleigh Arms.

CHAPTER IX

Although so pleased to see her fiancé
again, so happy to have him here with
her at last, Jenny did not feel altogether at
ease with him. As she chattered away at his
side or listened to his news, at the back of
her mind her conscience was nagging her.
Peter was so terribly good—so nice (a word
she knew could mean a bore but which so
aptly described Peter). He was no bore. He
was nice and he was also everything she
had ever wanted the man she loved to be:
kindly, considerate, decent, trusting and
trustworthy, and essentially masculine.

But it was one of these very attributes
that worried her now. It would not cross
Peter's mind to suspect that she might have
been unfaithful to him. He trusted her as
completely as she trusted him. Perhaps
they had both been wrong to take each
other too much for granted, she reflected
in a worried fashion. And yet, nothing
had changed. She still loved him—more,
in some strange way, than ever. Or was
it simply that she was more conscious of
her own deep emotions, after her recent
soul-searchings? She wanted to tell Peter,

not just the everyday events of her life at Marleigh Manor—but *all* the details; her reaction to Derek Barclay and his strange behaviour towards her.

She couldn't let Peter hold her in his arms and kiss her, as she knew he would do once they were quite alone together, with the shadow of her disloyalty lying between them. But how, she wondered, would she ever be able to explain it to Peter when she could scarcely explain it to herself? Would it, after all, be better to keep silent? To enjoy these two days with him and let them help her wipe out the memory of Derek's wild, passionate kisses?

It did not occur to Jenny that Peter, who knew her so well, might sense something of what she was feeling. But as he listened to her bright, gay words and her little bursts of laughter the first curious doubts and worries began to seep into his mind. Jenny seemed almost nervous in his company. He was sure that even her laughter was forced. And when she listened to his own news, he suspected that he held only half her attention.

He kept his counsel, however, until they reached the Marleigh Arms. Mrs Cottham had shown them into the little oak-beamed parlour which was to be theirs for the week-end. She left them with the promise to serve their dinner within half an hour. Then, at last, Jenny and Peter were alone, standing looking at one another, aware of an awkwardness—a shyness which had never before come into their relationship.

Jenny, suddenly afraid to speak, turned quickly away and went to the lattice-paned window; she stared blindly at the tiny garden, but Peter followed, put his arms round her and drew her gently round to face him.

'Kiss me, Jenny—my own darling Jenny!' he whispered, looking down into her eyes.

Her arms went round his neck as he drew her closer. He was unprepared for the passionate, emotional fervour with which she answered his kiss. Then, knowing how much he loved her, how many lonely evenings he had spent thinking of this moment when he would hold her in his arms again, he forgot his surprise and drew her even closer against him. He kissed her eager lips again and again with an effort to maintain that control over himself which he felt imperative whenever he and Jenny were alone together. Since neither of them believed in 'trial marriages', and both were normally conventionally minded, it had been obvious that their love-making must be kept within bounds during their long engagement, if they were not to become too nervy and frustrated. Often Peter had felt the strain and longed to give way to his feelings, but he respected Jenny too much, felt too protective in his love for her, to lose control. He knew that there were deep fires beneath that calm exterior which Jenny presented to the world in general; knew, too, that they were as yet unawakened. And until they were married he felt it best to hold the reins tightly, for if ever Jenny weakened, he might not have the strength to resist her.

Jenny, of course, had no knowledge of these thoughtful decisions on Peter's part. They had rarely discussed sex and its problems and Jenny had felt no need to do so. In the past she and Peter had always agreed on most points—except about the question of marrying right away—and they had drifted into their way of loving each other without stopping to think about it. It had been one of the beautiful parts of their love for one another—the complete naturalness of it. And yet now Jenny began to wonder if it were quite so natural. If Peter really loved her, would he not be more passionate, more demanding? (More—questioned her inner self—like Derek Barclay?)

She longed passionately and with every part of her being at this one moment for Peter to respond as ardently as she desired. Her lips strained against his. She wanted a reassurance that she could not name—a reassurance that he could need her physically as much as she knew Derek desired her. She wanted to feel again—but with Peter, whom she loved—that wild weakening of her senses, that shuddering rapture that she had felt in Derek's arms. She wanted Peter to make her feel that she was utterly desirable to him in every way; to rejoice in her own desire for him.

But Peter was unaware of these thoughts and with a great effort he struggled to remain calm, even while he longed to crush her against him, kiss her with all his own wild longing.

Jenny felt his restraint, and like a cold shower it cooled her ardour. She realized with acute disappointment that Peter did not understand the extent of her feelings. She felt suddenly ashamed of herself, ashamed that the physical side of their relationship should have taken on such importance; and that Peter did not seem to want her as she wanted him.

Frustration made her angry with Peter. She drew away from him with a hard, forced little laugh.

Peter, puzzled and strangely unhappy, put out his hand as if to draw her back into his arms, but she ignored him and went to the big armchair and lit a cigarette.

'Well?' she asked, her tone now purposefully light and casual. 'What other news have you for me?'

Peter shrugged his shoulders uncomprehendingly, and sat down opposite her.

'Nothing much, Jenny. I've been working hard. Done some quite good work, too. Then I saw your family yesterday. They sent their love of course. They'd only had one letter and were a little worried.'

Again that laugh from Jenny.

'Honestly, Peter, I don't know why anyone should worry. They must realize that I'm pretty busy; besides, they could get all my news from you.'

Peter smiled.

'I know, darling, but when people love you they do worry. I did myself in spite of your letters. It's a great relief to see that you are all right and hear that you like your job.'

Her face had softened at his first words, but now her expression became remote and thoughtful and he could not guess at her thoughts. It worried him even more. Was Jenny trying to hide something from him? Wasn't everything really all right?

'You *are* happy, aren't you, Jenny?' he persisted.

'Well, of course I am, silly. Why shouldn't I be?'

He gave a wry grin.

'Perhaps because you missed me? I've not been very happy without you, you know.'

Her face flushed a deep rosy pink.

'Of course I miss you, Peter. But you know what it is when you're very busy. There isn't much time to think. Last week-end there was this big house-party, and a dance on Saturday night—'

'You didn't say whether you enjoyed it,' Peter broke in.

'Well, I wasn't really there to enjoy it. I was acting as a kind of hostess.'

'Then you didn't get any dancing?' Peter asked innocently. He was amazed at the colour that had again rushed to her face.

'Well, once or twice. Sir Gerald asked me for a "duty" dance and also his stepson Derek Barclay....' Her voice trailed away into an awkward silence. Peter felt a sudden sharp suspicion, a pang of sheer jealousy. Had Jenny taken a liking to this fellow after all?

'You said in your letter that you hated him,' he said quietly. 'Why?'

Jenny bit her lip.

'Who? Derek?' Her voice was too casual. It frightened Peter as much as the sudden vehemence with which she said next: 'I *do* hate him! I think him despicable!'

'But why?' Peter questioned, again hoping his voice did not give away his sudden suspicions. 'I thought you said he was rather an attractive fellow.'

Jenny was spared an immediate reply, for supper was brought to them, and their hostess stayed chatting to them for a while as they ate. When at last coffee had been finished, and cleared away, and Jenny and Peter found themselves alone again, another awkward silence fell.

Jenny felt wretchedly unhappy. Something had spoiled this reunion—this evening that was to have been so marvellous. Something was wrong between her and Peter, and although she hated to admit it she felt deep inside her that it was her fault and not his. It was Derek Barclay's fault, too. But for *him* this sudden estrangement between herself and Peter would never have existed. She longed to throw herself into Peter's arms and sob out the whole story—the truth. But now she felt he wouldn't, couldn't, understand. He was such a sane, normal sort of person. How could she expect him to appreciate the fact that Derek appealed to something biological and fundamental to her, something she had not known existed—until he kissed her? How could she tell Peter, who loved her, that underneath her cool exterior she was terribly, wretchedly concerned with sex? It was an ugly word and she felt now that sex was ugly, too...it was horrible to long for physical contact with a man whom she disliked because his body caused some chemical reaction in hers. Jenny shuddered. Peter wouldn't want anything more to do with her; he might even hate her as much as she now hated herself.

Jenny wasn't to know that Peter would have understood very well that the same faculty for passion which she had discovered in herself, and thought abnormal, were the natural responses which he experienced all too often himself. They were both young, healthy individuals and Nature had meant them to love one another and had given them the power to respond physically to the fervour of mind and heart. It was the very fact that they were forced to live apart which was unnatural. Their engagement had been unusually long and it was obvious that, though they were not strictly aware of it—so gradual was its development—the strain left them frustrated and longing for fulfilment. And it had been Derek with his wild, sweeping, uncontrolled passions, who had jolted Jenny out of the rut and into that awakening Peter had hoped would remain dormant until they were married. He could so easily have explained all this to her, had he known the truth—had Jenny confided in him. He would not have blamed her;

thought any less of her. He might even have thrown his own ideas to the winds and asked her to marry him, as soon as possible—no matter whether they got this house or not.

But Jenny could not confide fully in him and Peter was left to his own suspicions: the belief that perhaps she had become interested in Derek Barclay in a far more serious way; that she might even be falling in love with him; and he, Peter, who had so much less to offer, be losing her. The thought was unbearable.

'Come and sit here beside me, Jenny,' he pleaded, beckoning to the little stool at his feet in front of the glowing log fire.

The leaping flames lit up the room. Mrs Cottham had not switched on the light, with admirable consideration for two young lovers, and the setting was adequately romantic, she thought. Peter would have agreed and Jenny, too, was aware of the soft light, the quietness, the sweet intimacy of the house. She longed suddenly to make everything right between her lover and herself again—to forget her worries and perplexities and just enjoy this moment.

Obediently, she moved across and settled herself against Peter's knees. His hand went to her head and softly stroked the shining, curly, burnished head.

'Jenny!' he said after a moment. 'Do you remember once we promised we'd never have any secrets from each other—not even if it was to say we had stopped loving one another?'

Jenny felt her heart jerk painfully. She nodded her head.

'Then you would tell me—if anything was wrong?' he added.

She hesitated. Could she tell him now? How much better it might be! Yet she loved Peter; loved him more, probably; than he knew. She could not bear to risk losing that love; risk him disliking her for what she was. She likened herself to those girls during the war who had let any man make love to them, no matter whom or of what nationality, in spite of the men who loved them and were fighting for them overseas, just for the thrill they got out of it. And yet, she hadn't really wanted Derek to make love to her. She had tried to avoid him, to struggle against him! But not for long, she thought with a shudder of distaste for herself. Only a moment's fight—then she had responded....

'Jenny, there *is* something wrong?' Peter's voice broke in on her thoughts, anxious, afraid.

She turned to him then, tears in her eyes, rolling down her cheeks. She held his hands tightly in her own as if trying to draw strength from him.

'Oh, Peter, yes, in a way. It's just something I've found out about myself. Something not very nice. Don't ask me any more. Just trust me if you can. I've got to fight it—alone.'

His face looked suddenly worried and drawn.

'Jenny...whatever it is, I'd like to help. Won't *you* trust *me?* It can't be so dreadful as you make it sound. And there might be something I could do.'

She shook her head, choking over her tears as she fought to control them.

'No, it isn't really anything to do with *us,* Peter. It's just something that concerns *me.* Don't make me tell you. You'd hate me if you knew what sort of a person I really was.'

He smiled then, for he knew his Jenny pretty well, and he knew without a doubt that he could never hate her.

'I should always love you—even if you committed murder and broke all the Ten Commandments and a few others besides,' he said gently.

She was in his arms then, sobbing against his shoulder.

'I love you too, Peter. I don't deserve anyone like you.'

'I deserve someone like Derek Barclay!' she told herself bitterly. Well, let Derek

Barclay try to trap her alone with him again. She'd show him once and for all that he meant nothing whatever to her; that she loved Peter truly with all her heart.

A little reassured but still strangely disturbed by this new Jenny, so unlike the cool, self-confident girl he had known these past long years, Peter decided to let the matter drop for the evening and perhaps see if he could find out what was behind this 'guilt' complex of Jenny's when he went to Marleigh Manor with her tomorrow. He would soon know when he saw Jenny and this Derek Barclay together whether the chap meant anything to her or not. And if Jenny really disliked him and he had been bothering her—why, he would kick young Barclay from here to Jerusalem!

When at last Jenny looked at her watch and realized with a shock that she was very late and must go, it was with considerable reluctance that she drew herself out of Peter's embrace. It had been a wonderful hour, sitting quietly here with their arms about one another, just dreaming into the firelight, talking of little things, making plans for the future. It was like old times together but with a new and precious awareness of each other's value. Everything was forgotten in this tiny world where there was only room for the two of them. Jenny hated the thought that it had to end, and she must leave Peter now and go back to the Manor, with its disturbing memories, and the possible presence of Derek Barclay, whom she dreaded meeting again.

But Peter insisted on returning with her, and when at last he kissed her good night outside the garden door to which Jenny had the key, she felt too tired and sleepy to worry about anything at all.

She went quickly to her room, and later, as she climbed into bed, lost herself in thoughts of tomorrow, when she would be with Peter again. Soon she was deep in sleep.

During the night Jenny had a dreadful and confused nightmare, from which she awakened shivering and inexplicably afraid. She could still hear the sound of screaming in her ears—screams which in her dreams had come from her own lips, though already she had forgotten the substance of the dream. As she lay there, breathing deeply and trying to shake off the effects of the nightmare, Jenny was sure that there was something wrong. It was just a reaction from the dream, she chided herself, and yet the longer she lay there trying to talk herself into reason, the more convinced she became that it was the echo of someone else's screams that had woken her.

Her mind leapt to the twins, and hesitating no longer, she slipped out of bed and, without making a sound, opened her door and went into the gallery. She did not, as she had feared, see any shadow at the far end by the oriel window. Gradually her fears lessened.

'There are no such things as ghosts, Jennifer Ames!' she told herself firmly, and without further hesitation hurried along to the twins' room.

As she reached the door her heart stood still, for she could clearly hear the sound of their low sobbing, muffled, no doubt, by the bed-clothes. Quickly, she pushed open the door and found the room in darkness. Had the night-light burnt out or blown out? She switched on the light.

Two tear-drenched faces peered fearfully at her; then, recognizing her, the children burst into tears again—tears which Jenny realized were this time of relief.

She hugged them to her, soothing them with gentle words, and telling them there was no need to be frightened now that she was there. Presently, when they were calmer, she questioned them.

'What happened to the night-light?' she asked.

'He blew it out!' Micky gulped.

'He? Who?' Jenny asked quickly, but already that brief look of warning had passed between the children and two little mouths closed like traps. She felt hopelessly inadequate to deal with the situation. How could she get to the bottom of all this if they wouldn't confide in her?

'You mean—the ghost?' Jenny asked.

Their white faces stared at her in surprise.

'How did you know about him?' Marie asked.

Jenny smiled.

'Never mind about that, Marie. But you know, darlings, there really and truly aren't any ghosts. Only in fairy-tales like the Giant in *Jack the Giant Killer*, and the wicked witch in *Snow White*.'

'This ghost is real!' Micky whispered, the words coming from his lips as if in spite of himself.

He was so obviously convinced that Jenny felt it better not to argue with him.

'Then you've really seen it?' she asked.

They both nodded.

'Just now?'

Again they nodded.

'What does it look like?' she questioned them eagerly.

But again that look of caution passed between them. Whatever they knew, they did not intend to tell her, she was certain now.

'Is it a man ghost or a woman ghost?' she persisted.

But it was useless. They would *not* say another word. They were damp with sweat and their faces so white and stricken that Jenny hadn't the heart to question them any longer. She tucked them up and relit the night-light, and switching off the main light, promised to sit with them till they slept. It was not long before they drowsed, and Jenny was about to go back to bed when she heard a noise that for one sickening moment caused her blood to freeze—the long low howl of a dog. Then, as suddenly, the howl changed to a furious barking, and as abruptly gave way to one short sharp yelp and was quite silent.

With an anxious glance at the children, who were, mercifully, still asleep, Jenny went swiftly to the window and leaned out. Through the trees she saw the dark shape of a man running, keeping in the shadows, darting from the cover of one tree-trunk to another until at last he was on the drive. With her gaze riveted on this sight, Jenny watched him until he disappeared round the bend of the road and was lost to sight.

Her heart was thumping wildly in her throat and she felt sick with fright.

So after all there was something going on in this house—something sinister and frightening and, she felt sure, something evil. Then her common sense returned. Whatever else it was, that figure was no ghost. There was nothing from the supernatural that she need face—but a human being.

For a long time she stood at the window, lost in thought, trying to find the answers to a hundred questions. Had the man she had just seen anything to do with the children's terror? Was he their ghost? Or was he one of the staff—the chauffeur, for instance, bent on some mischief? Or was it a thief?... Deep in her heart she felt that it was too much of a coincidence to suppose that the burglar had come on the one night the children's 'ghost' had appeared again. Had no one else in the house heard? Seen? Surely Derek would have woken again with the children screaming? Was he somewhere outside that door—wandering about trying to find what was up? If so, it was her duty to tell him what she had seen. For the children's sake, if for no one else's, it was high time this mystery was cleared up.

But she was woman enough to be afraid now to go out into that gallery alone. Nor did she wish to encounter Derek Barclay alone for her own personal reasons. He might take advantage of the situation and try to make love to her again. Fear, and what she felt to be her duty, fought equal battle until the matter was settled for her. A light tapping sounded on the door and she heard Derek's voice saying:

'Jennifer, are you there?'

She forgot herself then, and thinking only of the twins, slipped quickly through the door into the gallery. Derek was waiting for her, wearing a smart satin dressing-gown with black lapels.

'Then you heard the twins, too?' she asked him in a whisper.

He nodded.

'I thought you would go to them. Fact was, I imagined I heard footsteps, and they didn't sound like yours.'

'There was somebody about,' Jenny cried excitedly. 'Just a few moments ago I heard the dog barking, then it yelped as if someone had kicked it. Then I looked out of the window and saw a man running down the drive.'

'You're quite certain?'

She nodded.

'Perhaps I ought to throw on some clothes and go after him, whoever it was.'

'It's a bit late now. I ought to have sounded the alarm earlier, but to be honest, I was scared stiff!' she said.

Derek gave a low laugh.

'Poor little thing! I'm not surprised. Why, you're trembling. You must be frozen. What you need is a good stiff drink.'

'No, really, I'm quite all right now,' Jenny said, but she was suddenly aware that she was cold. Reaction had set in, and she started to shiver so violently that she could not stop her teeth from chattering.

'You're far from all right,' came Derek's voice. 'Now you'll do as I say. This is an order, Miss Ames!' his voice took on a pretended severity. 'We're going right down to the kitchen and I'll make you a nice cup of tea, and you'll drink it with a tot of the Pater's best whiskey in it.'

An inner sense warned her to refuse. A rendezvous with Derek was exactly what she had intended to avoid at all costs. She did not wish to be alone with him ever again. She had asked Peter to trust her, and when she did so she had resolved to put all chances of breaking that trust right out of the way. Circumstances might force her to see Derek from time to time, but she need not be alone with him.

He was aware of her hesitation and said quickly:

'You're not afraid of me, are you, Jennifer? I know you must think me an unspeakable cad for the way I behaved in the library this afternoon. It was a mean trick to play and an abominable way to carry on. I was just so damn' jealous because you were going to meet that fiancé of yours. Believe me, I realized then that you didn't want anything more to do with me in—*that*—way, but need that stop us from being friends?'

Jenny bit her lip. She eyed him doubtfully. She was considering what he said. She only hoped he meant it. For her own part, she felt as if he had suddenly lost whatever power he had had over her. She did not want Derek or any other man but Peter to make love to her and kiss her. But if Derek really wanted to be friends, her heart, always trusting and open, warmed a little to him. Besides, tomorrow Peter would be coming to the Manor. If Derek chose, he could make things rather unpleasant for her. And she did not want to give him the chance to blurt out things which, if Peter had to know, would be better coming from her. And she wouldn't put it past Derek to try and make some sort of scene in front of Peter, if he were in an ugly mood.

'Of course we can be friends!' she said, and did not pause to consider how impossible any platonic relationship would be *for him*. 'And I'd like that cup of tea without the whiskey more than anything in the world.'

With a faint sardonic smile on his face, which she could not see in the darkness, Derek took her arm and guided her through the swing doors and down the servants' staircase to the big kitchen. He seemed to know his way about perfectly in spite of the darkness.

In the kitchen however, coming through an open door, was a warm bright glow from the huge boiler which provided hot water and central heating for the whole house.

On this cold autumn night the heat was very welcome. A fire still burned in the kitchen grate.

Jenny sat down in one of the big old-fashioned wicker basket chairs and toasted her feet while Derek busied himself making tea. He had switched on a light. Already she felt better, calmer, less frightened by the night's events. Derek was being friendly and charming. He raided the larder, found a cold chicken and made sandwiches. Then he poured out tea and sat opposite her, making her laugh with perfect imitation of Cook and Mrs Minnow and old Robert. Jenny found a new side to Derek—a less serious and less bitter one. She found herself laughing with him, happy and relaxed in his company.

Derek, watching her, knew that she was now off her guard and feeling more friendly towards him. He waited an opportunity to bring the conversation to a more personal level. Presently he said casually.

'I think mother said something about your fiancé coming to tea tomorrow?'

Jenny nodded.

'Nursery tea, I suppose. Am I not to be invited?'

Jenny felt embarrassed. She really had not wanted Derek to be there—just the children and herself and Peter.

'All right, I understand,' Derek said, reading her thoughts. 'Anyway, I don't suppose I should be very civil. You know, Jennifer, if it weren't for the fact that you're so damned serious about this chap, I should have done my darnedest to make you love me.'

He spoke lightly enough, but with an underlying seriousness which made Jenny feel both nervous and embarrassed again. Once more Derek was putting his cards on the table, and she wasn't sure she wished to see them.

'You know you're not serious, Derek,' she said, with forced ease. 'Why, you yourself are engaged to be married, and she's very beautiful.'

'Oh, Cynthia!' his voice was hard with scorn. 'Lovely, but hard as nails, and too exacting to suit me. Besides, I've broken the engagement.'

'Oh, *no!*' Jenny cried involuntarily.

'Why not? I don't love her. I knew that

as soon as I set eyes on you. To be truthful, I've never been really in love before. Thought I was, of course, but I see now that I didn't know the meaning of the word. Oh, don't get all hot and bothered, Jennifer. I'm not going to attack you. I'm all too well aware that my advances aren't acceptable. But I had to tell you. I wanted you to understand that I wasn't just fooling around with you as you might have thought. You see, there's something about you that—well, something that does strange things to me. I've never been a decent sort of fellow—in fact I'm far more rotten than you know. But if you could have cared for me, I could have been better. And I'd have given you the earth—anything in the world you wanted, Jenny.'

There was no doubting the sincerity of his words at that moment, and Jenny was immensely touched—and sorry for him. She was strangely perturbed, too, by the thought: *'Suppose there had been no Peter—how should I have reacted to Derek?'* But she cast the dangerous thoughts quickly aside and said:

'I'm sorry, Derek—really sorry. I feel partly to blame—letting you kiss me the way you did—although I hadn't much alternative, had I? But...well, Peter and I do love each other and we're going to

212

be married when I leave here. Nothing can change that.'

Came Derek's voice, very low, almost inaudible:

'Even if you found you didn't love him after all?'

'That's not possible!' Jenny said quickly. 'We've been in love for a long time. I'll never change my mind.'

'How are you so sure?' Derek persisted, his strange eyes watching her closely. 'People do change. They grow up and sometimes grow apart. Then as one develops, he or she may find the other has been left far behind.'

'I am sure that I know where I am,' Jenny said quickly. 'Perhaps in the same way that you are sure you love me. I just *know* it. Peter is everything I want.'

'Everything?'

Why must Derek stress that word? Jenny thought desperately. Did he suspect that she had been worried about Peter? Worried about the physical side of their affair. Did he know, in some uncanny way, that she had found *his* kisses so much more disturbing, exciting, than Peter's?

He waited for her to speak, hoping he had laid the seed of doubt in her mind, wondering if he dared go further with his plans. She remained silent.

'I have the feeling that you're afraid,'

he went on slowly. 'Not of ghosts or burglars...' he gave a short laugh, 'but of *yourself.*'

'I don't know what you mean,' Jenny stammered, looking quickly away. How horribly near the truth he was!

'You see, you dare not look me in the face,' Derek went on remorselessly. 'If it weren't that you had stated so adamantly that you loved this chap, Peter, I should have been quite encouraged by your behaviour. You know, Jenny, I think you're afraid of *me!*'

CHAPTER X

Jenny looked at the handsome, faintly mocking face that leaned close to hers. Instinctively, she drew back, her mind whirling with indecision. She wanted to get up and leave the room—leave now before she could be dragged into further personal revelations and discussions. And yet she felt challenged and her pride would not allow her to give in to this man—to let him know she was afraid of him.

She gave him a look that was both anxious and haughty.

'Afraid—of you, Derek Barclay? Why should I be?'

He laughed.

'Come, Jenny, let's be honest. You know you're attracted to me even if you don't like me as a person. Admit that's true!'

'All right, I admit it. And what do you gain by it? Surely it does not flatter you to know that you attract me—that way? That when you choose, you can overcome my dislike of you by physical persuasion? I think it's hateful—something I'm ashamed of and of which you, too, should be ashamed. I cannot think what pleasure you get out of trying to force these reactions from me. You know very well I'm in love with Peter—that I don't like *you*. You know I don't want you near me, and yet all the time you try and devise means of getting me alone, hoping to wear down my resistance.'

Again he laughed and saw the swift rush of angry colour go to her cheeks.

'That all sounds very melodramatic, Jenny. You make me out to be quite the proverbial villain and you the frightened maiden and your Peter the brave hero lurking in the background. But I don't see things quite the same way. I have no evil intentions towards you. In fact, quite the opposite. You see, I want to marry you.'

Jenny gasped, her face now white and annoyed. The conversation was really getting beyond her. She no longer knew what she ought to do—to say.

'Does that surprise you?' Derek went on, his voice suddenly serious. 'Nevertheless it's true, Jenny. I knew it this afternoon when you ran away from me—to that other chap. But why shouldn't I fight for you? All's fair in love and war, they say. You're only engaged—not married. I've a right to try and make you change your mind, and I want you to do so more than anything in the world.'

'Don't—please don't!' Jenny whispered,

her head now buried in her hands. 'Don't you see it's hopeless? I love Peter. I want to marry *him*. Nothing can alter that—nothing, *don't you understand?*'

'Not even this?' Derek asked. Moving quickly towards her and taking her hands away from her face, he kissed her before she could prevent it. Automatically her hands went to his shoulders, trying to push him away from her—trying to free her mouth. He was covering her face with kisses. He held her in a grip like steel and she knew, as she struggled, that she was weak and powerless against him.

'Derek, stop!' she panted against his lips. 'You promised!'

He released her then, suddenly and completely; walked away from her in silence. She sat still, not knowing what to say—what to do.

'Now you hate me even more, no doubt!' came Derek's voice, bitter and angry. 'The trouble is you leave me no alternative. In fact I'm beaten before I begin *this* fight.'

'What do you mean?' Jenny gasped, the back of her hand against her bruised lips.

He gave another short laugh which held little humour. The sound was strangely frightening to Jenny, who longed to run from it and yet had to stay to hear what Derek was thinking. If only she could be sure of her own mind, her own wishes, and of really what lay behind her own conduct, then she might be able to cope with Derek and this new trend to affairs. But in her uncertainty she was unable to make any definite decision—she could not even run away this time.

'It's all so damned stupid!' Derek said violently, pacing round the room like some caged animal. 'You're wretchedly conventional, Jennifer. Because you're engaged to this fellow—because you've known him some years, that in your eyes is the end of us. You imagine you love him. Even if you *knew* you did not, you'd probably stick to him anyway. You're the type. Oh, don't think I don't admire you for it in a way, but what chance does it give me?—I've met you too late! Whatever I do or say you are adamant. Can you blame me for trying to kiss you the way I have? Trying to overcome your preconceived ideas on love, your beliefs that no engagements should be broken—that it would be dishonourable? It's the only way I have of reaching you—the real you behind the conventional Jenny that says *"Don't, Derek"* whenever I come near you. *"You mustn't! I'm engaged, remember, Peter!"*'

His voice was scornful, mocking and yet deadly serious.

Jenny shivered, afraid and yet not fully understanding the reason for her fear.

'I do love Peter!' she said, her voice low, almost a whisper. 'And I don't think you really love me at all, Derek. It's because you know you can't have me that you imagine you want to marry me. Why, you've only known me a fortnight! You don't learn to love someone in that short time. You know nothing about me really—not the real me. It's...' She hesitated for a moment and then plunged on in a desire to speak the truth, no matter who was hurt in the process. 'It's just my physical attraction for you and because I am unobtainable.'

He came to her then, his hands gripping her shoulders so that his fingers dug into her flesh, hurting her.

'Then you don't believe in love at first sight?' he asked. 'You don't think two people can meet and fall in love—all in one minute?'

Jenny bit her lip. His fingers were like steel. She winced under their pressure.

'No, I don't think I do believe in it,' she panted—'especially not in our case. I don't know anything about you, Derek. I don't think I want to know. I *am* afraid of you. There's some power in you that I can't explain but it frightens me. Instinct tells me it's an evil power—all wrong. It isn't just my conventional mind, as you put it—the wish to do the right thing by Peter, I think if I really met someone I loved more than Peter, I'd tell him, no matter how much it meant hurting him. I'd ask for my freedom and not hesitate, because I'd know it would hurt him more to go through with a loveless marriage. But you see, I happen to love Peter beyond all doubt and I still want to marry him.'

'Then you deny that there is anything at all—between *us?*'

Jenny longed to deny it as he dared, but her innate honesty forbade it, and as she spoke aloud it was also a means of sorting things out in her own mind.

'No, I think there *is* something between us, as you put it...but I regard it as a physical attraction. When you held me in your arms the other night I hated you and yet I wanted you to go on kissing me. Afterwards I was sorry and I felt horribly guilty about Peter. I resolved tonight that it would never happen again. You see, I think I believe that two people can be bodily attracted, and this means nothing more than that—just chemical reaction. Nothing more. I'm certain that if Peter kissed me in the same violent way I would respond just as violently. It is a normal woman's response to any man who happens to appeal to...to her senses!'

Derek released her. A curious light came into his eyes as he turned from her and walked over to the window, staring out into the darkness beyond. His voice was contrastingly soft and gentle when next he spoke.

'I don't know how much of what you say you believe yourself, Jennifer. But your attitude is far from being that of a normal woman. The average girl has to *love* before she feels as you admit you feel towards me. It is usually men only who love one woman and are attracted by another simultaneously, without it detracting from the greater love. You say that you hate me, but you give me no reason. Haven't you heard that hate is akin to love? You think you hate me *because you are afraid of loving me.* You know, Jennifer, you are surprisingly ignorant of human nature. There is evil in the world such as you wouldn't credit—wouldn't understand. I'm not so many years older than you, but in experience, a hundred. For your life has been a humdrum, everyday affair. For me—it has been a series of adventures...not amorous ones, as you might be thinking. I'll admit there have been a few women in my life—but never one I loved until now: never one I really wanted to marry. Cynthia just does not count. I've never in my life before told a girl I loved her. I asked Cynthia to marry me for reasons best left unexplained. If you knew me at all—the real me—you'd realize how serious

I am. I had plans for the future, the ambition to make a successful marriage for money alone. I wanted to be rich above all things—to be able to live as I would have done had I still been heir to the Barclay fortune. Well, I still want it—I shall have it, too. But more even than that, *I want you.* And I'm going to fight for you—fight with every weapon I have. I'll prove to you that you care for me—that already you do so and won't admit it!'

Again Jenny felt the impulse to turn and rush from this man. Again some curious impulse led her to stay. There was something about Derek Barclay and the things he was saying that intrigued as well as frightened her. She felt almost hypnotized by the expression in those fathomless green eyes of his. In his presence Peter, and everything connected with him, receded into the background. Against all her instincts (for she seemed to have no control left when Derek Barclay chose to impose his will on hers) she was utterly fascinated by his words, his expressions and her own sensuality, which he was trying to rouse.

Was it true that if she loved Peter as much as she thought, she could not have wanted to kiss Derek as he kissed her? Would she not have felt attracted by him? Was it true that there was more behind this than mere physical response? Was it possible that she did not hate him after all—that her hate was but an expression of her fear and the hypnotic power he exerted over her? Oh, it was easy enough to assure herself that she disliked him once she was out of his sight! But why then, as soon as she saw him again, did she find herself giving in—allowing herself to be forced into such a discussion as this—forced into doubting her own sincerity? What would have happened had she never known Peter—never been engaged to him? *Would she have fallen in love with Derek Barclay?* Would she have been flattered by his ardent proposal of marriage, thrilled by the thought of being his wife?

She gave a little shiver. No, she would never have wanted to marry him. There were other sides to marriage besides love-making; much more important issues. A woman must be able to respect the man she married, as she, Jenny, respected Peter—able to trust and confide in him, now that there was true companionship between them as well as passion. With Derek she could be sure of none of these things. There was little enough that she did know about him—good or bad—and yet instinct would not let her trust him. Perhaps because he was the son of a woman she really did dislike

223

both in type and person. Lady Barclay was a hard, sophisticated, almost cruel woman—when one started to probe deeply into her treatment of Amelia and of her own little children. It was under her influence that Derek had been brought up—by her that he had been spoilt. He was an incredibly selfish man—ruined by his mother's adoration, and although Jenny knew so little about his principals and ambitions, she was positive that they were quite different from her own or Peter's. He had admitted his main ambition to be money and position. Even while she understood the reason for this—she could not agree with it. She had no desire for riches—for a place like Marleigh Manor. She and Derek Barclay lived in different spheres and had nothing in common—except their physical interest in one another as a man and a woman.

'I'm sorry Derek!' she said at last. 'Sorry things are the way they are, and although I'm distressed that you should think you love me—it's quite hopeless. You must know it deep in your heart. Nothing you can do—*nothing*—will make me stop loving Peter. You can make me hate myself, feel unworthy of his trust in me. You can make love to me by force. But there can be no real happiness for you that way. The victory, such as it is, would be empty. And every kiss you take from me can only increase my dislike of you, for I should blame you as well as myself for my disloyalty to the man I love.'

It was a brave speech, a proud one, and Derek, for a moment, did indeed feel that his quest was hopeless. It was true that he really loved this girl—loved her as much as a complete egotist could ever love anyone. He was prepared to risk his mother's disapproval—perhaps even the loss of her interest and help with his ambitions. He was prepared to take Jenny, penniless, unimportant socially, and give her everything she desired. Her very lack of response only increased his respect and longing for her. In the past, women had been his for the asking. Cynthia, for all her wealth and position, would marry him tomorrow; had cheapened herself in his eyes by forcing her love on him even when she knew that he was tiring of their affair.

Now Jennifer, quiet, sweet, passionate Jennifer, had walked into his life with a complete disregard for him—with only one spark of physical attraction, which meant nothing in her eyes. He knew he was considered fascinating to women. He knew that his superior off-hand manner intrigued them, encouraged them to fight for his favours; knew that he could rouse a girl like Cynthia to passionate heights where other men left her indifferent. He had been proud of such achievements and conquests until now, when he saw how little they meant to a girl he really loved—the first girl he had *ever* respected.

Bitterly, he cursed the fellow to whom she was engaged; wishing him dead, knowing that in this moment of defeat he would willingly destroy Peter if he could get away with it. In mad pride he told himself that he was the more worthy of Jenny's love—the more truly alive; the better able to appreciate Jenny's nature. He had no illusions as to his moral worth; he knew that he had frequently trespassed against the law, but had no scruples about that. In his abnormal opinion ordinary people did not know how to live—they merely existed. Their lives were conventional—humdrum, diffident. But with him Jenny would know excitement, achievement, glamour and a world in which she would shine as he personally intended to shine. She would have a position thousands of other women would give the world to possess and he would love her as no other man was capable of loving...certainly not Peter.

Derek's dreams gave way to the more bitter truth of reality. Jenny had turned him down; she had admitted she disliked him; sworn she still loved the other man.

Then his determination got the better of him. He had not lost her yet. He had the advantage of the other chap in that Jenny would live under *his* roof for the next year. He would find some way of winning her—of convincing her that she did not love Peter. If he had to appeal to her in the one respect only where she knew herself to be vulnerable, then he would do so. He would *make* her love him, prove to her that her need of him was as great as his desire for her.

In that moment, looking through half-closed lids at the small figure in the blue silk dressing-gown through which the charming lines of her slender figure were so clearly visible, Derek knew an instant's madness. He felt the desire to snatch her in his arms, force her with his caresses to surrender—now...feel her weakening, feel his power over her *make her belong to him.* No other man should have the pleasure of teaching her the delights of love. That should be his prerogative. He would show her a world which she did not know existed—dear innocent little Jennifer. Her very innocence in itself was a challenge which Derek all but had to accept. He took a step towards her, his breath coming quickly, his face distorted with the half crazy emotion that surged through him. And then Jenny turned and looked at him. The distress in her eyes deepened into fright as she read what lay in his eyes. Her hands went to her throat and he saw a pulse there beating quickly, nervously. It seemed like a voiceless protest. This was not the way to win her. He would gain nothing by assault. Even if she surrendered she would feel sullied and guilty, and would despise him with every part of her. No! First he must win Jenny's affection—win her sufficiently to make her surrender at length of her own free will. Then it would be but a step to chain her to him by the depths of his own passion and art of loving.

With an effort he forced a smile to his face and said:

'Don't look so frightened, Jenny. I made you a promise and I shall keep it until you allow me to do otherwise. Now it is late and we ought both to go to bed. But before you go, please, Jenny, will you do something for me?'

Jenny was so relieved that Derek was ready to be reasonable that she felt willing to promise him anything. She looked at him enquiringly.

'Will you promise?' he said.

'Without knowing what it is? I can't do that.'

'Are you still afraid?' Derek asked.

'Need I be?' Jenny countered.

'Not if you really love your Peter. You see, I want you to be quite sure you do, and if you are sure, to convince me that I am wrong.'

'Then you still don't believe I love him!' Jenny cried. 'I think I'd do anything to convince you, for then it would mean an end to all this. I don't want it to go on. I want you to leave me alone, to forget this ever happened. I was quite at peace with myself until I came here. Now already I feel guilty and unsettled. You've no right to make me feel like this. I don't want to leave Marleigh because Peter and I have so much at stake. But I'm beginning to feel I shall have to go—for all our sakes—unless you and I can find a way to be friends.'

'You know I can never feel "just friends" with you,' Derek said, mimicking her in that old mocking tone she was beginning to know so well. 'Don't ask me the impossible, Jenny. I've told you I loved you. But I'm willing to *be* "just friends" if you will convince me that you wish it so.'

'How can I convince you?' Jenny cried urgently. 'I'd do anything to make you realize how much I love Peter...'

She was totally unprepared for his next words, although, had she known Derek Barclay better, she might have guessed them.

'Kiss me, Jenny,' he said.

She stared at him aghast.

'You're breaking your promise!' she shot at him.

'On the contrary. I'm not forcing you to—only asking. I am asking you to let me kiss you. Show me that you don't care for me...show me that you are proof against another man's love-making. Prove it to me by your ability to remain impassive in my arms. Or don't you dare?'

Jenny flushed a fiery red. She knew that he was trying to trap her. If she refused, it would be an admission of weakness; if she let him kiss her she might give in—could not be sure of her own emotions. It was cruel—hateful of him. 'And yet,' argued Jenny's inner sense, 'is he right after all? With Peter's kiss still warm on my lips—should I not be quite immune to this man? If I close my eyes and think of Peter...'

The memory of Peter sent a swift shudder through her body. How he would despise her for her feelings! How he would hate Derek Barclay if he knew what he was doing! This was but a cheap trick to get his own way.

She stood up, her head high, her face disdainful.

'I'm afraid that is something I won't do, Derek, and not for the reason you think.

It is not my own weakness I am afraid of. I will even admit that I *might* weaken. But from now on there must be no more of this sort of thing. It's cheap and beastly and I wonder you lower yourself to such petty conduct. I really *do* dislike you, and for that reason I have no wish to kiss you. I adore Peter and you know it. Now I'm going to bed. I think the less we see of each other in the future the better!'

Anger surged through him—anger because her barb had struck home; because he knew that behind his actions had been little but an insane longing to have her in his arms again, irrespective of whether she wished to be there or not. The very truth of her remarks, her disdain and the fact that he could see he was losing his battles all too quickly, made him vicious. He dropped his natural caution. This time he did not hesitate to give way to his true feelings; and to his desire for her was added a powerful desire to have his revenge—to hurt her for the blow she struck at his vanity.

As she tried to pass him, he caught hold of her and swung her round towards him, gripping her fiercely; she had no hope of avoiding him. She stared up at him, her face white and horrified. As he bent her body against his own and forced his mouth down on hers she did not cry out, did not struggle, but he knew as he felt the touch of her mouth beneath his own that this time she was not weakening. There was no response to him in lips grown hard and cold. Pride in his own strength and desire of mastery swept through him as he crushed her mouth with his own, pride and an uncontrollable primitive urge to take what he wanted no matter what happened afterwards.

Terrified, really afraid at last, Jenny held herself rigid in his grip. She no longer felt the old strange, thrilling sensuousness—only a white-hot anger coupled with hatred for this man. In that moment, while she was physically his captive, she knew herself to be free of him for ever—free of the mental hold he had once held over her. Whatever he might do to her now, there was mercifully an end to her own indecision. Even in her moment of horrified fear of what this man was about to do, Jenny felt her own pride give her courage. She would not cry out—would not even let him know that he was hurting her. His victory would be a bitter and empty one.

It was, without a doubt, a blessed and timely stroke of Fate that Mrs Minnow, suffering from insomnia in her old age, had lain awake for some hours, and at last, unable to find release in slumber, decided to go down to the kitchen to make herself a cup of tea. Mumbling to herself, she went slowly down the staircase to the kitchen. Her carpet slippers barely made a sound on the stone floor; she opened the door to a blaze of light which temporarily blinded her.

In that split second, Derek released Jenny. Free at last she fled from him, still unaware of what had brought about her release, and bumped into poor startled Mrs Minnow. She steadied the old woman, uttered a brief apology and rushed out of the room. Derek's mocking, derisive laughter following her up the stairs.

'He can explain in any way that he wishes,' Jenny thought, as she lay trembling on her bed. 'Tomorrow I shall go to Lady Barclay. If she does not give me her word that this will stop, I'll hand in my notice. And tomorrow I shall tell Peter—everything. Oh, how mad I've been! How utterly crazy to give Derek Barclay a moment's thought! He is vile—beastly, bestial! If Mrs Minnow had not come...'

Relief and reaction caused her to burst into a storm of tears. Into her pillow she sobbed out her own regrets; her apologies to Peter, whom she felt she had defiled even as she herself felt defiled. It was useless to say it had all been Derek's fault. In one sense, she had encouraged him, even if her response had been unintentional; until this last episode when he had kissed her by force, knowing it to be against her wishes, knowing her decision; and in spite of his promise. She had trusted him—crazy fool that she was—and it would have been her own fault if Mrs Minnow had not appeared on the scene to put an end to whatever might have transpired. Jenny could not bring herself to think of it. The idea was now as revolting as before his kiss had been stimulating and exciting. She saw Derek now exactly for what he was—a man who considered women only in the light of their sex and what he could get out of them. She did not believe that he sincerely wanted marriage.

'Oh, Peter, Peter!' she sobbed. 'Will you ever forgive me? Will you ever understand?'

It was a white, drawn Jenny who went downstairs after breakfast to find Lady Barclay. Her hands were trembling with nervousness and she felt exhausted. It was only the thought of Peter which sustained her.

Lady Barclay was, as usual, in her writing-room, dealing with her morning mail. She seemed annoyed by Jenny's request to speak to her 'on a private matter' and Jenny's heart sank. Perhaps after all it would be better to give in her notice with explanation.

To her unutterable surprise, it was Lady Barclay who broached the subject, before Jenny could speak.

'I hear you had some trouble with my son last night, Miss Ames. He told me all about it this morning. Very remiss of him. I hope, however, that you are going to look at the whole thing reasonably and not make a scene. I'm off to town in a few moments and I really don't want to be bothered with any explanations.'

Jenny bit her lip.

'I was not aware that...your son had already spoken about it. But I'm surprised that he has done so if he has really told you everything. Since you do know, you won't be surprised if I say that I'm afraid I cannot stay on here if there's even a remote possibility of such a thing happening again. Your son promised me this some—some days ago. He broke that promise. Now I have come for your assurance.'

Lady Barclay looked up from her blotter and gave Jenny a cold, unfriendly stare.

'Very well, you have my word. I'll speak to my son. But I want no fuss. I understand that your fiancé is coming to the house to tea. I am sure you will understand that I can't risk any scenes between him and my son. It would be too undignified and most undesirable. Under these circumstances, I would like your assurance that you will not tell your fiancé anything whatsoever about last night.'

Jenny gasped. The coolness, the colossal *verve* with which this woman was trying to control *her* personal affairs!

'You mean you are asking me to keep confidences from my fiancé?' she exclaimed.

'Why not? I really cannot see what would be gained by discussion of the stupid affair. Your young man would only be furious and jealous. He will no doubt ask you to resign your post. You will be forced into the part of a guilty person. And I shall have the immense trouble of finding another governess whom Amelia will like and who can control my children. No, since the matter is closed and will not be repeated, I think it is better for us all to ignore it. Later on, when you leave, tell your fiancé what you choose. By then I feel you will have thought better of distressing him for no practical reason. I pay you extremely well, Miss Ames, and I'm quite aware that in return you have a difficult task to perform. You've proved your worth and I shall give you a consequent rise in salary...say another two pounds a week from now on.'

'She's buying my silence,' Jenny thought, aghast. 'It's sheer bribery.'

'Well?' came Lady Barclay's voice. 'Surely, my dear girl, you do not wish to be unreasonable? No doubt you feel that the rise I have offered you has come at a very timely moment. Have no such qualms that I'm trying to buy your silence. You're at liberty to do as you wish. But you are useful to me and I don't want to lose you, added to which Derek is a foolish boy whose actions should not be taken too seriously. I'm prepared to pay what I think you are worth to *me*. You must look on my offer in that light.' Her voice became more persuasive. 'And the *twins* are so fond of you. They would be heartbroken if you left—Amelia too. Now be a sensible girl and forget my son's temporary lapse of manners. He is hotblooded and impulsive and I dare say I—and a lot of other women—have spoilt him. He shall not bother you again, I assure you. I have his word for that. Now, are you satisfied?'

Before Jenny could argue, she found herself dismissed. She walked slowly upstairs again, deep in thought.

'It's amazing how imperious and egotistical these Barclays are. No, not Barclays, for Lydia Barclay and her son are of some other blood. They command, order and expect to get their own way. When necessary, they bribe to

achieve it, lie to achieve it. They are both quite unscrupulous. Why didn't I realize sooner what they were like?' Jenny asked herself, with a little shiver of apprehension. 'If I had—I would never have come here—never.'

Then she saw Amelia, beckoning her from the top of the stairs, and her face softened. Poor Amelia—who was a true Barclay—as nice, as simple and unaffected, as her father.

'Oh, Jennifer, what shall I wear for your tea-party? I want to do you credit with your Peter. Should I wear the grey frock you like me in? And the coral necklace?' Amelia asked breathlessly.

'I couldn't go and leave her,' Jenny thought as she made some automatic reply. 'Poor, poor Amelia, living in this house with such a stepmother—and Derek! I must try to persuade Sir Gerald to send Amelia away, abroad perhaps, before I go. The child can never be happy here alone.'

She followed Amelia slowly and thoughtfully into her room.

CHAPTER XI

It was nearly eleven o'clock when Jenny walked down to the village to find Peter. He was already half-way to meet her.

'I was far too impatient to see you, darling,' he greeted her, linking an arm in hers and turning towards the Marleigh Arms.

Jenny pulled him back a step, quickly.

'Let's not go on just yet, Peter. Stay here with me. I want to talk to you.'

He did not raise any objections. There was something in Jenny's voice that puzzled him as much as her whole behaviour had done ever since his arrival. She had been so mysterious—so *different.* He could not have named what it was exactly that seemed different about her, and yet he knew there was *something.* Perhaps Jenny wished to tell him now, at this moment, and he was only too ready to be silent and listen to her.

They sat down in the stubbled cornfield, leaning their backs comfortably against a haystack in order to shelter from the chilly breeze. Out of the wind, in the sun, it was wonderfully warm for October. The atmosphere gave each of them a relaxed feeling of peace and happiness. Jenny was loth to spoil it all with words which, since she had given her promise to Lady Barclay not to tell Peter the whole truth, must necessarily worry him. If only she could find a way in which to show him how sorry she was for her disloyalty *without* betraying Derek; to let him know that she had been afraid of herself, even subconsciously! She was absolutely certain in her mind now that those stolen kisses which had disturbed as well as aroused her were nothing but the most primitive emotions; that Derek Barclay as a person repelled her more than she could ever say. Last night had shown her at last Derek's true nature. He was utterly abhorrent to her and would, she remembered with a shudder, have forced himself upon her without any respect for her wishes had Mrs Minnow not interrupted him just in time. Had it not been for Lady Barclay's assurance that Derek would not trouble her in the future Jenny would have been afraid to remain in the house another hour with Derek Barclay. It horrified her to think that she had once felt herself respond to those violent kisses; to the sensuous way he held her as he danced.

It was so easy, now, to name Derek's type—the kind of man who had no control over himself because he desired none. His only laws were those of what he wanted and what he did not want. No doubt in the past the type of woman with whom he associated had been only too willing to acquiesce to his demands. Then he had met someone who still respected moral conventions; who was, deep inside her, morally minded; whom he knew to be engaged to another man. It had seemed to him, no doubt, a challenge to his ability to seduce her. Her very antagonism had only served as a stimulant, and the more obstinately she tried to elude him the more intrigued and determined he had become. Perhaps, had she been the sort of girl to give way to him easily, he would not have long interested himself in her.

Jenny shivered, remembering the words with which he had tried to gain his own ends. He had attempted to convince her that she was attracted to him as a person; to convince her that she did not really love Peter at all; that in her inexperience she was not in a position to judge—that he could see her real self and *knew* she cared for him. It was horrible to contemplate now—difficult to believe that she could ever have been so blind to the truth. But his charm—and he could, undoubtedly, be charming when he chose—had dulled her instincts; her pity for him as a disinherited heir had softened her judgment; and that curious, hypnotic, impassioned way in which he had made love to her had almost succeeded in making her doubt herself...and Peter.

'You're very quiet Jenny Wren!' Peter said gently, worried by the frown that creased her forehead, by her lassitude and pallor.

She turned to look at him, noting the clear, sparkling blue eyes—a sailor's eyes; the lean, handsome face; the curly, somewhat untidy hair that gave him such a boyish, unguarded appearance. Her gaze travelled over the contours of his face. She seemed to see him now with a new awareness; the strong, sturdy frame that was such a contrast to the lithe grace of Derek Barclay; the long, sensitive fingers that were all artist; the straight, honest lines of jaw and width of forehead. Peter was what he looked—essentially English, decent, honest, uncomplicated. There would never be dark hidden depths in him—unless they were depths of unselfishness, kindness, goodness, and she already knew all these attributes. It would be beyond Peter to do a dishonest thing; to lie or cheat or hate. He was strong—in character as much as physically. How she needed a little of that strength herself!

'Peter, I told you there was something

important I had to say to you. Well, it's hard for me to know where to begin. Perhaps it all really started when I came down here. We'd been seeing so much of each other in town that I hadn't any time to think—about us, I mean. Well, here I have had the time in which to think. I know it's only a fortnight since I left London and yet it seems years and years longer. You see, in this short time I began to doubt whether we really were as much in love with one another as I'd always thought. I began to imagine that we'd reached an almost indifferent attitude—that we'd let our love become matter-of-fact, commonplace; taken each other too much for granted. It made me afraid—afraid that we'd drifted into a state of passivity from which neither of us had the power to arouse the other; that we were in fact almost like brother and sister.'

Peter did not interrupt her and she had turned her face away so that he could not see her expression. Likewise she could not tell what he was thinking.

'Perhaps I am not explaining very well, but I wanted to tell you this so that you'd know how small and beastly I've been. I've felt so guilty, so disloyal for doubting—us. Then something happened...I can't tell you because I promised I wouldn't...not yet, anyway; and I think it's better not to tell you yet in any case even although I do want to...to confess everything. Well, it gave me a new angle on everything. I've seen things in a new light, in a different light. I know now I was wrong to doubt; that the things I'd begun to think matter really didn't matter after all. I know now that I could never doubt that I love you. Deep in my heart I never did doubt that—only that our love was *everything* it should be. Well, I don't want any more than it is...not now—'

Peter's voice, quiet, controlled, interrupted her.

'I don't want to press for your confidences,' he said, 'but in order to understand, I think you must tell me what it is you thought our love lacked.'

'I can't tell you!' Jenny cried. 'I'm ashamed to tell you. You'd hate me so much if you knew.'

She was unprepared for Peter's response to her remark. His arms were round her, holding her tightly against him with a strength and tempestuousness which were quite foreign to his usual behaviour.

'I could never hate you, Jenny!' he was saying fiercely against her lips. 'And I think I do understand what you're trying to tell me. There's nothing wrong in it—you were right to think as you have done. You were suddenly shown—by some means I mustn't ask—that the fire and eagerness and passion had gone out of our love-making. That's it, isn't it?'

Jenny nodded, feeling the tears falling down her cheeks.

'I'm so ashamed!' she murmured.

'Oh, darling, darling, Jenny, you have no need to be ashamed. Why didn't you speak of this sooner? I didn't understand that you felt this way. We've been engaged too long—that's our trouble. I felt that since we weren't to be married for yet another year, then I must keep a rein on our feelings—that it was up to me to see that they didn't get out of control. Many a time I've longed to give way—to kiss you and hold you and take you for my own. At times I felt that it was beyond my power to conceal those feelings from you. You see, my darling, I never realized that you felt the same way. I imagined that you were content to carry on as we were doing, kissing one another good night as if, as you say, we were brother and sister rather than lovers! Just to hold one another's hands; and occasionally a caress—a brief embrace. But all the time, I wanted more—I'm only human, Jenny, as you are. You belong to me and yet I have not the right to have the whole of you—not yet. I knew you loved me—I hoped you knew that I loved *you;* I thought that you were content to be as restrained as I was—that you needed nothing more—and for your sake I did not want to upset you with the sleepless nights and torment of longing I myself have sometimes suffered. Oh, Jenny, Jenny, how blind I've been! But not now—I see everything so clearly.'

She longed to give in then—to feel, as he did, that nothing in the world mattered now they had rediscovered their love for each other—and discovered something new as well—their need of each other as man and woman. But she could not do so. Between her and Peter seemed to stand the ghost of Derek Barclay—of her guilt. Until she could tell Peter everything, she could not accept the love he was trying to impress upon her. He might, when he knew, feel differently. He might even not want her any more. This was her punishment for her weakness.

Feeling her restraint, Peter released her and his hands went to her face, turning her so that she was forced to look into his eyes.

'There's still something wrong, Jenny.... can't you tell me?'

She longed desperately to do so— wondered if, after all, her promise to Lady Barclay was so very binding. It had been mainly for Peter's sake that she had agreed to say nothing, and yet Peter, she felt certain now, *would* understand. He would not force her to leave her job if she did not really want to go. As for Derek, it could not affect him—nor Lady Barclay—since Peter certainly would not repeat what she told him, and Peter would not make a scene with Derek, no matter how he took it. He would not belittle himself by using physical violence on a man he would only despise, once he learned the truth.

She was in an agony of indecision. Her word—which she had given really against her will—was still binding, and yet was it not more of a duty to tell Peter, from whom she ought to have no secrets?

'Oh, Peter! I don't know what's right and what's wrong!' she cried helplessly. 'I want so much to tell you but Lady Barclay made me promise. I didn't think it would be so hard to keep that promise. I was in such a turmoil at the time and there seemed no point in worrying *you*. Then, before I knew what was happening, I found myself promising and at the same time receiving a rise in salary. I didn't want to take it, but I had no alternative. She's such a difficult person to deal with—so dictatorial and imperious.'

'She had no right to buy your silence, Jenny,' Peter said quietly. 'But in any case, I think there is no *need* for you to tell me. Already I have guessed part of it and the rest completes the puzzle. It's Derek Barclay, isn't it? He has tried to make love to you. There was some kind of compromising situation which Lady Barclay wants hushed up. And you are feeling guilty because of what happened. That's why you aren't at ease with me—why things are so different; why you're so upset.'

'Oh, Peter!' Jenny cried helplessly, the tears pouring down her cheeks now. 'You are so far-seeing. If you only knew how I hate myself—what a fool I've been! Are you *very* angry?'

He gave a twisted little smile.

'No, not with you, Jenny, but with myself,' he said quietly, not trying to touch her now. He let her cry, for he felt that it must relieve all her pent-up emotions—that it would do her good. 'You see, darling, I ought never to have let you over-persuade me when you decided to take this job. We ought to have been married then—in spite of the house. In fact, we ought to have been married years ago—when you wanted. It was plain stupidity for us to go on waiting—year after year. When you do that, tomorrow never comes. We were too sure of each other—too casual about something of supreme importance to both of us. We were *too* careful. There is a happy medium in all things—especially the

248

length of engagements.'

He drew a deep breath and added:

'You know, Jenny, I'm almost glad this has happened. It has shown me how precious you are to me—how terribly I should have cursed myself if I'd lost you after all this time. You do still love me, don't you?'

She was in his arms again and he was raining kisses on her lips, her hair, her tear-wet cheeks.

'You know I do, more now than ever.' She sobbed unrestrainedly now.

'Then listen to me, Jenny. We're going to be married now—next week. Give up the job—give up the house. We'll find another. But we aren't going to wait for each other any longer. Tell me you will, Jenny. Say yes!'

She drew away from him again her tears drying, her face pale and drawn. Every part of her longed to give in—to do as he suggested—and yet a queer, perhaps misplaced, sense of duty prevailed.

'Peter, I couldn't. I took the job and I can't let everyone down. It isn't Lady Barclay so much...I've little respect for her. But there are the children. I feel responsible for them. It wouldn't have mattered so much if I'd never known them, but already they have found a place in my heart and, Peter...they *need* me.'

Peter's voice was tinged with bitterness as he said:

'And don't *I* need you? Don't you need me?'

'Oh yes! Yes!' Jenny cried. 'But you don't yet understand, Peter. They are in some kind of danger. I know they are. Last night it happened again, and this time I know I saw someone. Amelia is frightened, too, and she has no one else to turn to but me. She trusts me. So do the twins. I must get to the bottom of this mystery first—before I leave.'

'Steady on!' Peter said, realizing how distraught she was, how on edge. 'Start at the beginning, Jenny. Remember this is the first I've heard of any danger. Are you in danger, too? If so, you're most certainly leaving Marleigh Manor immediately.'

Jenny smiled shakily.

'I'm in no danger,' she said. 'But I think the twins are. I don't know. It's all so muddled, Peter. I was warned the first evening I came that they had tantrums! I didn't know what this meant until one night they refused to go to bed. Then I discovered that they were frightened out of their wits. I thought it was "of the dark", and obtained them a night-light. But it can't be just that. They woke in the night screaming and crying and were quite hysterical. It was dreadful. I was woken by the noise and was going along the gallery to them when I could have sworn I saw a shadow by the window. The twins wouldn't tell me anything and I didn't like to persist as they were in such a state. Since then I've tried again and again to question them, but a look passes between them and they close up like clams. They either won't or daren't tell me. Amelia thinks it's a ghost. The house is said to be haunted, although Lady Barclay denies it and Mrs Minnow, who's been here years, swears no one has ever seen a ghost. I *know* it isn't a ghost—you see, the same thing happened last night. I didn't wake up immediately and, when I did, the gallery was empty. But after I'd calmed the twins down and they were dozing off, I heard the dog barking and went to the window. Then he yelped as if someone had kicked him and when I looked out I saw a man darting amongst the trees, keeping under cover. He disappeared down the drive. I know it was a man—there was nothing ghostly about him—his movements, his clothes—anything.'

'Of course it wasn't a *ghost!*' Peter said firmly. 'That's all my eye. It looks as if someone has been trying to break into the house. Perhaps a burglar trading on the ghost story and trying to find something he wants.'

251

Jenny shook her head.

'He wouldn't come back again, surely? Besides, there are a hundred and one valuable things lying around—Georgian silver left on the sideboard in the dining-room—paintings all over the walls worth thousands. Jewellery worth as much, if not more. Nothing is kept under lock and key. Amelia has emeralds, diamonds and rubies which belonged to her mother in a case on her dressing-table which are a fortune in themselves. And yet it is the twins' room which is being searched—I'm sure of it. Don't ask me why because I've never seen anyone in or near them, but they are so particularly afraid, Peter. They've seen *something* and I know *they* are much too frightened to get up at night and wander about the house.'

Peter frowned.

'Have you told Lady Barclay?' he asked.

Jenny shook her head.

'I don't like to, Peter. She puts it all down to this "haunted house" rumour and would call me hysterical and as stupid as the last governess. Besides, she isn't the sort of person who'd be interested. She doesn't seem to care about anything but her eldest son, and the large parties she gives. She lives for Derek. The other children count for nothing. At times she's almost cruel to poor Amelia, and the child is scared stiff of her.'

'Then Sir Gerald. You said in your letter that he was charming. Couldn't you tell him?'

'I never thought of that,' Jenny admitted. 'You see I don't often talk to him. He's so vague and dreamy. He locks himself up in the library and we rarely see him except at mealtimes, when he wanders in late. His wife hates him—I'm sure she does.'

'I think you ought to tell someone,' Peter said. 'If there is something of particular value hidden somewhere and somebody is after it, Sir Gerald ought to be told. For your own sake as well as the children's, something should be done. You may be in danger, Jenny. Good heavens—to think you've been here all this time—anything might have happened!'

At last Jenny could smile.

'Only two weeks, Peter, and I'm sure I'm not what they are looking for! I'm not even sure *they* are looking for anything.'

'You mean, someone is merely trying to frighten the twins?'

'I don't know. I haven't really sorted it out in my own mind. It was only when it happened again last night that I began to worry at all. Then—the other business, and you being here, took it out of my mind. But you see, Peter, if something *is* going on, I ought to protect the children. I can't just leave them to their fate.'

Peter bit his lip.

'It's all very well for you to assume the rôle of protector, but that's their parents' job,' he argued.

'Their parents don't concern themselves. I know Lady Barclay would dismiss the whole question—if I tried to tell her—as nonsense. And if I tell Sir Gerald, what can he do? What can I tell him, anyway? I've no proof, no facts. It is possible that I could have been mistaken about the man in the garden—or Sir Gerald might think I was.'

'But you are sure?'

'Yes,' Jenny said quietly. 'I am sure.'

'But who could want to do the twins any harm—or the girl? What could they gain by it?'

Jenny put a hand to her mouth, looking at Peter in horror as a sudden thought struck her.

'Derek Barclay! He has been disinherited by Micky. Oh, Peter...that can't be it. Besides, he was there, in the gallery. He came to see what was the matter...' Her voice trailed away. The same suspicion had struck her even while she was speaking, a suspicion that was also in Peter's mind.

'And supposing Derek wasn't coming—but *going*?'

Jenny shuddered and then a look of relief crossed her face.

'It couldn't be possible. He was in the gallery just a few seconds after I had seen the man in the garden. It couldn't have been Derek!'

Peter stifled the pang of jealousy and concern that rose at this revelation of midnight meetings between Jenny and Derek Barclay. But he could not bring himself to question her about them now. She had said that it was all over—whatever had happened. She had told him quite a lot of her own accord. He would not blame her. He still trusted his Jenny. With an effort he put his own feelings in the background and tried to help her fathom this mystery.

'Tell me, Jenny, honestly, is Derek Barclay capable of doing a small boy—his own half-brother—any real harm?'

'I don't know,' Jenny whispered. 'Perhaps. After last night I'd believe him capable of anything....'

Peter trod on the desire to rush up to the house and strangle the fellow with his own bare hands. Whatever Derek had done to Jenny, he should pay for it one day—Peter silently vowed.

'Then could it have been an accomplice in the garden?' he asked.

'I suppose so.'

'Then what I don't understand is what game he is playing at—supposing it was Barclay,' Peter said. 'I mean, he has had ample time to get rid of the child—push him over a wall or off a horse or find some means of getting him out of the way that might seem accidental. Why risk roaming around the house in the dark with the child screaming and anyone liable to come in and find him? And if he means to do the thing, why hasn't he done it already? None of this really makes sense!'

Jenny agreed. Whatever she might believe of Derek Barclay now, she could not think he meant murder. There were no facts to prove this or any of their suspicions.

Peter took her hand and held it in a tight grip.

'Jenny, let me take you away. I'm afraid now for you. You may find out more—and then be in danger yourself. For my sake, leave this place today. I don't want you to be dragged into...anything sordid and dangerous. It isn't worth it. I can't allow you to take risks—'

'Peter, don't ask me. If I went now I wouldn't have a moment's peace of mind, worrying about those children. I know they aren't really my responsibility and yet in a way they are. They trust me. And they are children. You'd risk your life, if necessary, to rescue some child from drowning, wouldn't you—no matter how hard I tried to stop you and if you'd never seen it before in your life? That's the way I feel. And I don't truly believe *I* am in danger. We're letting a lot of crazy ideas and unfounded suspicion run away with our common sense. Derek wouldn't commit murder...and suppose I did leave, and later something awful *did* happen, you'd feel responsible, too, for influencing me. Don't you see, darling? I *must* stay at Marleigh Manor—until I feel sure the twins are all right.'

His disappointment was only equal to his admiration of her courage. Another woman might have left already. But not his Jenny. And in a way she was right. If only he could stay here—be near her—see that she didn't come to any harm!

'Darling, here's a grand solution—for us, anyway—and perhaps it will help you in another way. We'll get married—quietly, down here somewhere near, without telling anyone...not even our families...and certainly not the Barclays. You could get a week-end off—say in two weeks' time. We'll spend it together in one short sweet honeymoon. Then you shall go back to Marleigh Manor and together we'll try and clear up the mystery. If nothing happens in three months from now, we'll assume that this so-called ghost was just a burglar and you'll resign your post. Unless you still really want to finish the year. It won't matter, you see, because I shall come and live down here, in the inn. We'll be able to spend every spare moment together and you can get time off—a week-end—a night. It will have to be enough and it will certainly be better than nothing!'

Jenny looked at him, her face flushed, her eyes radiant.

'Oh, Peter, *darling,* what a heavenly plan! Do you think we could? What of our wonderful ideas about a white wedding —bridesmaids—all the main reasons why we didn't get married in wartime?'

'And darned stupid we were not to do so!' Peter said. 'What, after all, does it matter whether you are married in white or blue as long as you're my wife!'

She smiled at him and lent her cheek against his.

'Oh, Peter, you angel, I do love you so much,' she whispered.

He could not resist asking then:

'And you're quite sure about—the other chap?'

'Oh, yes, *yes!*' Jenny cried. 'I must have been utterly crazy. But...I don't know what it is about him—a kind of hypnotic attraction which just attacked me in a weak moment, I suppose. I feel so guilty, Peter. I feel I've let you down, and the way you've taken it has made me feel even worse. You've been so wonderfully understanding.'

'Darling, Jenny,' Peter said, 'I don't think any the less of you. It's only human that you should be attracted if the chap has that sort of effect. And our over-long engagement has left us both a little thwarted, I've no doubt. Perhaps I ought to admit that I've not been entirely immune to the opposite sex. I don't mean I've ever given way to it, because I didn't have the same opportunities. With a man it's different. He makes the running, and, of course, I thought better of starting anything of that sort. But say a darned attractive girl *had* thrown herself at my head—done her best to force some kind of reaction out of me—I can't say I'd have been proof against it. There was once an artist's model.' He bit his lip and flushed. 'She was very beautiful physically, but mean and calculating and the type of woman I fundamentally dislike. She appealed to the senses only, and none of it had any effect on my love for you. So you see in a way I've been through the same thing. I'd have made love to her probably if we'd ever been alone together. I wanted to even while my mind fought against it. I was very ashamed of myself and felt guilty, but such a thing could never have happened if you and I had been married when we should have been married. Nor would this doubting of yours ever have taken place. We've never bothered to discuss sex much, have we, and yet it has an important effect on our feelings because we're normal, healthy human beings. Well, all that is over now. We shall be free to love each other as we both want to, instead of trying to find someone else to receive our surplus emotions.'

Jenny drew a breath of relief. Her eyes danced at him.

'Oh, Peter, I'm so thankful I'm engaged to you—that I love *you*. You're so very wonderful. There is no man in the world like you. I don't deserve your love. I can't believe we might really be married in two weeks' time—after so long, so very long.'

'Well, it's time you started to believe it,' Peter said, laughing happily.

'But, darling, how can you live down here? We never thought about the difficulties—your work, the expense—'

'I can free-lance from here as well as from London,' Peter said firmly. 'As to the expense, we'll manage somehow. I'm doing quite well, you know, darling, and work is pouring in. You are really going to marry a man with prospects!'

'And, Peter, I've got a rise. You won't need to save at all!'

'There, then that's settled. And when you leave, we'll go on a long glorious honeymoon before we settle down at the cottage.'

Jenny relaxed against him, soothed and, at the same time, wildly excited.

'Oh, if only there were no mystery at the Manor, how wonderful everything would be!' she thought.

As if reading her mind, Peter said quietly:

'And now we're going to get down to solving this mystery of yours, Jenny darling. I'm going to see what I can find out. Local gossip can be a blight, but in this case it might be a blessing. And, sweetheart, if you ever think you're in the slightest danger, you're to come straight to me—no matter what has happened to the children. Promise that! Promise!'

'Of course I will. It'll be a wonderful relief to know you are so near. It's only ten minutes' walk to the inn from the Manor and I could run all the way and be with you in five minutes.'

'Yes!' said Peter thoughtfully. And to himself he added: 'But five minutes is a long time if she *is* in danger. I must find some way of protecting her, of getting closer to the scene of the trouble. If there really is any trouble afoot. And somehow I think there may be. Jenny isn't the type to worry unduly over trifles and she is so concerned, so anxious and nervy. I wonder if that chap Barclay *is* at the back of it?' Aloud, to comfort her, he said lightly: 'Perhaps it's nothing after all. Let's forget it for the moment, Jenny. I want to kiss you now and it's of far more importance that I should do so than discussing any old ghost you can name.'

And this time, Jenny felt free to go to him with no thought of Derek Barclay between them.

But it was Peter who felt his presence— not as a rival, but in a curious way, as some sinister influence, that threatened the happiness and well-being of the girl whom he held so lovingly in his arms.

'I'd kill him first!' Peter vowed passionately, and then forgot everything as Jenny's lips met his. All other thoughts vanished from his mind in the wild ecstasy of their reawakened love.

CHAPTER XII

It was with a light heart and eager footsteps that Jenny led the way towards the Manor, her arm linked in Peter's. It was really a perfect autumn afternoon, sunny and warm now that the wind had dropped. The leaves were a carpet of gold, patterned in reds and browns, beneath their feet, and it seemed that in such a world of beauty and peace, there could be no place for fear, for ghosts or sombre mysteries.

Even Peter began to feel that, perhaps after all, Jenny had been suffering a little from nerves, and wondered if by chance she could have *imagined* what she had seen in the gallery.

As they neared the house two small figures came racing to meet them. They wore bright green dungarees and scarlet jumpers and they looked at a distance like two small elves laughing and racing one another between the trees.

'We've come to meet you!' shouted Micky, and the next moment they were jumping round Jenny and Peter, showing no sign of shyness—full of childish inquisitiveness and good spirits.

'Is this Uncle Peter? Why hasn't he got a sailor's clothes on? Did you meet any pirates?'

Peter grinned at them, winking at Jenny over his shoulder as he bent down to swing Marie high above him on to his shoulders.

'You're Micky, aren't you?' he teased her.

She pouted.

'I'm not! I'm Marie. Can't you see I've got *long* hair?'

'Oh, yes, I'm sorry. But you really do look alike, don't you? Well, what's new in this part of the world?'

'There's chocolate biscuits for tea,' Micky informed him seriously. 'And we had to promise Mrs Minnow we'd keep clean if she let us come to meet you.'

'And we're not to be a nuisance!' Marie added.

Jenny, seeing Peter's laughing face and kind, twinkling blue eyes, felt a surge of happiness within her. He was clearly enchanted with the twins, and his manner with them was perfect. It made her very happy to know that Peter loved children as much as she did—that one day soon perhaps they would have children of their very own.

A little of her happiness faded, however, as they neared the house. She hoped desperately that Derek was not about—that she wouldn't be forced to introduce Peter to him. Instinctively she knew the two men would not like each other and she wanted nothing to spoil their little tea-party.

For this reason, she suggested they should go in through the garden door and up to the nursery by the back staircase. The twins sensed nothing odd in this, but Peter looked at her curiously as if trying to guess her reason.

In the nursery, Amelia was waiting for them. She smiled shyly at Peter. He soon put her at her ease and she began to chat as happily as the twins. Tea was a gay affair and it was all Jenny could do to prevent the twins getting too excited by Peter's lurid and slightly exaggerated tales of his days at sea. Pirates appeared out of the ship of his imagination, 'sailing ships' laden with treasure. Even a desert island evolved. The children were enthralled and delighted with this new Uncle, and Jenny could have hugged Peter for entertaining them so charmingly.

When tea was over, she managed to drag Peter away for a short while to show him over the house. In the gallery, where twilight now had gathered in the dusky corners, a moment's eeriness was felt by them both and Peter was no longer so sure that Jenny had imagined her fears. The long dark passage, in the half light and deepening shadows, was a sharp contrast to the noise and laughter and brightness of the schoolroom. It seemed suddenly as if the house were deserted with no other occupant besides themselves. No light shone from the hall downstairs, no sound broke the silence except for the steady ticking of the big grandfather clock.

A door banged suddenly and they both started involuntarily. Jenny gave a nervous laugh.

'So there is someone about—in the kitchen, I think. I wonder where Lady Barclay is!'

Robert, the butler, came into the hall and, seeing the two figures on the landing, came up to meet them.

'M'lady said to tell you that she and Mr Derek have gone to London and won't be back until Wednesday,' he said. 'And Sir Gerald wishes you and the young gentleman to join him for dinner unless you have other plans.'

'Thank you, Robert!' Jenny said, looking enquiringly at Peter.

'I'd be delighted to meet Sir Gerald,' Peter said, and the old butler went slowly down the stairs again towards the library.

'Well, I think that's jolly decent of the old baronet!' Peter said with a smile. 'You look pleased about something, Jenny.'

Jenny gave a quick laugh.

'I am! Somehow I feel happier when Lady Barclay isn't here. And I've no need to tell you I'm glad *he's* gone, too.'

He gave her hand a quick squeeze and then said gaily:

'Come on, darling, let's have a look at the rest of the "haunted house." Show me your room, first.'

Peter was as impressed as Jenny had been by the luxury and extravagance that was in evidence everywhere they went. They did not go into Lady Barclay's suite, naturally, nor into Derek's rooms, but Peter was interested in the general layout of the house. In the twins' night nursery he spent some time looking around as if trying to puzzle out why anyone should want to come in here. Jenny knew what was in his thoughts.

'There's nothing to explain it,' he said. 'Unless whoever it is—if there is someone —intends harm to the children. Couldn't you arrange to sleep nearer to them?'

'Lady Barclay won't permit it. She calls it pampering the twins. But I can leave my door open....'

'You know, darling, this place does give me the creeps!' Peter admitted. 'It's so darned big and deserted and gloomy. I don't like to think of you here—alone—'

'I shan't feel lonely with you living so near by,' Jenny reassured him. 'And it may be nothing at all, Peter. I know only too well that I've no facts to go on—except I *know* I did see someone in the grounds. The rest is just instinct; I am certain something peculiar is going on. But of course it may be just the atmosphere of the old place.'

Peter put his arm round her shoulders and gave her a quick hug.

'You're not to worry too much, Jenny darling. We'll find out soon enough. And tonight, with your permission, I intend to bring the subject up with Sir Gerald. It's a great opportunity and it can't do any harm, if he's as decent as you say. He would surely respect our confidences.'

Jenny nodded.

'I only hope he won't think we're both half-witted!' she said with a nervous little laugh.

They rejoined the children in the schoolroom and until bedtime Peter kept them entertained and enraptured. When at last bedtime came he joked with them until they were safely tucked up in bed, the little night-light glowing between them. Jenny kissed them both good night.

Watching her, Peter knew that he loved her more than ever at that moment. He saw her suddenly as the mother of his children, kind, sweet, loving and patient. He knew then that he wanted more than anything in the world to take her away from this house—from the evil influence that seemed to pervade it when night fell. He was increasingly afraid for her, and however ridiculous that fear might be, he loved Jenny too much to risk any harm coming to her. But at the same moment he knew that he could not now ask her to desert these two small children. They were wonderful kids—and they loved and trusted Jenny as if *she* were their mother rather than the woman who had gone to London without even bidding them good-bye. Looking down at the flushed little faces, into two pairs of glowing greenish-blue eyes, at their curly black heads, his own protective instincts were aroused as much on their behalf as on Jenny's. They were so innocent, so helpless, against whatever danger might threaten them. Now he had met them, he himself would have no peace of mind until he could be sure that no evil was threatening them.

Amelia, too, he noticed, was pathetically attached to Jenny. He felt sorry for Sir Gerald's elder daughter and wondered what kind of a life she must have, living here in this big house, friendless, lonely, lost, dreaming in a little world of her own.

His feelings were vaguely resentful as he went downstairs with Jenny to meet the children's father. He blamed Sir Gerald as much as Lady Barclay for not caring more about the children's happiness. When he met the old baronet, however, his attitude changed. The man was so obviously a dreamer, buried in his library of books—living in a bygone age—and hardly aware of what went on around him. But it was soon clear that, although his natural reticence and shyness prevented any demonstrations of affection, he was devoted to his daughter of his first marriage.

Sir Gerald gave them both a glass of sherry and the first awkwardness was soon overcome when he started to question Peter about his wartime experiences. In turn, Sir Gerald told him of some adventures he had had in the First World War.

'Times have changed a bit since then, though,' he said with a regretful sigh.

'Well, they've brought you one great asset—or rather two,' Peter said, cleverly twisting the conversation into the channels he desired.

'You have a son and heir now, and little Marie! Those twins are really delightful, sir.'

'I know, I know,' agreed the old man. 'I bless the day they were born. But I sometimes wonder if it was so important after all!'

'Having the heir, you mean, sir?' Peter asked.

'Yes! I ask myself whether it is so important that the name of Barclay should continue. These are changing times. Taxation and the present Government are ruining the country—destroying the old ways of living. I ask myself what there'll be left for young Michael to inherit!'

'Oh, Father, that's a gloomy outlook!' Amelia chided him gently.

'Well, it's true. We're not very rich any more, Amelia—not by the old standards, anyway. Of course, there'll always be the Manor—but Michael might not want it by the time he inherits! It will be more of a liability to keep this place going, than of an asset to the boy. Oh, well, I hope I shan't live to see the day the place changes hands.'

'Jenny tells me that the Barclays have lived here for a good few hundred years,' Peter remarked, lighting the cigarette the baronet had offered him.

'Indeed they have, my boy. I've got a book somewhere on the family history. Been some good Barclays and some rogues too.' He looked suddenly happier.

'And does the book say anything about the ghost that's supposed to haunt the

271

house?' Peter enquired innocently.

'Yes, indeed! Though, mind you, I've never seen it myself. Don't really believe in them. But Amelia does—don't you, my girl?'

'Yes, I *know* there's a ghost!' Amelia said quietly. 'I've heard it, Father. And once I thought I saw it.'

'Sheer imagination!' said Sir Gerald with a good-natured laugh. 'Now run along and see if dinner is nearly ready, Amelia. I want to talk to Miss Ames alone for a moment.'

As Amelia obediently left the library, Sir Gerald turned to Jenny and said:

'Hope your young man won't object to my talking like this for a moment. Truth of the matter is I'm worried about my girl... Too lonely here for her. That ghost nonsense...too much time for brooding and all that. What do you think I ought to do about her?'

Jenny looked surprised. Surely this was a matter to be discussed with Lady Barclay—she was Amelia's stepmother. Yet Jenny was only too eager to help Amelia.

'I think you're right,' she said eagerly. 'It's not natural for anyone as young as Amelia to lead such a life. Wouldn't it be possible to—well, perhaps send her to Switzerland for a year or two, where she'll be with other girls?'

'Hum! Might be a good idea. Should miss her, though. Wouldn't seem the same without her. Wish I could have taken her abroad myself but...' His voice trailed off into silence. Neither Jenny nor Peter spoke, and after relighting his pipe Sir Gerald continued: 'Perhaps there's no need to send her away now you're here, Miss Ames. She's very attached to you and I'm grateful for the interest you take in her.'

'I'm very fond of her,' Jenny began, but Peter broke in:

'The point is, sir, that Miss Ames won't be here indefinitely. I mean Lady Barclay only engaged her for a year, until the twins go to school. And as a matter of fact, Miss Ames and I...well, we intend to get married as soon as possible. I'm hoping I can persuade her to give up the job even sooner.'

Sir Gerald peered at Jenny from beneath his bushy eyebrows.

'Well, I can't say I blame you, young man. But I should be sorry to see her go.'

'I shan't leave just yet,' Jenny said quickly. 'I feel it's my duty to stay because I arranged to do so when Lady Barclay engaged me and I don't want to let her down.'

'Quite! All the same, under the circumstances—'

'There's another reason, too, sir,' Peter put in quickly. 'My fiancée feels it's her duty to stay here until she can assure herself that the children...well, that they aren't in any danger.'

'Danger!' Sir Gerald's, thin, aristocratic face turned to Peter, wide-eyed with sheer amazement. 'What *can* you mean by that, young man? What *sort* of danger?'

'That's just it. We don't know. There's nothing much to go on, but I think you ought to know about it,' Peter said, taking courage in both hands, although he was beginning to feel he might sound rather ridiculous. 'Twice Jennifer has been woken in the night by the children screaming. Once she thought she saw someone in the gallery, as she ran along to their room that night. Admittedly it could have been imagination. The second time—last night to be exact—she *knows* that she saw someone in the grounds. The dog had been barking and she looked out of the window and saw this fugitive, whoever he was, running down the drive. She is convinced that someone goes to the children's room, but the children won't tell her what has frightened them.'

'Well, bless my soul!' exclaimed Sir Gerald. 'I hope you are not right, my dear young lady. Have you told...my wife?'

Jenny shook her head.

'To be truthful, I didn't like to approach her. You see, I think Lady Barclay would think I was imagining it...that I was influenced by the ghost story. *But it isn't a ghost.* I'm sure of that. I don't believe in spooks, anyway. But *something* has frightened the twins. And I believe it's the same thing that Amelia is meaning, only she *does* believe it's a ghost.'

Sir Gerald waved a hand in the air as if to dismiss the 'ghost theory'. 'How long do you think this has been going on?' he asked, frowning over his horn-rimmed glasses.

'Since before I came. When I arrived the twins were scared to go to bed. They *know* something, but it's hopeless to try and force it out of them. They're determined not to tell. If only I knew who could possibly want anything from their room!'

'Or wish them any harm!' Peter added bluntly.

Sir Gerald coughed. He looked vaguely distressed.

'This is very worrying—very worrying indeed. You're sure you're not mistaken, Miss Ames?'

'I could be,' Jenny admitted. 'But I'd swear to having seen that man in the grounds last night. And you could see for yourself how frightened the children are.'

'Well, it's best not to take any chances,'

Sir Gerald said slowly and thoughtfully. 'I shall have to look into it. You've no idea *who* the fellow was?'

Jenny shook her head.

Sir Gerald added. 'A burglar perhaps—but no thief would come so often or so regularly. It seems as though it's someone who knows the house well and is looking for something. But why in the children's room? Nothing valuable there.'

'That's what we thought, sir,' said Peter.

'One of the servants, perhaps. But for what reason? Doesn't make sense.'

'Let's hope I'm wrong,' Jenny said fervently.

'Very glad you told me,' Sir Gerald said. 'Tell you what, Miss Ames—next time anything suspicious happens, come straight along to me. You know where my room is. Wake me as soon as you hear anything; before you do *anything* at all. Don't like the sound of this.'

'You have no suspicions yourself, sir, if I may ask?' Peter enquired.

The old man shook his head.

'Afraid I wouldn't be the person to know. Rather keep to myself I'm afraid. Fact is I bury myself in my books and forget the rest of the world! Very remiss, but it's peaceful and quiet. Amelia and I have some good times here with our books.'

Peter felt suddenly that the old man was infinitely pathetic. He had so much in the way of worldly goods and yet so little. He knew from Jenny how shabbily Lady Barclay treated her scholastic husband—how much he had loved his *first wife who had died.* No wonder he lived amongst his books with Amelia for company.

'I hope there isn't anything in all this,' Peter repeated Jenny's remark. 'But if there is, I should be grateful if you'd keep an eye on my fiancée, sir. I should feel happier if I knew she wasn't tackling this problem alone.'

'Certainly. Very brave of her to stay on in the circumstances. Understand the last governess left because she was scared out of her wits—but I was told she *did* believe in ghosts! This is probably just some hoax, no doubt. Anyway, we'll see. Now, we mustn't be morbid when my Amelia comes back. Tell me, when do you two plan to be married?'

When Amelia returned to say dinner was ready she found them all talking and laughing together as if they were old friends. She stood beside Jenny, her eyes on her father, and once leant over to say very quietly:

'It's the first time Father has laughed for years, Jennifer. I *do* like your Peter!'

'So do I, Amelia!' Jenny whispered, a mixture of pride and pity mingling in her heart.

Dinner was a surprisingly gay affair compared with the more official meals normally held in the huge dining-hall. Although the massive silver candlesticks were out as usual and all the beautiful Georgian silver, cut-glass and Crown Derby dinner service—the meal served by Roberts as impeccable and staid as ever —somehow or other the atmosphere had changed. It had become an intimate family party at which Amelia and her father played host and hostess to Peter and Jenny.

Sir Gerald, it appeared, was not always dreamy and vague. Tonight he told his young audience some exciting stories of his own adventures and those of the Barclays long since dead; and when he was on this favourite topic—the history of the Barclay family—he proved himself an amusing and interesting *raconteur*. Amelia, too, was far more talkative than usual, and Jenny saw a new side to the girl whom her stepmother believed so dull and unintelligent. She was very well read—due to her father's library and influence no doubt—and she seemed as *au fait* as Sir Gerald with the past history of her ancestors.

Peter and Jenny were enthralled listeners.

There was something romantic and inspiring about this family as there was about any long lineage of the aristocracy. There had been the bad Barclays who were pirates, robbers, highwaymen; there had been the good ones, even one reputed to have been a member of Robin Hood's outlaws. There were the great Barclays who had won distinction in wars, at court, in private duels...in all the spheres in which honour and fame were to be won. And Sir Gerald himself, Amelia told them with pride, had gained distinction and had been mentioned in despatches in the First World War.

'Now it's up to young Michael to carry on the traditions,' Sir Gerald said thoughtfully over his port. 'The boy has spirit and intelligence and I have every faith in him. You've no idea how pleased I was when my dear wife presented me with an heir at last—after all this time. In fact, I don't know who was the more pleased, Amelia or myself.' He gave his daughter a brief intimate smile which she returned radiantly. 'Perhaps you will think it just a silly old-fashioned whim to be so concerned about another Barclay coming into the world to carry on the line, but family tradition is strong in me, and I can't agree with the modern idea that blood and breeding are unimportant. No doubt I'm biased, but I feel it was the old families who were as much responsible for England's greatness as the "Yeoman stock".'

'I agree with you, sir,' Peter said heartily. 'And since I don't come from a long line of any particular note, I am unbiased. Mind you, I do approve of a lot of the socialist ideas. The poverty and misery that used to exist was unbelievably frightful. Even now there are far too many slums, and tenements and misery, particularly among the kids in big cities. And yet surely social reforms could be achieved without destroying the pride and hope of old families.'

'That is entirely my own attitude,' Sir Gerald said with enthusiasm. 'I've made it my business to see that anyone who works on this estate—no matter in how menial a job—should be well housed, and paid sufficient to give him and his family a decent living. I have arranged a pension scheme, too, for all my old retainers. As for unemployment, no man has ever need fear that he would be discharged so long as he worked well. If he does not, then I consider it wrong for him to be able to claim his keep. I disagree with the dole in such cases. If the State will keep him—no matter whether he works well or badly, or at all—it encourages idleness. Let us have unions by all means, if employers are not to be trusted. No man should work more than a certain number of hours a day. The days of slaves are, mercifully, gone. But to ensure a man a means of living, no matter how lazy or inefficient he is—that is madness. It destroys all incentive—all wish to do well.'

'I trust young Micky will have the same sentiments as yourself, Sir Gerald,' Peter put in warmly.

'Indeed, I hope by the time he is of an age to take my place that there will be something left for me to hand on to him!' Sir Gerald said with a smile. 'If taxation continues at this crippling rate, my son may find himself a very poor man.'

'But, Daddy, if we've not got so much money now as we used to have,' Amelia asked with a slight frown, 'why don't we economize?'

Her father smiled again indulgently.

'It hasn't come to that yet, Amelia. I'm still rich. But as a matter of interest, my dear child, how would *you* start to economize—suppose you had the running of the house in your hands?'

'Isn't that rather a difficult question, Sir Gerald?' put in Jenny, smiling. 'After all, I doubt if Amelia has ever had anything to do with household accounts!'

'Maybe not,' Amelia said swiftly. 'But I'm sure, for one thing, that the parties my stepmother gives must cost a fortune and are a terrific extravagance. And we have them so often.'

There was a moment's embarrassed silence for Jenny and Peter, but Sir Gerald seemed quite unperturbed by Amelia's somewhat tactless comment on her stepmother's behaviour.

'Now, Amelia, how many times have I told you not to judge others by yourself?' he chided her gently. 'You don't like parties, so the first thing you'd do is put an end to them. But your stepmother does like them and so does your brother Derek. This house is run for the comfort and enjoyment of everyone in it. You young children have your horses and they run up quite a big bill, but I don't notice your suggesting you should do without them, my child!'

Amelia hung her head but Sir Gerald patted her shoulder kindly.

'Dear little Amelia, don't bother your head about such things any more. Fortunately, as I said, we've not reached the stage where we need cut down on our little personal luxuries. When the time comes, I shall discuss the matter with you seriously. Now, my dear, I think we'll adjourn to the library for coffee, after which I feel certain Miss Ames and Mr Barrington would probably like a little peace and quiet. We must not take up too much of their time.'

'Oh, we shall have plenty of time to be together from now on, sir,' Peter said. 'I'm coming to stay at the Marleigh Arms for a bit and I shall work there.'

'Oh, are you really coming to live down here?' Amelia asked eagerly. 'Then Jenny can see you as often as she wants, can't she?'

'As often as I can be spared,' Jenny put in quickly.

Sir Gerald smiled.

'Well, I dare say there'll be plenty of times when the twins can do without you. We shall have to arrange our routine accordingly. We don't want to lose you yet, do we, Amelia?'

'Oh, *no!*' Amelia cried. 'You wouldn't really leave us, would you, Jennifer?'

'You see how indispensable you are already, Miss Ames!' remarked Sir Gerald, as he lit his cigar and puffed at it peacefully.

'I'm very happy you should think so,' Jenny said with a quick look at Peter.

'I shall just have to curtail my own demands,' Peter said with pretended unhappiness. Amelia was immediately contrite.

'Of course, we wouldn't want her to stay unless she really wanted to herself.'

'I'm sure Jennifer prefers your company to mine, Amelia,' Peter teased her.

They laughed together, and as Peter

linked his arm through hers, Jenny gave a sigh of contentment. The house seemed to be very care-free and happy when there was just themselves in it...when, in fact, Lady Barclay and Derek were out of it. It was strange how their very presence cast a shadow on the place. Could Sir Gerald really not have noticed, or was it just a figment of her own imagination? she wondered.

She slipped away before coffee to see if the twins were asleep and found that all was quiet in the room. Their deep regular breathing was the only sound. She added a little water to the saucer in which the night-light flickered, and for a moment leant over the two little sleeping figures, lost in thought. Their small elfin faces were childlike and rosy in repose, their lashes curly and black against the pink cheeks. They looked very cherubic, very innocent and good. It seemed hardly possible that harm threatened them. Could that also be her imagination? Were they nothing more than a pair of naughty children who were 'playing her up'? She rejected the idea immediately. Their screams and tears had been all too life-like and their terror very real. If only they would tell her what it was they feared! If only she could persuade them to trust her sufficiently to let her into their secret...for there was a secret between them...those queer little looks they exchanged and the way they became almost furtive as soon as she started to question them. They were hiding something from her for some reason of their own and she meant to find out what it was. They were very young—scarcely out of babyhood—but if this continued, and the dark remained menacing and fearful, their highly strung nerves might tauten, and who could tell what damage would result to their health? In another year they would be going to school—perhaps the best thing for them—but until then, and during this very impressionable year of their lives, it was her duty to care for them, spiritually as well as physically.

'It's strange,' she thought, 'but I don't think I've ever heard them say their prayers. Tomorrow I shall teach them a prayer to say at bedtime.'

As she went downstairs, closing the door softly behind her, she could not help but think that it was her mother who had taught her her first little prayer—not a strange, impersonal governess. It was her mother's soft lap in which she had buried her head to confess the day's misdeeds, in *her* gentle loving arms that she had wept and been comforted. But who could imagine children kneeling at Lady Barclay's feet, little voices stumbling over long words of prayer, eyes raised questioningly to those slanting green ones with the cold aloof expression so often tinged with contempt?

Jenny gave a wry smile at the improbability of her thoughts.

'I ought not to condemn her ladyship,' she told herself. 'It may not be her fault. After all, she is not young and the twins were born so late in her life. Peter and I will have our children when we are young,' she vowed suddenly. 'Then we shall belong to them and they to us.'

With a lighter heart she quickened her pace down the stairs and hurried back to the sound of Peter's laugh and Peter's voice.

'Soon,' she told herself exultantly, 'we're going to be married. In fourteen days' time I shall be Peter's wife. I don't deserve such happiness—such a wonderful husband. I can hardly believe it's true—in two weeks' time I shall be Mrs Peter Barrington....'

But Jenny, as she walked with a light step and singing heart towards the closed library door, was not to know that once again fate intended to intervene in her life; yet again postpone her marriage to Peter. She could have no inkling, at that happy anticipatory moment, that before the two weeks had passed, the mystery which surrounded the house and the people in it, was to deepen with frightening intensity, involving Jenny herself in a way from which there could be no extraction. She had no premonition of what the next ten days would bring, but Peter, looking up as she walked into the room, felt a sudden twist at his heart. She looked so very beautiful, so very desirable, so very endearing as she came towards him with that tender smile on her face. Was it possible that now, at last, she was really to become his wife? If only these Barclays had no claim—no need of her! he sighed, and yet even while the thought crossed his mind he knew that he asked the impossible. Jenny had taken the job, and he had allowed her to do so. Now she had become attached to the children—they to her, and she believed them to be in danger. He could not ask her to leave them, would not do so himself, and yet in that instant's queer premonition of coming disaster he longed to be able to pick her up and carry her away like some knight of a bygone age rescuing his lady from her prison tower!

Then the absurdity of his thoughts brought a smile to his lips and the face he turned to her was cheerful, loving, humorous...all the things Jenny liked to see. How proud she was going to be when she wore his wedding ring and could call herself his wife! she reflected.

'Everything all right, darling?' he asked

her softly as he took one of her hands in his.

'Everything!' said Jenny, looking deep into his eyes.

So for the moment, anyway, their happiness was complete.

CHAPTER XIII

The remainder of the week passed without incident of any kind. Peter had returned to London after the week-end, to pack up some clothes and painting materials, see one or two editors to collect a further batch of work, and most important of all, obtain a special licence and a wedding-ring. In a fit of extravagance and excitement, he also bought, for a wedding present for Jenny, a beautiful baby seal fur coat—a silvery, grey, gleaming thing.

In the meantime Jenny led a quiet, uneventful life at Marleigh Manor. The weather had turned suddenly wet and cold and it seemed as if summer had departed overnight and that winter had taken its place, heralded by a big gale which had brought down most of the leaves still left on the big beeches. The flowers, too, had been flattened by the heavy rain, and looking out of her bedroom window, the fine old garden seemed to Jenny cold, bare and deserted. The great lawns were sodden with water. The ornamental lake was a dull metallic hue.

Indoors, however, fires were lit and logs

crackled cheerfully in the big grates. For all the size of the Manor, it was kept beautifully warm by central heating as well as open fires, and by five o'clock, when the curtains were drawn and lights shone warmly in all the rooms, it was cheerful enough.

The children seemed content to abandon their riding and long rambles, for the nursery fire and their new scrapbooks which Jenny had helped them start. Amelia spent most of her time with them, knitting a jumper and cardigan with Jenny's help. And once, during the week, Sir Gerald joined them for nursery tea. It was a happy family party and Jenny felt more than once, that if only Lady Barclay and Derek would stay away in London, this friendly, cosy atmosphere might continue indefinitely.

But their privacy was short-lived. A telephone call from Lady Barclay announced that she would arrive with her son and numerous week-end guests on the Friday evening. Jenny was to prepare for the house-party as she had done so successfully a fortnight ago. There would be no dancing this time, but card-tables were to be put up instead. Obviously it was to be a week-end of heavy gambling. Lydia Barclay liked poker.

Jenny accepted her orders quietly but

with an inner irritation she could not quite banish. On Friday evening Peter, too, was due to arrive and she had hoped to be able to get the evening and perhaps the Saturday afternoon off and spend them with him.

When Sir Gerald heard that his wife was arriving and that there was to be a big party, he sent for Jenny. She joined him in the library. He told her to sit down as he had something he wished to say to her.

'It concerns this question of the younger children,' he said. 'I've been thinking about it quite a lot since you and your young man mentioned your concern to me. Tell me, nothing has happened since?'

'No, I'm glad to say,' Jenny told him.

'Then there is a chance that it might have been a burglar and the danger you feared of no real foundation. However, it has occurred to me that the last time this thing happened was on the night prior to the last party. There were many people in the house at the time. I'm not suspecting anyone, you understand, but I'd like to make absolutely certain that it doesn't happen again. Now I thought it might be a sound scheme if your young man came to stay in the Manor this weekend. He could have that room next to the night nursery—nobody occupies that at the moment, do they? Then he could keep an eye on them in that way. Do you think he'd agree?'

Jenny's eyes shone. What a relief! she thought. Dear Sir Gerald!

'I'm sure Peter would!' she said. 'You see, he has been in London all week and I had been looking forward to seeing him this week-end. Now that there is to be a party I shall be pretty busy and could not easily leave the house. If he could come here, too, it would be simply wonderful.'

'Then that is settled,' Sir Gerald said. 'There may be a perfectly logical reason why the children were frightened, and the idea of someone actually bent on doing them harm or purposely frightening them still seems to me rather ridiculous. However, I do not intend to take any chances where my children are concerned— nor do I think your young man would appreciate it if I let *you* come to any harm! So we'll arrange for him to be here to keep an eye on the lot of you!'

'You're very kind,' Jenny said with feeling. 'I hope that there will be no real need for Peter's protection and that I merely imagined what I saw the other night. There's just one thing more—will you explain what has happened to Lady Barclay or shall I tell her?'

'I see no reason in worrying her unduly,' Sir Gerald said. 'I doubt she would be very concerned by our fears. She is a woman of great courage and sound common sense and I feel sure she would merely reject the idea as absurd. I'm half inclined to do so myself. Once such tales of haunting and ghosts get around it is so easy to imagine one sees things, hear things. But I believe you also are a person of great common sense and that you would not have spoken of this to me unless you believed there really was something wrong. Well, we shall see. The fewer people to learn of our suspicions, the more likely we shall be to get to the bottom of the mystery. Lydia, my wife, would consider the matter in a humorous light and, perhaps, think the whole thing a joke to be related to her guests. So I will simply tell her that I have given my permission for your fiancé to join our house-party. She won't raise objections, I'm sure.'

'You're very kind,' Jenny said again. 'Now, if you will excuse me, I'll drop a note in at the Marleigh Arms and tell Peter what has been decided.'

Jenny felt it wiser not to inform the twins of Peter's visit, for they would be bound to discuss the matter, since he had become their new hero. They asked innumerable questions about him, told Mrs Minnow everything he had told them and pestered Jenny to let them have a drawing Peter had done for her of Marleigh Manor—a brief pencil sketch he had amused himself with during their nursery tea-party.

Amelia, however, would be sure to see him at the party, so Jenny said simply that Peter would be coming, and trusted to the girl's customary reticence not to broadcast the fact. Amelia, in fact, was far too concerned with her own excitement to think for long about the strangeness of the governess' fiancé being invited to one of her mother's house-parties. The afternoon post had brought a letter from Charles saying that he and his mother had been invited down to Marleigh Manor again this coming week-end, and that he was looking forward to it because he knew that *she* would be there.

'What shall I wear, Jennifer?' she asked, her face radiant. 'Oh, it's strange to think that until now I've always dreaded Mother's parties. Now I'm as excited and as happy as I could be!'

'And should be!' Jenny thought, remembering her own first grown-up dance and how thrilled she had been even although it had been quiet and dull compared with the exotic parties Lady Barclay gave.

She, too, was pleasantly excited and was glad that she had so much to do that the time flew by and almost before she knew it, Friday evening had come, and Peter, impeccably dressed, wearing a dinner jacket he had packed at the last moment on impulse, arrived as the first 'guest'.

She took him to his room, and for a moment he held her in his arms and kissed her.

'I shall see something of you at the party?' he asked her eagerly.

'I hope so, darling,' Jenny whispered against his lips. 'After everyone has arrived, I shouldn't be too busy.'

'I'll probably be in the library with Sir Gerald if he doesn't object,' Peter said. 'You'll find me there. I want to thank him for letting me come here for the week-end. It was a superb idea. Whatever motives for your safety and the children's, it has also given me the opportunity to see more of you, and that's what really matters.'

'Oh, darling!' Jenny cried, feeling his arms tighten around her and her own heart beating swiftly in response. 'I was afraid I shouldn't see you at all. I *couldn't* have asked for time off so soon after last week-end.'

'And now we needn't worry,' Peter agreed. 'Oh, Jenny, darling, this week has crawled by! It was only the thought of coming back to you today that has kept me sane. It's strange, but when we used to see each other so often, the importance of doing so seemed so trivial. We *had* allowed our love to become too commonplace, you know. I feel now as I used to do in the war—that every second I have with you is vitally important and to be treasured and that every moment apart is hell! Whatever happens now, I think I shall be glad you took this job and showed me what an old dullard I was becoming! It served me right that I so nearly lost you to young Barclay—'

'You certainly did not!' Jenny interrupted. 'I never would have stopped loving you, Peter, no matter what happened. It was just—oh, I don't know—a strange new thrill, I suppose, and Derek is or was attractive to me in a rather devilish way! You'll meet him this evening.'

'And I'd better curb my feelings,' Peter said. 'I shall be livid if he so much as looks at you!'

'He won't dare!' Jenny said smiling. 'I feel quite safe from him with *you* here.'

He put his arms around her and would have kissed her again except that there were footsteps stopping outside the door and Amelia's voice called:

'Are you there, Jennifer? Some of the guests have just arrived and Mother is asking for you.'

With a quick pressure of their hands

Peter and Jenny parted their different ways, each happy and eager for the moment when they would be together again.

It was, however, with some trepidation that Jenny descended the stairs into the hall below. Somewhere amongst the crowd of people gathered there was Derek Barclay, whom she had not seen since that night in the kitchen. What would he say—if anything? Would he cut her dead or else make some biting comment?

Nervously she surveyed the gathering and was instantly called by Lady Barclay.

'Ah! There you are!' she said in her cool, imperious voice. 'Will you show the guests their rooms?'

'Ah, Miss Ames!' said a voice at her elbow. 'How nice to be welcomed home! I trust you are pleased to see...all of us?'

Derek's voice, as she had suspected, mocking and sarcastic...carefully lowered to a tone that would reach her ears only. She bit her lip, refusing to meet his gaze—forcing herself to ignore his greeting. She moved quickly away from him towards the dowager, whom she recognized as Charles' mother. Behind her back she heard Derek's short sardonic laugh and her face flushed with annoyance. Why could he not leave her alone? she wondered. There was something a little cruel and sadistic about him—something even vicious and untrustworthy. She felt it now in his presence indubitably.

She did not see him again until the guests were seated in the hall, drinking, laughing, talking. Peter had already gone to the library, having introduced himself to Lady Barclay, who appeared disinterested in his reason for being there or in himself as a person. Peter had not yet been able to pick Derek out from the other fellows. They all seemed to him of a similar type which he did not care for...hard drinking, hard living—even degenerate; as slack in manners and voice as in morals. The women, too made up, too hectic and excitable. He was glad to escape to Sir Gerald's library. He liked and admired the intellectual old man who had made such a mistaken marriage.

Derek, however, had noticed a new face and enquired of his mother the name of the stranger. When he learned that the tall, good-looking young man was Jenny's fiancé, he was furiously angry, consumed by unreasonable jealousy.

'Who the hell asked him to stay here?' he said violently.

Lady Barclay laid a placating slim white hand on her son's sleeve.

'Now, Derek, don't fuss. You know very well that you've cooked your own goose with the girl by your own conduct last week. So what does it matter whether her young man is here or not?'

'It certainly does matter!' Derek said, his face white with anger. 'This is my house, and I will not put up with the servants' boy friends walking around as if they owned it.'

'My dear boy, do not exaggerate. In any case, Jenny Ames is hardly a servant—you are not living in the past. This is a socialist age. She is an employee. As to it being your house, I'm afraid that it is still your stepfather's and *he* invited the young man. So there's nothing you can do about it.'

Derek swore under his breath and turned swiftly on his heel.

Someone was going to pay for this. If he couldn't have the girl, he certainly didn't intend to stand by and watch her stupid young man enjoy her favours under his very gaze.

There was a revengeful angry look in his eyes as he singled Jenny out from the crowd around him. He went straight up to her and bluntly interrupted the conversation she was having with another man.

'I'd like to speak to you a moment, Miss Ames!'

She could hardly refuse him without making a scene in front of one of his guests, so perforce she followed him to a deserted corner of the room.

'Well?' she asked, facing him with a courage she was far from feeling.

He relaxed a little, taking a cigarette out of a flat gold case and lighting it casually while she waited. His long slanting green eyes surveyed her rather as a cat might watch its prey. Jenny forced herself to meet that gaze, holding firmly to the thought that Peter was only a few yards away and that she could run to him in a matter of seconds....

'Well?' she asked again, when the silence became unbearable.

'You're looking as lovely as ever!' Derek spoke at last. But they were words which she would have preferred not to hear. She turned as if to go. He caught her arm and held it in a vice-like grip. She could have cried out at the pain of his finger-nails digging into her flesh but would not give him the satisfaction. Head high, cheeks flushed, eyes sparkling with anger, she said coldly:

'If that is all you have to say, may I please go?'

Derek laughed—a laugh that was an insult in its very tone.

'I'm afraid I have more to say. Firstly, I want to know if this handsome young man of yours truly appreciates your perfect beauty. Does he, Jenny?'

'Really, I cannot see that it is any of your business. And now, if you don't let go of my arm, I shall—'

'Run to my mother and tell a few more tales?' Derek finished sarcastically and laughed. 'Oh, no! Not yet awhile, Jenny. You see, I don't intend to stand by and watch you make another escape, not yet! Besides Mother will not help you. All you can say is that I am talking to you in public. You should be honoured, my dear girl. Or has your head been turned a little too far? Perhaps you thought you could play with me and get away with it? Did you? Did you? Answer me!'

'You are insufferable—despicable!' Jenny cried. 'Let me go this instant!'

'Yet once you seemed to enjoy my kisses!' Derek continued as if she had not spoken. 'I wonder what your young man would say if I were to tell him just how quickly your heart beat, just how passionately you returned those kisses; how near you were to giving way to me—*completely!*'

She went crimson to the roots of her hair.

'I was mad ever to think you attractive!' she said through her teeth. 'I didn't know then that you were so vile—beastly, *revolting*. I even thought you charming— once. And I was sorry for you. How I loathe myself for the way I behaved! That may give you satisfaction—to know you made me hate myself. But fortunately there are some decent people in the world—men unlike yourself who can see further than their own horrible desires. Peter knows *everything*. He guessed the truth and I wouldn't lie to him. So you see, you can do no further harm by telling him.'

His face whitened in fury as he realized that now indeed he had lost his last weapon over her. He knew only too well that he dared not use force to take her in his arms and kiss her as he wanted to do. The more unobtainable she became, the more he knew he wanted her; the greater grew his sense of frustration. It was maddening to him that he, Derek Barclay, rich, good-looking, a man whom women had never yet been able to resist, should find that he had lost the one he most desired—if indeed one can lose something one had never really had, he thought ironically.

He hated her now—even while he desired her. She seemed even more beautiful now that her fair, sweet, passionate beauty was beyond his reach. If it hadn't been for her fiancé, he told himself furiously, he might have won her. His hate turned to the man this girl loved.

'I'll make him pay for it!' he vowed silently. 'I'll find a way to make him suffer!'

He released his hold on Jenny. His eyes narrowed as he saw the expression of relief that crossed her face as she turned away from him. Then suddenly he laughed, a cruel mocking laugh that seemed to follow her out of the room. Jenny shivered as she heard that sound. There seemed something threatening and ominous in it. Subconsciously she quickened her footsteps and was almost running by the time she reached the library.

Peter was the first to notice her pallor.

'Aren't you feeling fit, darling?' he asked quickly.

Jenny forced a smile to her lips. In front of Sir Gerald she could not tell Peter what had happened. He must never know the truth about his stepson—the boy he had once intended to make his heir. How little Derek Barclay was worthy of that fine name, of the wealth and power he might have had!

She squeezed Peter's arm and sighed.

'I'm just a little tired, dearest,' she said with forced lightness.

'Perhaps you've been overdoing it, Miss Ames,' Sir Gerald said kindly. 'I'm sure there is no need for you to remain at the party if you would like to retire. You have worked so very hard on my wife's behalf all day.'

Jenny grasped at this offer of release from any further possible encounter with Derek.

'Thank you Sir Gerald. Then I think I will go to bed!'

'I'll see you to your room,' Peter said, glancing at her white shadowed little face with concern.

'Are you sure you're all right,' he persisted as he walked with her up the wide staircase to the gallery. 'You look quite upset, Jenny.'

She clung to him for a moment, glad of his strength, his kindness.

'I had a few nasty words with Derek,' she told him. 'Oh, Peter, I never thought I could dislike anyone so much. He's utterly vile! I know it's a hard word, but it's not bad enough for him. He's jealous of you and resents your being here.'

Peter put his arm round her and gave her a quick hug.

'Well, I can't blame the fellow. It must be maddening to have such an attractive young woman within arm's length and yet have no right to make a bid for her! Honestly, I'm quite sorry for the chap!'

She gave a shaky little laugh.

'You don't know quite how horrible he is, Peter. He's beyond pity. And I'm frightened of him. I think he might do you some kind of injury. I'm sure he's planning some kind of revenge!'

'Now, Jenny, take hold of yourself, my sweet. What harm could he do me? After all, I won the boxing championship in the navy, didn't I?'

He was glad to see the colour come back to her cheeks and the smile to her lips.

'Come now, sweet, kiss me good night and run along to bed. You look tired out, and small wonder with all the work you do!'

'I'll just look in on the twins—' Jenny began. But Peter cut her short.

'You'll do nothing of the sort. I shall see that they are all right. You forget, darling, that tonight *I'm* looking after them—and you. And doctor's orders are—straight to bed.'

'Oh, Peter, I'm not really tired. And I wanted to be with you.'

'Well, so you shall—tomorrow!' Peter said firmly. 'And soon—for a lifetime. Then you'll be fed up to the teeth with my company and wonder how you could ever have turned down an attractive fellow like Barclay.'

She had to smile but her lips trembled. Peter was so wonderfully good to her. And she knew she need have no fear for the children or for herself when his room lay between theirs. She knew he would be alert for the least sound; knew, too, that in a house so full of guests Derek could not possibly make a scene or do Peter the harm she felt certain he intended.

He kissed her good night, swiftly and passionately, and she clung to him for a moment, savouring his calmness and strength. Then she forced herself to leave him and, with a little sigh that was part contentment, part fatigue, she went quickly into her room to bed.

Once the door had closed behind her Peter's expression changed. He had not wanted Jenny to know how bitterly angry he was to know that Derek Barclay had been annoying her—had upset her again. He had forced himself to treat the incident lightly and with a certain amount of humour, but underneath his nerves were jangling with irritation, and a longing to give the other chap the thrashing of his life.

Of course, his position in the house made such action devilishly awkward, he told himself with a wry grin. Firstly Jenny was employed by Derek Barclay's mother. Secondly, he was, himself, Sir Gerald's guest. He could hardly assault the fellow in the face of such facts. On the other hand, he felt that nothing could stop him from rushing downstairs like a mad bull, charging into the room and finding the man and giving him a quick punch in the jaw.

However, he could see that it would get him—and Jenny—nowhere to behave like an enraged schoolboy. There would be some way of settling this score, and if Jenny's suspicions were right, Derek himself would soon give him the opportunity. Meantime, he would play a waiting game, and his first course of action was to find out which of all these dapper drawling young men was young Barclay.

He mingled with the other guests and, before long, noticed a tall dark young man talking to a raven-haired girl who was apparently either annoyed or extremely agitated. Her hands fluttered about as she spoke and he could see by the expression on her face that whatever she discussed was of vital importance to her. In a hard, sophisticated way she was quite attractive. But Peter thought her mouth ugly—like a scarlet gash in her pale face, and she was painfully thin. She looked a bundle of nerves.

The man, however, held Peter's attention. He knew at first glance that this must be Derek Barclay. The description Jenny had given him fitted the fellow perfectly and there was no mistaking the long slanting green eyes that were also Lady Barclay's most arresting feature. The twins, too, had those emerald, almost oriental, eyes. It was a family feature.

A high-pitched voice sounded at his elbow, some woman chattering to another:

'Oh, deaaarling, do look. I think Cynthia and Derek have made it up. We all thought he'd got tired of her, but they seem to have lots in common, don't they!'

Peter had not meant to eavesdrop, but he could not help overhearing these words. He found himself listening for further information.

'Of course, she's as mad as a March hare, but you must admit she *is* attractive. Still, she ought to have more control over...*you know what.*' The voice dropped on the last words and Peter only just heard them. 'Cats!' he thought. The couple behind him moved away and, as the room emptied, he found himself almost alone with Derek and the dark girl.

It seemed that supper had been announced, and as Peter turned to go into the dining-room Derek likewise saw *him*. He took Cynthia's arm and walked her swiftly over to Peter.

'You must be Jenny's fiancé,' he said in a loud clear voice which was both insolent and patronizing.

'That is so. And you must be Mr Barclay. I've heard a lot about you from

Jenny,' Peter returned calmly.

The thrust went home and he saw the other man's face tauten.

The girl beside him put a hand on his arm.

'Oh, do come along, Derek,' she said, her voice nervous and irritable. 'You *promised!*'

Derek threw her an amused, slightly bored smile.

'My dear Cynthia, there's plenty of time, and you haven't been introduced. This is the worthy boy friend of our new governess, Mr...er...?'

'Barrington,' Peter put in, biting his lip in an effort to keep his fist from smashing into that white mocking face. He would not allow the man to know his insults were finding a mark. 'And to whom have I the pleasure of being introduced?'

'My fiancée, Cynthia,' Derek said calmly. The girl shot Peter a quick disinterested look and turned back to Derek. Her hands were shaking and Peter, noticing her impatience, her ghastly pallor under hectic spots of rouge, felt curious, and interested.

'Derek, are you going to keep your word or not?'

Her voice was high-pitched and cracked on the last word.

'She's close to the border-line of hysteria!'

Peter thought. 'In a minute she'll be out of control. What the devil's wrong with her?'

Derek, it appeared, seemed equally aware of Cynthia's hysteria. He gave an exaggerated sigh.

'The impatience of women is past understanding!' he said. 'Oh, well, come along, darling.' He turned back to Peter and for a moment their eyes met. 'No doubt I'll be seeing you later,' he said coolly and, with a curt nod, led his fiancée by the arm out of the room. Peter could hear a muffled voice outside;—Cynthia's—whining, pleading, wretched. It made him feel curiously sick. He sat down and drew out a pipe. The room was empty now. He needed a moment or two alone in which to digest his thoughts. He puffed quietly and without enjoyment as he considered this first encounter with the man whom he knew to be his enemy, even before they had met. It was easy to see why Jenny had thought him attractive. Even by masculine standards, the fellow was handsome in a compelling way. The incredible green eyes beneath the dark lashes and brows, the smooth dark hair—he was as striking as was his mother Lydia Barclay—but in an utterly *un*-English way that immediately arrested the attention, but left Peter unmoved.

Derek's character lay in his mouth, Peter thought. With his artist's perception he had noticed the thin long lips, with their curiously sensuous, cruel curve. It was the mouth of a man of violence, one who could be both tender and passionate but always vicious. The mouth and face of a man Peter would never trust even had he known nothing about him until this moment. All the same, the man undoubtedly had charm when he chose to exert it, and a lithe, graceful body that might be attractive to women; a certain haughty aloofness, even a pride of bearing, that would hold a girl's attention.

An interesting face to paint, Peter decided. The fiancée, too. What was there about Cynthia's face that reminded him of *someone?* Of some woman he had once known perhaps? He searched his memory, but could not find the answer. 'I'll think of it later,' he told himself. After all, it couldn't be difficult. He had not known many women of her kind. He did not move in her set. He puzzled a bit longer trying to find the clue and then gave it up. After all, Cynthia was unimportant really, he told himself. It was Derek who interested him. Meantime he was hungry.

He went through the brightly lit hall to the dining-room and joined the circle round the buffet.

Some hours later, lying awake in his bed, Peter found himself thinking again about the girl Cynthia. But try as he might, memory eluded him until at last he forgot her in a sound dreamless sleep.

It could not have been more than a couple of hours later that he awoke with a start, quickly and suddenly awake, as he had had to be during the war. His six years in the navy had trained him to this complete regaining of consciousness the moment he was stirred from sleep.

Instantly he knew what it was that had roused him—footsteps creeping stealthily past his door. There was no mistaking the soft sound. His hearing was very acute. He waited only long enough for whoever it was to pass his door, then in a flash was out of bed and, without stopping to fling on a dressing-gown, he flung open the door and plunged into the darkness of the gallery.

He looked quickly at Jenny's room and beyond—then towards the far end, where he saw a shadow moving swiftly towards the swing door. Without stopping to speculate, Peter raced down the gallery towards the figure, his breath coming in quick jerks, his bare feet noiseless on the polished floors. But the sound he had made in opening his door must have warned the intruder that someone had heard him, and before he had taken more than a few steps the shadow disappeared through the door, and when Peter reached it the staircase beyond was, as he had suspected, deserted.

Peter swore softly under his breath, knowing that this time he had been too late to surprise the 'ghost'...he had only succeeded in frightening whoever it was into instantaneous flight. Well, that, at any rate, was one thing, for there was no sound from the children's room and a quick glance inside proved them to be sleeping soundly. He went quickly along to Jenny's room and listened for a moment outside the door.

He could just hear her faint but regular breathing and knew that she, too, was sleeping undisturbed. He closed the door again.

With another little oath for his lack of agility and silence, Peter went back to his own room and sat down on the bed. He lit a cigarette and smoked slowly and thoughtfully. This proved all that Jenny had told Sir Gerald and himself. That figure was no ghost, he was quite convinced. It was the figure of a man wearing some long garment or other—a dressing-gown perhaps. It could, possibly, Peter corrected himself carefully, have been a woman, for it was too far away for him to see the face or hair—and too dark. But something about the build seemed to suggest a man.... The shadow had been so tall.

But the solution to the mystery was no nearer, he told himself. If he had been quicker, quieter, he might have been able to follow and surprise the 'ghost' in the act of doing whatever 'it' intended to do. Had 'it' meant to go to the twins' room? If so, why pass *his* door? Or had he only imagined the footsteps to be so near? A board creaking—why, it could have been further along the gallery—nearer the twins' room. But why, *why?* Peter asked himself.

He finished his cigarette, and turning out his light, climbed back into bed. He came to only one decision before at last he slept again, and that was to inform Sir Gerald at the first opportunity in the morning that 'the ghost had walked again'. And next time he would be more careful in his attempts to exorcize it. First round to the spook, he told himself drowsily, but the next round would be his.

He was not to know that inadvertently the 'ghost' had laid the seeds of the second round and that it would be played before even Peter woke to a new day.

CHAPTER XIV

It was quite some time after breakfast before Peter so much as caught a glimpse of Jenny. She had been up early, dressing the twins and giving them their breakfast before placing herself at Lady Barclay's disposal. As had happened the previous week-end, Lydia sent for Miss Ames while she breakfasted in bed at nine-thirty, and issued her instructions for the day...numerous tasks to ensure the comfort and pleasure of the guests, things Lydia was either too lazy or too disinterested to attend to herself!

Peter had had his breakfast with Sir Gerald, Amelia, and young Charles Vagne —the only other early risers. He was later persuaded by them to tour the stables and see the lovely mounts that Sir Gerald kept for himself and the members of his family. There was, also, a trophy-room in which hung many ribbons and rosettes, as well as a shelf of silver cups, all won at some time or other by hard-riding members of the Barclay family. It was an imposing array and Peter was fascinated by them as much as by the saddle-room, which might have been that of a racing stable.

His fingers itched for a pencil, and when Amelia suggested he might like to do a pencil sketch of her horse for her, he jumped at the opportunity.

For this reason, the morning passed quickly and pleasantly for him, and when glancing up from his sketch to the clock, to find that it was nearly one o'clock, he reluctantly stopped work and made his way back to the Manor.

Then only did he feel a little guilty that he had, in his pleasure in his work, forgotten the more important duty of seeking out Jenny and Sir Gerald to inform them of last night's events.

As he entered the house, Jenny was the first person he met. She came running down the wide staircase, her face flushed and a look of acute anxiety on her face. She nearly passed him without stopping, she was so agitated.

'Hey, steady on, darling. What's the hurry?' he asked, catching her arm with a smile.

'Oh, Peter, it's you!' she cried, clinging on to him as if for support. 'I'm so worried. Have you seen Lady Barclay?'

'Why, no!' Peter answered. 'I've been in the stables all morning. Why, darling, is anything the matter?'

She looked at him anxiously, biting her lip.

'It's Micky!' she said. 'He's ill. I don't know what's wrong with him. I must tell Lady Barclay and ask her if I can send for the family doctor. I don't know his name or I'd 'phone first.'

'Well, try and calm down, Jenny. It can't be very serious. And Lady Barclay is bound to be somewhere. We'll go and find her together.'

'Oh, Peter, hurry then. I think it *is* serious. He was perfectly all right when I gave him his breakfast. I left him and Marie playing with their toy cooking set. They said they would make some "special cakes" for tea. When I went to them at eleven they were having their milk and biscuits and were as good as gold, so I rushed off again. Then just now, Marie came crying to me that Micky had gone to sleep and wouldn't wake up. I dashed along thinking he might have fainted or something and found him full length on the nursery floor, as white as a sheet. I loosened his blouse and put his head between his knees and bathed his face, but he's right out. It's most extraordinary. Oh, Peter, I'm so worried!'

'Steady up, darling,' Peter said again, a little of her anxiety reaching him. The symptoms sounded so peculiar. Could this have anything to do with last night's events? he asked himself suddenly. *Had someone tried to poison the child?* He laughed away that melodramatic suspicion. Now he was being ridiculous he told himself severely. Anyway, this was no time to bother Jenny with futile worries.

He accompanied her and within a few minutes they found Lady Barclay in the little writing-room with two or three guests. Jenny went up to her employer and asked if she might have a word with her alone. Peter saw the older woman frown, then she shrugged her beautiful shoulders and moved across to another corner of the room with Jenny. As Jenny explained, he saw the frown on Lady Barclay's face give way to a definite look of annoyance. Jenny's face looked up into the cold, disinterested one as if she were pleading for something. Lady Barclay shook her head and after a few more minutes of conversation Jenny turned and came back to Peter.

Outside the door, he took her hand. Already he knew that Jenny was even further upset. Her fingers trembled in his grasp and her face had an angry flush.

'Peter, she refused!' she said indignantly. 'She won't let me get the doctor. Says Micky is probably playing me up and, if he isn't, then it can't be anything serious. She won't have Dr Medows bothered at the week-end and I'm to put Micky to bed and nurse him myself. That's what I'm here for, she said.'

Her voice broke and she seemed near to tears. Peter's own face reddened in indignation.

'Well, that's the absolute end!' he agreed. 'Any normal mother would send for a doctor without hesitation, or at least go and see for herself. Would you like to see Sir Gerald?'

Jenny hesitated and then shook her head.

'Perhaps I'd better go back to Micky and find out if he's come to—before I do anything further. I don't like to go over her head, but if he isn't better soon I must go to his father.'

'Of course!' Peter said comfortingly. 'Come on, then, darling, I will see if there's anything I can do. Have you taken his temperature?'

Jenny shook her head.

'I just put him to bed and went straight to Lady Barclay.'

They found Micky still with closed eyes, still ashen pale, and Marie, who was by his bedside, said he hadn't moved. She was weeping and frightened and would not speak to Jenny.

Jenny sent the little girl back to the schoolroom; Amelia was there to look after her. Then Jenny and Peter bent over the little boy.

'Mick—Mick—wake up,' she said, shaking him. 'Micky—wake up.' His long lashes fluttered and he opened drowsy eyes.

'I'm so tired....' His voice was blurred. 'Ever so sleeeepy!'

And the beautiful eyes closed again as if indeed he found it hard to keep them open.

'Tell me, Micky, when did you first feel ill?' Jenny asked, carefully keeping her voice calm and unflurried.

'Don't know!' Micky said, and she could get no further information from him. He appeared to be semi-conscious again.

Jenny looked at Peter helplessly. It was difficult to diagnose a child's ailment under ordinary circumstances. But this drowsiness and his bad colour terrified her.

Peter drew her over to the window. He said in an undertone:

'I don't think he's in any pain, Jenny. He'd be bound to say so if he was. And he hasn't actually been sick, has he? Maybe he's just sickening for measles or mumps or something.'

'Perhaps we ought to let him sleep,' Jenny whispered back. 'He doesn't seem to have much of a temperature—his wrist and forehead are rather cold.'

'I suppose he couldn't have eaten anything to upset him internally?' Peter asked tentatively.

'But Marie had the same. They both ate cereal and boiled egg for breakfast. And both had a glass of milk at eleven. I'll go and ask Marie if he had anything else.'

The little girl shook her head in reply to Jenny's question.

'Are you quite sure, Marie—nothing at all? Not even one of the "special cakes" you and Mick were making.'

'Well, Micky did have one,' Marie said at length. 'We found some *ever* such nice icing and Mick had just *one*. But I didn't...you aren't cross, are you?'

'No, of course not, darling,' Jenny said quickly, anxious not to reprove her for this act of disobedience. The children had a toy grocery shop and often made puddings and cakes and things for 'pretend tea-parties', as they called them, but they had been forbidden on any account to eat what they made. 'Tell me, Marie, why didn't you eat one, too?'

'Because,' said Marie, 'I was afraid to. Micky dared me, but I said you'd be cross. But you aren't *are* you?'

'I'm sorry that Micky disobeyed me,' Jenny temporized. 'But I'm not going to punish him because you have told me the truth. So you needn't be afraid to answer me. What did you make the "special cakes" of, Marie? Something from your grocery shop?'

'Nooo!' Marie said slowly, eyeing Jenny somewhat dubiously.

'Then what was it, darling?' Jenny asked again, trying to curb her impatience.

After a moment's thought Marie said:

'It was just paste and special icing what we found. Meely brought us the paste for our scrapbooks, what we wanted to do, but we thought we'd cook some instead.'

'Flour and water!' Jenny murmured to Peter. 'They often have it for sticking pictures into their scrapbook. That couldn't have made him feel like this, surely?'

Peter said:

'I doubt it, darling. Might have made him sick, but that's all.' He turned to Marie. 'Look here, kiddy, what was the wonderful icing you say you found?'

'Just icing!' Marie said, hanging her head.

'Try and remember where you found it and what it looked like, pet.'

'On the floor in the gallery,' Marie said after a pause. 'It was ever such nice white icing all done up in a little parcel. Micky says Father Christmas might have brought it. Do you think he did, Uncle Peter?'

'Maybe!' Peter answered, his mind working furiously. *Powder, in a little packet!* Could someone have dropped something —*medicine?* But surely that wouldn't make the child so queer—so dopy. *Dopy!* The word spun in his mind and he gave a swift exclamation. Suppose that was it—a strong drug—possibly one of the guests had some sedative powder—for headaches—hangover—something which might be poison to a small child. He went back to the little boy and gently lifted each of the drooping eyelids, peering at the pupils to see if they had contracted. The result was astounding. On the contrary, the pupils were dilated.

Following his train of thought, Jenny watched anxiously.

Peter looked puzzled.

'I wonder what that powder was,' he said under his breath, low enough to escape the child but reach Jenny's ears. 'Strange! Why, his pupils are *enormous*. They can't normally be as big as that.'

'What causes contraction?' Jenny asked helplessly.

Peter said:

'Morphia for instance. But cocaine... Jenny, *cocaine*—'

He broke off, the word hung in the air between them while they stared at one another, not daring to think they had found the solution—not wanting to think it. Then Peter put a hand on Jenny's arm and drew her out of the room. In the gallery he said:

'We've got to make sure, Jenny. I know it

seems pretty far-fetched, but it is possible. I once had a model who was a cocaine addict. I'd swear, on that kid's eyes alone, we've found the answer. The lassitude, too. That's a typical effect. But if he has taken it, then he must have had a quarter of an hour or so of extreme excitement—a sort of wild exhilaration. Marie could tell us. Great Scott, Jenny, if he has had hold of some of that stuff we can bless our lucky stars the kid isn't dead or poisoned. It's deadly stuff taken in large doses—and through the mouth, too.'

Jenny drew a deep breath.

'Peter, you don't think...someone was trying to *poison* him?'

'I don't know, dearest. Let's cross one stile at a time. We must make sure first.'

'Then if it's true, he's not in any danger?'

'Thank heaven, no!' Peter retorted. 'He'd have collapsed by now. At this stage he's in, he must have had the stuff quite an hour ago. He'd be dead if...come on, darling, let's talk to Marie again.'

Jenny followed him to the nursery, forcing herself to assume an air of calm she was far from feeling; making her tone light and casual as she questioned the little girl.

Marie was unwittingly helpful.

'Micky was just ever so noisy!' she said

with a little laugh. 'He danced about and sang and said he was a canary. He did look funny, Jamie, and he wobbled all over the place, too. He pretended he was walking the plank like the pirates in Peter Pan. Jamie, isn't Micky coming to lunch? It's his very most favourite blackberry and apple tart, and I know 'cos Meely said so.'

'Micky is having a little sleep,' Jenny said. 'He'll have his lunch when he wakes up.'

The little girl looked doubtful.

'But if Micky's sleeping, I want to. I'll have my lunch later, too.'

'No, precious, not today,' Jenny said. 'You see, Micky isn't very well. He ought not to have eaten the "special cake". Now he has tummy ache.'

'Ooooh!' said Marie. 'Are you going to punish him?'

'No, because he's ill and that's his punishment. You were a good girl not to eat one, too. Now tell me, Marie, where are the little cakes you were making? I'd like to see them. Are they nicely cooked?'

Unsuspectingly, Marie took Jenny to the nursery cupboard and showed her a little row of damp floury mushes, one or two of which were covered in a white sugary-looking powder.

'There!' she said proudly. 'And that one is for you, Jamie. I saved it specially 'cos it's got nice icing on.'

Curbing her desire to snatch the object from the child's hand, Jenny took it gently and said:

'Thank you. Now could Uncle Peter have one, too?'

'There's only one icing one left!' Marie said, her dark little head on one side like a little robin.

'Well, suppose I give you a piece of chocolate instead to have after your lunch?' Peter suggested.

'Pretend chocolate?' Marie asked.

'Real!' Peter replied. And the bargain was struck. Peter and Jenny looked at one another triumphantly. Then Peter said:

'Isn't there any more icing for the other cakes, Marie?'

'It's all used up,' Marie said sorrowfully. 'We spilled some on the floor and it's got trodden into the carpet.'

The danger now out of reach, Jenny and Peter hurried away to Jenny's room, where they surveyed the sticky mess which was Marie's special cake.

'How can we tell?' Jenny asked.

'There isn't enough here to test ourselves!' Peter said with a grin. 'However, I dare say I could send it to London and get it analysed. Or come to that the local doc could probably tell us.'

They sat in thoughtful silence, each

326

following a train of thought.

'We should tell Sir Gerald,' Peter said at last. 'Someone in this house has cocaine—*or did have*. There may be more. Oh, blast, there's the gong for lunch. I'll stay and have mine with you—could I?'

'Yes, I suppose so, but, Peter, perhaps you ought to go down. It might look odd when you've been acting as one of the guests. We don't want anyone to think there's anything wrong... I mean, whoever lost that packet of cocaine must have missed it by now.'

'You're quite right. Until we've decided what to do, best keep on as usual. Jenny, I wonder if it's possible that Lady Barclay *knew* and that's why she wouldn't let you 'phone for the doctor?'

Jenny looked at him horrified.

'But she couldn't... Oh, Peter, I don't think I like this. One's mind sort of runs away on the subject. Maybe it's *hers!*'

'No I don't think so. I'd hardly have thought her a cocaine addict, Jenny. She's much too level-headed and cool. Now stop worrying, darling. We've got the whole afternoon to think this out. Then we'll go to Sir Gerald when it's as clear in our own minds as possible. After that it's up to him.'

'Oh, Peter, I'm so glad you're here,'

Jenny cried. 'I'd never have known what to do on my own.'

He put his arm round her and drew her close.

'I'm glad to be with you, sweetheart,' he said tenderly. 'To think of you muddled up in a house full of cocaine addicts...great heavens!'

She smiled at his exaggeration and he knew that she felt a little better. He dropped a kiss on her hair and said:

'Oh, and give that small boy an enema, and if he isn't better we'll send for a stomach pump. I'll be with you as soon as possible.'

The time before Peter returned from lunch was full of hard work for Jenny. It took her two hours to get Micky back to full consciousness. And she had had to be cruel to be kind. At length, after a bout of sickness and sobbing and a hot drink, he was fully awake and considerably better again. Only then was she able to relax and behave normally with Marie and Amelia. She told them Micky had had a bilious attack and left it at that. She left the small boy in bed, chastened, pale but content to look at his scrapbook.

When Peter returned from lunch, however, he was far from cool and calm. As soon as they were alone he grasped Jenny's arm and cried excitedly:

'Jenny, I've discovered something—important. Stupid of me not to have thought of it before. I must be slipping. It was at the back of my mind, and I just couldn't remember it.'

'What?' Jenny asked eagerly. 'What on earth are you talking about, darling?'

'That girl...Cynthia whatever her name is!' Peter cried. 'She was at lunch just now. Well, I met her last night for a few minutes with Derek. He was talking to her when he caught sight of me and came over to make a few scathing remarks. He introduced her but she wasn't interested in me—only in something she apparently wanted from him. Well, I thought at the time that there was something vaguely familiar about her. Thought I might have seen her somewhere before—or someone like her. I know I puzzled about it for some time. I couldn't make out why she seemed odd and yet at the same time familiar. Now I know. As soon as I saw her today I remembered.'

His voice was triumphant. Jenny shook him impatiently.

'Remembered what, Peter? It gets more and more confusing.'

'That she reminded me last night—although I didn't realize it at the time—of that model I used to have—the cocaine addict. I told you I know the symptoms anywhere! Well, she was fidgeting about and begging him—Derek, I mean—to keep his promise and give her something. That's all she was interested in. She could barely conceal her impatience even in front of me, a complete stranger. Well, that's a symptom, too. When they can't get the drug, they go nearly crazy and every caution goes to the wind. I've never seen anyone else except that model—June, I think her name was—get like that: agitated to a degree and that brilliant glazed look about the eyes...wonderful to paint, but tragic in effect. I remember now I did her portrait in oils and called it *Coquette and Cocaine.* It was the best thing I ever did. Unfortunately, she slashed it to pieces one night when she was...well, not quite herself.

'However, that's unimportant. But the fact is, Jenny, that I believe this Cynthia to be a cocaine addict, too. And assuming she is, I'm pretty certain that Derek Barclay either supplies her with it or else knows where she can get hold of it.'

'Peter! But this is...*amazing!* I can't take it all in.'

'I know, Jenny. And part of it is only guesswork. But I feel we might be getting somewhere if we keep probing. For instance, suppose we go a step further and assume our deductions are right as regards Derek and his girl friend, then what of the rest of the household? And what if it connects up somewhere with our other mystery—the ghost in the passage?'

Jenny sat round-eyed, trying to follow Peter's racing thoughts. It was so hard to remain cool and reasoning when such terrific and terrifying issues were raised. *Cocaine*—smuggling or supplying drugs was a crime in this country. She knew that if Derek Barclay had been supplying Cynthia with the dope, then he could be convicted and sent to gaol.... It was horrid. He was a Barclay by name, if not by blood, and it would break Sir Gerald's heart if any such scandal took place.

'Peter, we must go to Sir Gerald—now!' she said. 'We've no right to jump to conclusions. But it's up to us to tell him, and let him do the thinking and the deciding.'

'I agree up to a point,' said Peter. 'But it isn't going to be easy to say these things to the old man. After all, it's his family and his house, isn't it, darling? He's going to feel pretty rotten about it all. And besides, we haven't any real proof—only our suspicions and, of course, Marie's "special cakes". We shall have to ask him if he wants the stuff sent off to be analysed. It'll be a difficult decision for him to make. I shouldn't care to be in his shoes.'

'Nevertheless, Peter, if it *is* cocaine Micky has taken, then I'm sure Sir Gerald won't hesitate to take some action. Micky might have died. I know Sir Gerald will bear that in mind first and foremost.'

'Then we'd best go and find him,' Peter said. 'Come on, darling, let's get it over.'

Each felt reluctant to take the first step, but having made up his mind, Peter persuaded Jenny to follow him to the library, where he felt sure Sir Gerald was to be found. Amelia and young Charles Vagne were with him.

'Could we possibly have a word with you alone, sir?' Peter asked gently.

Sir Gerald turned to Amelia, who said quickly:

'Charles and I were just going off for a ride. We'll see you at tea, Daddy.' She bent and kissed him good-bye and with a smile at Peter and Jenny, the two young people left the room.

Sir Gerald told them to find themselves a seat and offered Peter a cigar, which he refused.

'Not just at the moment, sir, thank you. Jenny and I have something rather important to tell you...'

'The boy—Micky—he's not worse?' Sir Gerald asked quickly. 'Amelia told me he wasn't well. Has the doctor been sent for?'

'No, and Micky is not worse!' Jenny reassured the old man quickly. 'In fact, he's sitting up in bed quite cheerfully reading at the moment, and I think he'll be all right tomorrow. I'm not certain of course, although I would like the doctor to see him. *It might have been very serious.*'

'What do you mean? Why hasn't the doctor seen him?' Sir Gerald asked quickly, staring at her. 'Surely it would be safer to make sure?'

'Lady Barclay did not think a doctor was necessary,' Jenny said gently. She wanted to spare this charming old man as much as she could.

'Oh, then if Lydia said that it is nothing much, I'm glad. Naturally you are anxious. I am very fond of them, my dear, but children do get these minor ailments, don't they?'

'The point is, sir, if I may put this rather bluntly, if Micky is suffering from what we imagine, it could have been very serious indeed,' put in Peter.

Sir Gerald looked at Peter from beneath bushy eyebrows. His face looked concerned, anxious.

'What exactly do you mean? Don't be afraid to speak out, my boy.'

'I hardly know how to put it, sir,' Peter said awkwardly. 'You see, we think...that is...well, I suspect that Micky, a few hours ago, was suffering from the effects of a small dose of cocaine.'

'*Cocaine!*' Sir Gerald echoed, a look of amazement on his face. 'But how on earth did he get hold of that? You must be wrong.'

'I'm not absolutely sure,' Peter admitted. 'But very nearly. Look here, sir, the twins found a little white paper packet on the landing—the gallery, I think it's called. They were making some kind of cakes for a dolls' tea-party and thought the white powder inside the paper would make nice icing for the cakes. They had been forbidden to eat these little pies they make from time to time, but I gather Micky thought he'd try one all the same. Marie was frightened to disobey so she didn't touch one herself. Immediately afterwards she tells us Micky became very excited and peculiar. This was followed by the depression and lassitude which I happen to know is a symptom of cocaine dosing. Then came drowsiness. When I looked at the boy's eyes I found the pupils were dilated, I happen to know something about these things. Had it been morphine the pupils would have been contracted. It seems to point to cocaine.'

Sir Gerald looked stunned. 'This is appalling!' at length he stammered. 'Who on earth could have such stuff lying about or have it in my house? Who on earth could have dared to bring cocaine here into Marleigh Manor?'

'That we don't know, sir, of course,' Peter said hastily. 'But we felt you might wish to find out.'

'It's incredible—incredible!' the old man muttered. He was obviously very upset and duly half credulous.

'It could be untrue,' Jenny said, longing to comfort him. 'We are only guessing.'

'Then we must make sure at once,' said Sir Gerald. 'You say it could have been serious for young Michael. I know there *is* such a thing as cocaine poisoning. A white packet? Good heavens! If it is a dangerous drug... Whoever has let my child in for such a risk is going to pay for it. We must make certain at once.'

'We managed to keep two of the "cakes" with their icing on them,' Peter said. 'That is in case you would like the local doctor to analyse the powder. Or if you prefer that it should be done in London, I could run up tomorrow and take them to one of the hospital laboratories...on some pretext, of course. Your name and address need not be mentioned. I know a medical student who would fix it all up for me so that there would be no questions asked.'

'I should be very grateful. Don't want any scandal,' said Sir Gerald quickly. 'If it's one of the guests in this house, then they must go immediately. You've no suspicions, I suppose?'

Peter bit his lip.

'I hardly like to make any accusations when it's all so vague,' he said quietly.

'Nevertheless I'd like to know. I trust you, my boy, to keep nothing back from me—nothing at all.'

'Well, sir, it did occur to me that your stepson's fiancée had the symptoms of a cocaine addict. I couldn't be sure, of course....'

'My stepson's fiancée!' Sir Gerald cried. 'Oh, this is indeed awful. However, as you say, we mustn't do anything until we are certain. I wish I could be sure no one else is involved.'

'I've been thinking, Sir Gerald, that if I'm going to London, I could take a list of the guests in the house with me. Please excuse this unpleasant way of putting things, but I presume you will consider them all under suspicion, so to speak, since any of them could have dropped it. I have another friend—an ex-naval officer, who is now an inspector at Scotland Yard. If I asked him for information of anyone on the files known to be a cocaine addict, it might help discover who was responsible. There would be no need for it to go any further. You can take my word that this whole matter will be entirely confidential.'

'I shall be deeply obliged,' Sir Gerald said. 'This has all happened so suddenly I can't think just for the moment what action I should take if we did find the culprit. However, let us hope that we are all wrong and the child is not suffering from more than a slight chill or something. In the meantime, I know you will not repeat a word of this to anyone—no one at all, you understand. I don't wish my wife to be worried about her guests until we are certain.'

'Of course!' said Peter. 'Then I see no point in wasting time. I'll catch the next train to town.'

An hour later, Peter slipped out through the garden door and made off for the station, leaving a forlorn and anxious Jenny behind him. When he kissed her good-bye he held her tightly for a moment, knowing a sudden unreasoning fear at leaving her alone in heaven knew what danger. If anyone had or did guess that they were suspected, they might even do Jenny some harm to keep her from talking. It was a horrid thought which Peter did not share with Jenny for he had no wish to frighten her unduly. He did, however, ask her to promise to lock her bedroom door and on no account whatever stir from it till morning.

This Jenny had refused to do. She could not, she told him, neglect the children's safety for her own. It took courage to say this, for the same fears that beset Peter regarding her own safety had occurred to her, and she longed to be weak and beg him to stay with her whatever Sir Gerald thought about it!

'Then there's only one answer. Sleep with the children and be sure to lock their door,' Peter said, breathing a sigh of relief when Jenny agreed to do this, in spite of Lady Barclay's orders to the contrary.

There would be time enough to explain to Lady Barclay tomorrow when Peter would be returning and, it was to be hoped, the whole affair sorted out. She could hardly complain under the circumstances.

Nevertheless, Jenny chose a moment when the gallery was deserted to move her night things into the twins' room. Micky had had his tea and already seemed more his usual self. She noticed that the pupils of his eyes were quite normal again and his colour, too, more rosy and fresh. By bedtime, he was chattering to Marie as if nothing had happened. He did not talk about his illness, no doubt because he had an attack of conscience for disobeying Jenny so flagrantly over eating the 'cakes'.

She went to bed early, leaving the usual crowd of laughing noisy guests in the rooms below, where there was dancing and drinking and a continuation of the card games of the night before. No one noticed her departure, and she hoped that she would not be missed or wanted.

Having locked her own bedroom door after her and taken the key, she then locked herself into the twins' room and made herself as comfortable as possible on the camp bed she had erected there, much to the children's delight. Her presence was easily explained by Micky's indisposition, and neither the maid who brought up their supper, nor Amelia, who came to say good night to them, questioned it.

The twins were sound asleep as she turned off the little bedside lamp and settled down for the night. She listened to their soft breathing, drawing comfort from the sound. For some time she lay awake thinking about Peter and his mission in town, about the day's events and what they might lead to. At the back of her mind she felt certain that they linked up in some way with 'the ghost' and the children being so frightened. It seemed to her as she lay there in the dark that she ought to be able to sort out the puzzle; that, like a jig-saw, it only needed one little piece for the whole thing to make the complete picture. But try as she might she could not find the answer. Even if, as Peter had wondered, Derek had been supplying Cynthia—perhaps others—with cocaine, why should he, of all people, come to the twins' room to frighten them? It didn't make sense. In any case it couldn't be Derek who played at being a ghost, for twice she had met him searching for the 'ghost' himself.

Then suddenly another piece of the puzzle fell into position. Derek hadn't been prowling round the passage because he had heard the children crying—he had been there because he had caused it and hadn't had time to get away before she appeared on the scene.

She felt her scalp prickling and her body grow cold with a horrible fear. She recalled that she had been out there in the dark—alone with this man who must be some frightful kind of maniac to want to frighten two small children for no reason at all. She had allowed herself to be kissed by him—had even imagined herself attracted to him in some queer way. Oh, it was horrible, horrible!

She buried her face in the pillow, trying to still her nerves, which were jumping all over her body. 'Oh, Peter, Peter,' she thought, trying to bring back his image in place of that other dark, sinister one.

She remembered Peter's fair curly hair, the bright honest blue eyes, the square jaw and humorous, generous mouth. And then, quite suddenly, the image left her and her mind became paralysed with fear. There was a soft footfall outside in the passage, and a second later she heard the slight squeak of the latch as someone outside slowly and softly turned the handle of the door.

CHAPTER XV

Hardly daring to breathe, Jenny lay perfectly still, ears straining for further sounds. Whoever it was at the door must have realized it was locked. She was just about to climb out of bed and go to the door to convince herself that the gallery was empty, when she heard a voice which, although barely a whisper, caused her to draw in her breath sharply with a new fear—this time even more horrifying than her recent terror.

'Micky, Marie, are you there? Open this door at once!'

Jenny gripped the edge of the bed trying to shake off the horror of her suspicions. Even had she wished to do so she could not have moved or spoken. That was Derek's voice, she was convinced. It must also have been he who tried the handle. And if tonight, why not the other nights when the twins had been frightened?

'Micky, Marie, do you hear me? I'm sure you're awake. Why did you dare lock this door?'

She knew then that he had no knowledge of her presence in the room. He had possibly already been to her room, and finding the door locked, assumed she had barricaded herself in there! For a moment she wondered if she had the courage to call out and ask him what he wanted; or else fling open the door and surprise him. But her courage failed her. Peter had made her promise to remain where she was—whatever happened. No harm could come to the children while the door remained locked, and what good would come of opening a conversation with Derek now? He would find some excuse for being there. Far better let him go away. He would have to return some time and tomorrow night Peter would be there.... Peter, who would know what to do.

It was fortunate for Jenny that the twins did not stir and call out to her and betray her presence. Presently she heard the handle sliding in the lock again, a muttered exclamation, and then soft footfalls disappearing along the gallery.

Jenny relaxed a little and pulled the bed-clothes round her trembling body. She could not recall ever having been more frightened or nervous, and knew at last what it meant to feel real terror—the awful weakening of all her limbs and the cold sweat that had dampened her whole body. It was some little time before she grew warm again and was able to relax and try to think. What could be the reason for Derek's wishing to come to this room? Could it have been he who had dropped that little packet of cocaine and come in search of it? He could not have come during the day, since Micky had been in bed and someone with him nearly all the time. It would have been too dangerous to risk such a venture even when Micky was alone, for at any moment he might have cried out and attracted attention. So Derek had waited until night, when he meant to steal into the room to search for the packet.

It seemed plausible until Jenny recalled that the children had found the cocaine in the gallery itself. Why should Derek come here to search for it? It was unlikely that the children would have taken the tiny packet to bed with them. The most likely hiding-place for all the twins' treasures was the schoolroom. Had he already been there and searched the room?

Again Jenny felt nonplussed. It stood to reason that he must have learned Micky had been curiously taken ill that morning. Lady Barclay would have told him—or one of the servants, or Amelia. He might have put two and two together and realized Micky had taken the drug. That being so, again what purpose would be served in his coming here tonight? To see if the child were all right? To try to force his silence? But that, too, was improbable, since anything Micky had to say would surely have been said already during the day.

Jenny tossed wearily in bed, unable to stop thinking and find relief in sleep. She felt as if she were on the brink of an important discovery, if only she could find the answer to this mysterious visit. One thing of which she felt almost certain was that it linked up in some way or other with the other visits—the 'ghost' she herself had seen; explained why the twins screamed at night for no apparent reason.

It was dawn before, at last, Jenny fell asleep, and not long afterwards that the twins woke her, begging to be allowed to get up early and go for a walk before breakfast. Micky did not appear to be suffering from any ill effects, and it was Jenny who felt hot-eyed and tired out.

With an effort she pulled herself together, and having made the twins promise not to mention to anyone that she had slept in their room, she agreed to the early walk, glad, once she was up and about, of the refreshing cold air of the autumn morning, for it seemed to clear her head and prepare her for the day.

Since it was Sunday, the morning passed quickly enough with a visit to church with Amelia and Sir Gerald accompanying them. Jenny found herself offering up a fervent prayer that, whatever came of this whole peculiar mystery, it would not hurt this old gentleman too much. He was the soul of goodness himself, of truth and straightforwardness. It would be bound to shake him badly to find that any of his family were involved in any kind of wrongdoing.

Not long after lunch, while the twins were resting, Jenny heard a knock on the schoolroom door and in walked Peter. The blood rushed to her cheeks, and she felt her heart thumping madly as she ran to him to be lifted into his arms.

'Oh, Peter, darling! I never expected you so soon,' she cried breathlessly. 'I'm so *glad* to see you!'

'Everything all right, I hope?' Peter asked anxiously, sensing the relief in her voice and a certain tension about her which was unusual in his cool little Jenny.

'Everything!' she answered, clinging to him, 'now that you're back. Oh, Peter, I've never been so appallingly frightened in my life. It was only the thought of you that kept me from having hysterics.'

He drew her over to the big nursery couch and pulled her down beside him, his arm still round her holding her close.

'Tell me all about it, sweetheart,' he said gently.

When Jenny had finished her story of last night's events Peter's face looked thoughtful and very serious.

'I, too, have made some discoveries,' he said gravely. 'First and foremost, It *was* cocaine. Not the shadow of doubt about it. So when I left the lab I went along to Scotland Yard and luckily found John in. He's the inspector I told you about. Well, I told him I had a list of names which I wanted to compare with his files on cocaine addicts, and although it was against regulations, he agreed to let me get on with it. He was dashed interested to know what I was up to, and I told him some story about a bit of private detecting. I'd like to have asked his advice, but as I'd promised Sir Gerald...well, that was that. Anyway, darling, the result was quite stupefying. Exactly eight of the guests at present in this house have all at one time or another been suspected or convicted of cocaine taking. Eight certains, Jenny, so heaven alone knows how many that weren't on John's files are in this too. I could hardly contain my excitement.'

'But, Peter, that means—'

'Exactly—that someone is handing the stuff out to them in this house. I thought it all out in the train coming back as well as most of last night. The way I see it is this—they manage to get themselves invited down to these big house-parties, which are only a cover-up for passing them the stuff. It's a dangerous game, but the chances of anyone finding out in a place like this, and under Sir Gerald's roof, too—are certainly remote. No one would suspect anything of the sort in Marleigh Manor, of all places. Now, if I'm right so far, then we can assume that someone in the house gives it to them, and that "someone" must be storing it here, and in some way or other receiving it. It's smuggled into the country by devious means, and the poor wretches who take it wouldn't deal direct with the smugglers. There's big money in it, Jenny. Everywhere along the line the men who get it in, the men who pass it on, the men who actually do the selling—they all get their whack and a pretty big one. The organizer must be clearing a packet. Now what we've got to discover is who has the stuff in this house and where does he or she keep it?'

Jenny looked at him helplessly.

'Oh, Peter, I wish we'd never got into this. Now we're so near to solving the mystery I'm really frightened. I don't think I want to know who is responsible.'

He pressed her hand encouragingly.

'Now buck up, sweetheart. It'll soon be

over and then I'm taking you away from here—altogether. I'd take you right now if I hadn't promised Sir Gerald I'd help. And to be honest I'm interested now—very interested. I'm like a hound on the scent of the fox. And Jenny, I think I'm beginning to see daylight after what happened last night.'

'You mean...Derek...?' She broke off, not liking to put her suspicions into words.

Peter nodded.

'It all ties up so well, Jenny. You remember that I saw that Cynthia of his begging him to keep his promise? I'd swear that she was asking for cocaine. And Jenny, it makes sense in other ways. He must be making a fortune—and in a way, one can understand how it happened—*if* it happened. There's always a motive for crime, and he'd been disinherited. I dare say he'd have got a reasonable legacy from Sir Gerald, but that's not the same as big money *now*, is it? It would give him power and a sort of revenge on fate, if you see what I mean.'

Jenny shuddered.

'He spoke of plans for his future,' she said, more to herself than to Peter. 'One day he would be rich... I can recall his words almost exactly. He said: "I want to be rich above all things; to be able to live as I would have done if I'd been heir to the Barclay fortune...." '

'Then doesn't that confirm my suspicions?' Peter cried eagerly. 'He's a psychological case, Jenny. I always felt there was something odd about him—something mocking and cruel from the first time you spoke of him. His mother, too, seems hard...calculating.'

'Peter, you don't think she's in it, too? Oh no, not Sir Gerald's wife—the twins' mother?'

'I don't know, Jenny, but I gather her eldest son is more important to her than anything else in the world. She mixes with these people whom we know to be addicts. She invites them here. He could hardly arrange all that without her knowledge.'

'Peter, what are we going to do now?' Jenny asked helplessly.

'Tell Sir Gerald the truth. Then it's up to him to decide. But whatever happens, Jenny, not a word to anyone else—anyone, at all. So far I don't think anyone suspects *our* suspicions. It might be dangerous if they did. These types can be utterly reckless when they think they might be discovered or that supplies might stop. Now buck up, dearest, and come with me. We'll face Sir Gerald together.'

The ordeal of telling their new discoveries and suspicions to the old gentleman was harder even than Jenny had imagined. When Derek's name was mentioned, Sir Gerald's face seemed to age another ten years—become drawn and heavily lined. But he insisted on hearing everything, and it was he himself who asked:

'Do you think my wife might know anything of all this?'

Neither Peter nor Jenny spoke. Sir Gerald coughed and spoke again:

'You will please oblige me by treating the whole matter as if it were entirely impersonal. I must get to the bottom of this—know the whole truth. I assume from your silence that you think my wife might know. I am forced to agree. These people you mention are her guests. The boy is her son. She never cared for the twins—never wanted them. She behaved, as far as possible, as if they weren't her children at all—only mine. I was too blind to realize how deeply she felt about her own son...how she resented her first born being supplanted—even though it was by her own child.'

Hearing the agony in his voice, Jenny laid a hand on his arm. She was filled with pity for him.

'It may not be true. We have no proof,' she murmured.

'Not as yet,' Sir Gerald cried harshly. 'But we must get it. We must think of some way to find out—everything.'

'Do you think, Sir Gerald, that it might be a good idea to get a private detective down here for a bit to look into it?' Peter asked gravely.

Sir Gerald looked startled.

'I hope I shan't be forced to such action. I don't want a word of this to escape beyond the house. I had hoped...that is, I know I'm asking a great deal, but couldn't you...?' His voice trailed into silence.

Peter stood up.

'If there's anything I can do, sir, please tell me. I'm entirely at your disposal.'

'That's just it,' Sir Gerald said wearily. 'I can't think what ought to be done next. I'm very grateful—very grateful indeed for your kindness...a complete stranger...perhaps you could suggest—'

'Will you leave it in my hands?' Peter asked, sensing the older man's wretchedness and concern. 'I'll think of something.'

'Anything at all—you have my permission to do what you think best. Only I would like your assurance that you will not pass this on to anyone, not a soul, until you have asked me first.'

'That's understood!' Peter said gently.

'What are we going to do?' Jenny asked when they had left Sir Gerald, looking old and bent, huddled in a big wing chair, a tired, disillusioned old man. 'We've gone too far to turn back.'

Peter followed her into the schoolroom, lost in thought. Presently he spoke:

'We'll have to take a chance, Jenny—a chance that Derek, if it was him, will return tonight. I'll conceal myself somewhere in the twins' room and leave the door unlocked—and watch. Heaven knows what I expect to see, but it might show us something....'

'There's a big cupboard where all their clothes hang,' Jenny suggested. 'Peter, are you sure it's safe?'

He gave a short laugh without humour.

'That's impossible to say. Anyway, I shall have the advantage of surprise. You stand by, if you can keep awake, Jenny, and at the slightest noise, come in and see to the children. We want to protect them as far as possible.'

'Then you think he will come?'

'I hope so!' Peter said grimly. 'And if he does he won't get away.'

The remainder of the day passed with agonizing slowness. Jenny, when at last she went to her room, felt doubly tired from the strain of awful anticipation and from lack of sleep the night before. It was only by the greatest effort that she could keep awake. Peter had slipped into the twins' room while they were sleeping and hidden himself in the cupboard with a torch and a flask of coffee. The light was burning merrily between the twins' beds and their door stood slightly ajar—to encourage the intruder, Jenny thought with horror.

The hours dragged by and gradually she found herself dozing off for a moment or two and then waking with a jerk and presently dozing again.

Peter, too, was finding it hard to stay awake. The cupboard was airless and warm and the whole atmosphere inducive to sleep. Even the coffee did not help much, and he, too, dozed in fits and starts.

Suddenly, however, he found himself wide awake, every nerve straining to catch a renewal of the sound that had startled him. Someone had pushed open the door and was walking quietly through the room.

Peter held his breath and very slowly leant forward until his eyes were to the crack he had left by not quite closing the cupboard door. By contrast with the dark interior, where he had been for some hours, the children's room seemed light—sufficiently light, in any case, to make out the back of a man's figure. Then the figure turned slowly round and with a furious effort Peter refrained from gasping. *So it was Derek Barclay.* His face, though shadowed, was unmistakably recognizable.

Peter's hands clenched on the long handle of the torch as he stood prepared to pounce should the man decide to leave.

Derek, however, had moved over towards the window, and then, his back once more to Peter stood facing one of the walls. He lifted his right hand as if he was feeling for something, and a second later a door sprang open, and before Peter had recovered from his surprise the figure disappeared into the darkness within the wall.

In a flash Peter was out of the cupboard and tiptoeing across the room, taking care not to wake the children, which he wanted to avoid if possible. He peered into the darkness of the passage which the sliding panel had revealed. Not more than two or three feet away he saw a thin square line of light and realized that there was a closed door facing him behind which was a lighted room.

Without further hesitation Peter went carefully forward and, tensing his muscles for action, wrenched open the door.

It was doubtful whose was the greater surprise: Peter's at what he saw—Derek's at beholding Peter in the doorway. In a glance Peter took in the little room, which was furnished with nothing but a square deal table on which lay numerous little packets—undoubtedly cocaine. Derek stood staring at him, a slip of white paper in one hand, a bundle of banknotes in the other.

It was only a matter of seconds before the two men recovered and went into action. Handicapped by what he held in each hand, Derek had no means of protecting himself against the stiff uppercut that Peter flung to his jaw. He was knocked flat and quite unconscious before he realized what had hit him, and Peter stood over him staring down at the inert figure covered in the deadly white chrystalline powder, the banknotes scattered around him like so many fallen leaves.

The whole thing was over so quickly that it left Peter unprepared for his next move. For the moment it sufficed to know that Derek was truly knocked out, and that evidence of his crimes were all around him—proof of all their suspicions, the answer to all their problems.

Peter had had sufficient experience of boxing to know that Derek would not remain unconscious much longer. Quickly he bent down and, unbuckling his belt, tied the man's wrists tightly together. In another minute he had fastened Derek's feet with his tie. He was, by then, already groaning a little and moving his head.

Peter had never in his life before hit a man who was down, but this time he had no alternative and no compunction in delivering a second knock-out blow. Only a few yards away were two young children who would be surely woken if he and Derek had a scene in here.

With his lips pressed tightly together, Peter stooped and lifted Derek's inert body on to his back, surprised that the man did not weigh more heavily for all his height, and went quickly back through the twins' room and into the passage. A moment later he had dumped the still senseless body of Derek Barclay on to his own bed, locked the door behind him, and run to fetch Jenny.

She was fast asleep, curled up in an armchair with a blanket over her. For a moment he hesitated, unwilling to wake her. His heart felt weak with tenderness for her. She looked extraordinarily young and helpless and childlike lying there lost to the world, her beautiful hair tumbling about her cheeks, her breast rising and falling softly as she breathed.

He watched her, knowing in this oddly unsuitable moment that he loved her more than life itself—that the longing to lift her into his arms and carry her to bed was almost overpowering. He smiled a little at the incongruity of such an emotion at a time like this, and with a return of humour, he hesitated no longer. He bent and touched her hand gently, calling her name.

She woke instantly, her face startled and then relaxing as she recognized Peter's face.

'Darling! What is it? I'm afraid I've been asleep.'

He put his arms round her then, waiting for her to wake to full consciousness, just holding her from where he knelt at her feet, his cheek against hers.

Then he told her gently all that had happened.

'I think we ought to get the twins into another room, darling,' he ended. 'Sir Gerald is bound to want to see this secret room we've found. Is there anywhere we could put them where they'll be out of the way?'

'They can have my bed,' Jenny said quickly. 'I'll find somewhere else later. Oh, Peter, this is ghastly! I hardly dare to think what will happen now.'

'Don't worry about it, dearest,' Peter said. 'It'll sort itself out. Now let's move those children before I go to Sir Gerald.'

She clung to him for a moment, savouring his calm strength and reassuring coolness. With Peter she need never be afraid—never at a loss to know the right thing to do. He was utterly dependable—utterly satisfying—and she loved him in a new way which had in it an element of respect for his male superiority that she had not realized before.

Then together, her hand held tightly in his own, they went back to wake the twins.

Jenny never fully understood how she managed to live through the next twenty-four hours. Somehow or other she had managed to do so, and once again the twins were safely tucked up in bed and she was sitting in the schoolroom alone with Peter once more.

Downstairs in the library Amelia was with her father, discussing their newly made plans for going abroad for a year or two. There was no one else in the house at all except for the servants. It was strangely quiet and deserted after the incredible bustle and noise of the day now past.

Jenny sighed wearily, leaning back in the circle of Peter's arm, her eyes looking thoughtfully into the blazing fire.

'I can't help remembering, Peter, that if I hadn't come here all this might never have happened,' she said regretfully.

'But, Jenny, darling, you can't wish it undone.'

'I suppose I ought not to, but it's brought so much unhappiness with it, Peter.'

'That is surely better than allowing such things to continue, my dearest. And remember, too, that the twins were suffering a great deal. Ever since they recognized their half-brother as the "ghost" he terrorized them to such an extent that they were literally dumb with fright. He even dared to say he'd kill them if they so much as breathed a word of what they knew, and they must have realized how serious he was, since they never did tell anyone until today. Believe me, darling, there's no need to waste any pity on that scoundrel—even if he was thwarted and unbalanced. After all, he's not the first man to be disinherited or lose a lot of money he'd expected to have: and others don't turn to crime—not to a drug which harms not only the wretched degenerate people to whom he sold the stuff, but two innocent children as well.'

'I don't think I have any pity for *him*,' Jenny said quietly. 'But for Sir Gerald, Peter, and for Amelia. How dreadful that poor old man must feel!'

'Perhaps. And yet he still has plenty to live for,' Peter said comfortingly. 'He admitted, didn't he, that he had married Derek's mother not from love but from the wish to beget an heir. Since he did so, he learned how cold and selfish and dictatorial she was...learned, too, that she had no intention of being the loving mother he had hoped for to take the place of Amelia's own mother. He cannot have had many illusions left about her, even if he received a shock to know the extent of her baseness. He is a human sort of fellow, Jenny darling, and he'll excuse her to himself on the grounds that she did it for her son. And I do think that he and not money was her motive.'

'I'm glad Sir Gerald didn't immediately phone for the police,' Jenny said. 'It would have been so awful for everyone...the twins—'

'And that's why!' Peter broke in. 'I think he is a sufficiently conscientious man to have felt it his duty to call the police no matter how great the scandal, had it not been for the children. I think he did the right thing when he gave Derek and Lady Barclay forty-eight hours to get out of the country—two days and nights before he gave full details to Scotland Yard. They may kick up a bit when they learn he's let them escape—along with the rest of the guests, but no doubt they'll catch most of them. And I think they'll respect his wish to keep all this from the public if it's possible to do so.'

'You don't think Lady Barclay and Derek will be caught?'

'I doubt it. They have plenty of money,

which will make the way easier for them. By now they'll be on their plane bound for some outpost where no doubt they'll change their names and start life afresh. Not much of a prospect in comparison with life here, but that's their punishment. They should have been content with what they had, which was, after all, considerable by our standards. Those sort of people always want more. Money becomes a kind of god to them and they must make more and more. It's an obsession, I suppose. Anyway, Jenny, Sir Gerald and Amelia will be in Kenya before the case breaks and that's all that matters. Two years out there, and by the time they return no one will remember if an occasional cocaine addict was put in gaol all that time ago and was somehow connected with Marleigh Manor. Sir Gerald will see that the Press keep it suppressed...he has influence.'

'Amelia will be nearly eighteen when they return,' Jenny said dreamily.

'Old enough to think of marrying her Charles!' Peter said with a smile.

'And the twins nearly eight!' Jenny added. 'Oh, Peter, I'm glad we're having them, although I think they'll be a responsibility.'

'Nonsense, darling, we'll cope. It'll be good practice for when we have our own brats one day!'

Jenny laughed, glad of the pressure of the hand which held hers so tightly.

'I still feel we ought not to accept all that money,' she said. 'Sir Gerald has been far too generous. He's practically set us up for life instead of just settling the cottage on us so we have a roof to put over the twins' heads!'

'I think he's so relieved to know they'll be in safe hands that he'd have given away a fortune,' Peter said. 'I tried to refuse, Jenny, but you heard for yourself how impossible it was. He just said we could keep what was over for a wedding present.'

'A wedding present!' Jenny echoed, smiling. 'Oh, Peter, can it really be true, after all this time? And we shall have a whole week's honeymoon before we return to collect the twins from Mrs Minnow's care to take them home with us. I suppose she'll stay on as caretaker. She's too old to do anything more.'

'And Marleigh Manor will be closed down,' Peter said. 'It's strange, isn't it, darling, to think that so much has happened to us all in such a short while? It's only a month since you left home to come here.'

'A month!' Jenny repeated. 'It seems more like a year. Oh, Peter, I think I'm glad I came after all. I've learned so much, and the most important thing of all is learning how very much I love you.'

She lifted her face to see the blue eyes smiling down at her. She saw the lean face, the strong determined chin, the humorous quirk to his lips, and then, as her arms went round his neck drawing him down to her, his mouth found hers and she forgot everything but the fact that this was the man she loved and to be kissed by him was the most exhilarating and glorious emotion imaginable.

'I love you, I love you!' she whispered, and heard his voice, passionate and demanding, utterly satisfying as he whispered back:

'Oh, Jenny, Jenny. Only a few more days and you will be my wife!'

And so for the moment the past and all its horrors were forgotten and within the big old house there was a new warmth and light—not bought by money or built by wealth, but a richness that came from two young people's hearts; and around them shone a golden haze that was the promise for the future and the coming fulfilment of their love.

This Large Print Book for the Partially sighted, who cannot read normal print, is published under the auspices of

THE ULVERSCROFT FOUNDATION